SHATTERED

STEPHANIE CARTY

BLOODHOUND
— BOOKS —

EIGHT MONTHS AGO

I 'm broken, waiting to be fixed. When are they coming back? My legs feel too heavy to move from the bed, as if I can no longer fight the force of gravity. I scratch at my temples to clear the fog inside. It seems as though I've been here by myself for days, but maybe time moves differently for me now? I'm missing something, someone, somewhere. The details hide in a haze.

I must ground myself, pay close attention to what's around me rather than panic. There's a dimly lit floor lamp in the corner of the room with no switch: everything is controlled externally. My suitcase sits next to a silver trolley with empty shelves. The window is covered with blinds that are decorated with a pattern of jagged little lines in clusters. They seem familiar. Breathe, breathe, it'll come back to me when I'm not so exhausted.

What the hell time is it? I'm in a velour tracksuit rather than my pyjamas. It could be morning or night, day one or day seven. My arm lifts clumsily, like it doesn't really belong to me. I reach up to my head to check the wired cap. It's not there as it should be.

In the corner of the room a red dot of light pulses. I'm being

1

watched. That's better than being ignored. I drag my body a little way up the bed. There's a bottle of water just in reach. I gulp so fast that some dribbles down my chin but it's no good, it doesn't quench my thirst.

With effort, I turn my stiff neck to the far wall. A map of London almost fills the whole space. *My* map. It sets off a kind of hunger, though not for food. I'm ravenous for that feeling, that knowing, that sucking up of information. The map starts to change right in front of my eyes. A yellow trail appears as I track the first taxi route from Manor House Tube Station, Hackney to Gibson Square in Islington, then fades. I can still do it! I shift focus to route fourteen which glows a rose pink: New Cross Station to the National Maritime Museum. Each stop along the journey is ingrained as clearly as a nursery rhyme. There are still a hundred more routes to learn. I close my eyes. The pink line stays in view, wriggling across the darkness behind my lids to show me the way. My lips move to the rhythmic chant of those places. I couldn't stop them even if I wanted to.

It's not enough.

My vision swims as two people enter the room. It's a chance to escape but my body won't obey my commands. The sound of their speech is muffled as though I'm under water: a deep male voice, a higher-pitched female. I desperately want to stay in the present with them but a mask is placed over my mouth, the air as sweet as talc. I stare up at the light with one, two, three, four, five, six, seven sides. Dizziness descends. My fists loosen, useless. My thoughts can't arrange themselves into order. They don't realise that I'm on the edge of understanding so much, I just need a little bit more of whatever it is they give to me – it's been too long without it. I wait for the gel to tingle my scalp through the spaces on the cap and for the coolness of pads on my temples.

It doesn't come. They don't give me anything at all.

I flinch at the sound of tearing paper. Don't touch it! Don't you dare take my map. Then, the thud of their feet as they leave me all alone, with nothing left to make me good enough.

1

The darkened one-way glass of Somni Company headquarters gives away no clue as to what goes on inside. Metallic panes reflect contorted versions of my face. Each storey is set back a little further from the one below, like the layers of sleep that are investigated inside. *Sleep architecture* is the focus of our research: all the components of sleep that form the solid building of a person. Unlike me for the last few months: a shattered-mirror version of myself.

I pause to clip my identity badge on my wrinkled blouse. The walk to work, curving along the Thames to Southbank, has cleared my brain fog but this relief is temporary. I push the rotating door. Add a smile to my face. Leave my northern vowels behind me. Now I'm only what my badge declares: Christie Langdale, Research Psychotherapist.

Receptionist Anja click-clacks at a keyboard with manicured nails. The water cooler next to her bubbles with pale pink liquid fortified with vitamins nobody asked for. Each wall holds a screen that flashes adverts for sleep-enhancing services. Hard chairs designed to prevent microsleeps line up below.

Anja, with her fantasy curves, has a face that can no longer frown. All plastic.

'Morning, Anja, are the night crew out yet?'

Anja lifts one finger and swishes it across to indicate *no*.

As I pass the front desk, she turns away from me and taps four digits: an internal call. This happens each morning since I returned to work from sick leave, as if she's been told to inform somebody from the department that I've arrived.

Even though taking the lift would save me from sapping my low energy reserves, I use the stairs. I struggle with the oppression of small spaces: a sense of being trapped behind doors so thick no one would hear pleas for escape. Ever since... what? My *episode*, or *breakdown*, or what did one of the company doctors call it? An *abreaction* to the research trial I was placed in. All those psychological tests that helped me to get a foot in the door of the company must have missed something. With serious consequences.

By the fifth floor where my office is based, my head spins. I lean an arm against the handrail to steady myself. The window ahead is divided into small concave rectangles of glass which bounce colours around like a bubble. Warped by the glass contours, the sprawling city below looks unreal. God's playset. During the Maximus research trial last year, I'd memorised the streets of London as perfectly as any taxi driver. Today, I can barely remember the passcode to get into my section of the building.

I pull back my slumped shoulders and get my everything-is-fine face ready before I enter the department. I've had three decades of practice to perfect it. At Somni, only positivity is permitted.

Through the door, yellow light streams from squares on the ceiling and marks a shift from the real world to a man-made dream: twenty-four-hour living. Night staff are preparing to leave after their long shifts in the sleep labs. For the science of sleep, they're expected to sacrifice their own. The foxes and owls.

My colleague Heidi is a fox: clever, glamorous and into everyone's business. The parting of her blonde hair is ruler-straight. Her silk shirt and fitted trousers skim her slight body in gentle shades of pink. I don't see her as much since she switched to night shift in a bid to climb the ladder. Nine years of friendship here at Somni have weakened a little lately.

'Hey, you look how I feel,' says Heidi from across the hallway, her nose wrinkled in concern. I doubt that. My friend is unlikely to be battling concentration and memory problems: the effects of weeks with only snippets of sleep, a brain that has forgotten how to log off for the night.

I quickly check if anyone may have overheard. She doesn't realise that someone like me could pay the price for her flippant comment.

'I stayed up late, how was your night?'

Heidi links my arm as if we're fifteen as we head to our shared office.

'Promising results coming through on the stroke trial.' Heidi packs up items from her desk and drops them into different sized pockets in her bag. Everything has its place. 'Definitely speeding up the recovery process. Looks around twenty per cent benefit at least.'

We research sleep engineering – we mess with the patterns of patients' sleep waves, all with the hope of a treatment for trauma.

I nod my approval as I glance over to my desk. Unlike other people's, there are no photographs pinned on my board. No picture of my mother whose grave lies unvisited. No picture of my brother who I haven't seen for so long to avoid a reminder of what I did.

Some people's traumas can't be cured by sleep.

Heidi squeezes my shoulder. 'Take it easy, you need a blast of those sweet, low waves.' She winks – most of her research focuses on the benefits of increased non-REM sleep, particularly the long, slow waves of deep sleep. Her kindness stirs something painful in me that dissipates into my toes as I press them into the ends of my boots. 'I'm off to the gym before bed.'

Heidi stands in front of me for one beat longer than I expect, as if there's more she needs to say. Since my return to work earlier this year, we've danced around the topic of what made me so unwell. It's not safe to discuss here. Then she swishes up her leather bag and is gone.

Through the open office door, sounds of night staff departure and day staff arrival mark another cycle completed. The less sleep I have, the more I feel these cycles physically: a churning. Day to night, slow to fast, here to gone. But like wheels, they keep me moving forwards. There's nothing for me in the opposite direction.

Ben – one of the sleep lab technicians – pops his head around the door. He always awaits an invitation into the office, no matter how many times I welcome him and his data. I beckon him in.

'Good morning, Christie. I've transferred the night's readings into file R224. Subject A became tearful at 03.34am with extended sleep latency and wakefulness after sleep onset. Shall I place him on your waiting list?'

My tension softens at his sleep speak. I'm at home here.

Ben is an owl. Focused, wise and made for the night. In the morning hours he seems out of place, his eyes dart about even more than usual. I imagine his head rotating one hundred and eighty degrees to check whether the crowd of staff in the lobby has dispersed yet. The reddish hue in his short beard warms his face. He's had that maroon cardigan since I first started here – a stark contrast to my boss Dr Harry Curzon in his Armani suits who strides through the building.

I'm drifting. Chains link one thing to another in my sleepy stupor. Ben moves his weight between his feet, ready to head home.

'I'm not working on that trial at the moment,' I say, as my body stiffens back into armour mode. Neither of us mention that I'm still on light duties and only permitted three therapy patients. The rest of my time is taken up with the drudgery of writing research reports. I'm lucky to still be employed by Somni at all – it's usually one strike and you're out. Not only out of the company but out of the job market across the whole of London, if the rumours I've heard are true. Those who leave rarely do so without a story breaking about them online soon after: truth or smear, it's impossible to know.

'You look different today.' Ben speaks his mind which means I can trust him. He can see how battered by sleep deprivation I am. But his honesty could be the end of him one of these days. How much longer can I cope with the wretched insomnia before it comes to the attention of those at the head of Somni?

Ben points to his left eye, then right.

'Ahh, you mean my new glasses! The woman in the shop said thick black frames were more professional than wire.'

Ben blinks his acceptance of this new version of me.

'They suit you. It's good to have you back at work, Christie. You're good at your job. You can focus on being a researcher now rather than being a research participant.'

My heart does one of those uncomfortable double-beats that the doctor said are palpitations. Normal. Harmless.

'Good researchers produce as well as analyse data,' comes out of my mouth automatically, learnt as dutifully as a prayer. The expectations are clear: as research department employees, we should volunteer to take part in any sleep studies at short notice.

He hesitates, a small frown creases his forehead. 'That's not typical for a research post.'

I don't tell him that I've already found that out by using online research forums under a pseudonym while I was on sick leave. There isn't a single other company or research lab that contracts its research staff to also be participants in studies. It doesn't fit with choice and consent.

'It's what I signed up to,' I say, miming a signature in the air to communicate what I need to without giving away anything that could be audio-recorded. I can't risk the conversation moving on to a dangerous topic such as ethics while we are in the office. Dangerous for more than one reason: to now-me and past-me. 'I've got a patient soon, I better get ready.'

Ben places his hand on the door handle. 'It's time for me to go home. Goodbye, Christie.'

I feel so heavy on the chair. I lift my feet off the ground to check I still can, then feel ridiculous for testing it out. My constant doubt drains me. *Can't you try to look normal, for God's sake.*

There's a shift inside at Ben's absence; I wish he was the type of person who said everything was going to be all right, even when it wasn't.

I push up on my heavy limbs to head over to the therapy room to prepare. In the foyer, the sheen of polished tiles hurts my eyes. I forbid a yawn and try to focus.

Photographs line the walls with images of models who smile as they sleep. One of the company mottos is Smile for Somni. This isn't what sleep looks like for the people who come here for help. It hides from them. Or overtakes them. It makes them dream the same trauma again and again until they are terrified to close their eyes. It jolts them awake and tricks them into believing night-time horrors exist in the day.

It isn't what sleep looks like for me. Not anymore. My sweat-soaked covers and sore eyes that refuse to stay shut until an hour before my alarm goes off are evidence of that. I thought I had left all that behind when I reached my teenage years and numbed my guilt, turning myself into cool glass. But that made me vulnerable to breakage.

The lift doors are closing as I pass. A middle-aged woman with hair in a dishevelled bun and glasses on a chain around her neck stands alone. She reminds me of one of the participants from the Maximus research trial I was in a year ago. Could it be her? The trial was abandoned part way through so what's she doing here? With my go-slow brain, it's too late to call a halt to the lift. I don't have the energy to run down flights of stairs to catch up. Besides, I couldn't risk the receptionist reporting my unusual behaviour.

I stride through the corridor to try to appear sure of myself. People believe what they see. Once inside the nest of my therapy room, I shut the heavy door behind me, then flop into my black leather chair. I push my back against the padding. The arms hold me steady. A red light blinks in the top corner of the room on the video camera that records therapy sessions for research. It's not recording at the moment but the sight of it helps me to keep my composure. The threat of being observed helps me to shut off from distress, to settle into numbness. My shoulders drop. The chair feels as warm as skin behind my head; like lying on the chest of someone safe.

My heart slows back down after the shock of seeing someone who looked so much like another research participant. As much as I don't wish to recall the impact of being in Maximus, it gnaws at me for attention. All the changes to my thinking and behaviour. And then a black hole of memory where I lost two weeks of time, my boyfriend, my life as I knew it. For the second time, I lost who I was.

I push the thoughts back. I need to focus. Perhaps that lady wasn't from Maximus at all; it could have been another older woman with similar style? My memory plays tricks on me. I let my eyes close.

I love this job. It's a privilege to be part of research that can be life-changing for people. There won't be opportunities like this anywhere else, the HR team explained to me that my 'breakdown' will be on my record now, it's mandatory that they would have to inform any other employer. I'm lucky to be here and despite everything, I mustn't forget that. Plus, I need the money to send to Jake – it's the very least I can do for him given it's my fault that he needs it. It's too late to repair anything with my mother, so I can't fail my brother again.

With half an hour until my patient is due to arrive, I have time to reset myself before I have to break some news to her. The clock ticks its reassurance. This room is the one place where I have a purpose and feel worthwhile. I mustn't do anything to compromise that. Each therapy session I deliver gives me a new chance to reach in and heal a patient. And perhaps to heal myself a little, too.

2

I sobel sits on the therapy chair opposite me as her feet dangle above the floor. She's in her late twenties but has the dark circles beneath her eyes of a woman twice her age. Her timid voice is an apology for existing. I have unexpected news to share from her sleep study results. The weight of it presses on my chest.

'Isobel, lovely to see you again. I'm wondering if there's anything you took from our assessment session last week?'

She searches my face for the right answer. Isobel is a people-pleaser who suppresses her own needs so often that she no longer knows what they are. She was referred for adult-onset sleepwalking which puts her and her child at risk. She walked a mile from home in her nightie at two in the morning, leaving her young son home alone.

'It was helpful, yes, thank you.' She scratches the back of her hand.

'That was only the assessment, Isobel – me gathering information to help us to make a plan for therapy.' I mustn't let my nerves show about the results. Isobel's gaze is fixed on me. She's used to taking her cue from others, unable to monitor her own emotional state that's been squashed down since childhood with messages of *be grateful for what you have*. At assessment, we wrote out every significant event that had happened since she was a child onto a timeline. The end result was a crammed page full of loss, change and stressors.

'Did anything strike you as interesting or come as a surprise from the timeline of your life that we wrote out?'

Isobel's neck muscles tense as if this is a test and failure will cause rejection. Another life lesson she's picked up along the way. Her focus is on saying the right thing. That uses up so much of her attention that she hasn't registered the real meaning of my question or allowed herself to reflect. What happens in therapy is a mirror image of behaviour in the real world. She lives for others. I want to take her hand and hold it between mine. Instead, I weave my fingers together. My urge to rescue is unhelpful and would only add to her sense of being someone with no agency in life.

'There was a lot of writing on the page by the end?' she says and smiles – an attempt to neutralise a painful feeling. It's not the right time to address this pattern of disallowing her emotions, we're still in the early stages of working together.

'Yes, I noticed that too! You've actually been through a lot of tricky times in your life.' I lean forward. 'So often you were the one being strong and helping others, but it didn't really ever happen the other way around, with you getting support for yourself?'

She nods, but there's no rise in her anxiety: the sad truth of how she's lived her life always sacrificing herself for others has not yet sunk in. She sees it as simply the way things are. Inevitable. Never expecting anything or desiring to change.

'The results came in from the sleep studies.' I slow my voice down so it doesn't waver. This is important for her recovery. I feel like I'm about to crush a small creature in my palm.

'Interestingly, your results are unusual. I think it was explained to you that sleepwalking usually takes place in non-dreaming sleep? It's not acting out dreams as people presume but more like being on autopilot in half-sleep, half-wake.'

An old memory tries to resurface at this phrase but I push it down by focusing on observing Isobel as carefully as I can.

She is completely still: freeze mode. Her fear response has kicked in.

'Well, the study shows that when you appear to be sleepwalking in the lab, Isobel, you're not actually asleep at all. You're awake.'

My heart rate quickens. I need to keep it together for her – this will be helpful in the long run.

'I'm not saying you're faking it, please don't think that. Part of your mind chooses these actions, even though it doesn't seem so. The behaviour isn't really sleepwalking, it's psychogenic, probably linked to...' I can't think of the right word. Stress? Trauma? A crappy life where you've been a dogsbody to your whole family growing up, and now you're a single mum in a shitty flat and you don't know when your son's dad will next come over to threaten you, and the government has ripped away your benefits so you hardly eat because you love your son and spend what little you have on him, but also you really, really want to run away from it all? I cough to hide the delay. 'Linked to stress.'

Isobel crumples then, the mask of adulthood slips to show the girl who was never cared for. A fluttering of her pain reaches me as if it could transfer in the particles of air. *Transference* – in training, none of us questioned how that happens, the pain of one into the other. It's inexplicable but real. I hope that none of my own pain leaks out to echo back into her.

I've retreated into my head. I need to get my focus back on Isobel.

'I'd never put my Riley in danger.' She sobs into her sleeve.

Why have I got no bloody tissues in here? Why didn't I check?

'No, no, I know you wouldn't. You didn't choose it with your *thinking* mind. Your *feeling* mind acts on an impulse. An impulse to escape?' I phrase it as a question, trying to pull back from being certain. I could be wrong. I could move too fast for her. Or I could be confusing something from my own past with her longings. But on the word 'escape' she looks up and connects with me. There, right there, is an acknowledgement. It stabs me.

Now is the time to offer structure and hope. A reparenting of sorts.

'I suggest we do two things, Isobel. Firstly, we look at your stress and how to soothe your mind and body. Secondly, we let the team put video cameras in your house to see what we can learn about you from these night-time behaviours.'

For a moment, I wonder what my night-time behaviour would look like if it were being filmed. In bed, I feel how I imagine jet-lagged people do – as if the clocks and night sky tell me it's night-time but my body says no it's day, keep moving. I twist and turn, move my covers, dangle one arm, then one leg out to try to regulate my temperature changes. I long for a sense of refreshment in the morning. A video camera in my bedroom would surely show an agitated insomniac over recent months. At times, I get the sense that I *am* being watched at night, just as I'm asking Isobel to agree to. But paranoia is a known side effect of lack of sleep that I've seen often enough in my patients. It could also explain the blue car that seems to track me some days. But there are plenty of blue cars. I can't trust the messages from my mind.

'If you think so,' Isobel says, dragging me back to the present moment.

'Yes, let's start with some rehearsal in soothing your system down with some breathing techniques.' My voice sounds calm and confident despite the dryness in the back of my throat.

It feels good to have a plan for Isobel even though I don't yet have one for myself. We can figure it all out another time. I'll hold her with my voice and my hope, as I try to believe that things will get better for both of us.

3

The sash window behind my headboard rattles with each car that passes. It's too late to be considered night-time, too early for morning: a space between that should be slept through. I lean my head back towards meagre curtains that don't block the light pouring in from streetlamps.

My eyes won't stay closed. A nervous energy refuses to let me shut down and escape into the arms of sleep anymore. Knowing the mechanics of sleep doesn't seem to help me to get enough. The urge to move position is a whole-body version of restless leg syndrome, so different to my learned behaviour to keep still so as not to disturb anyone. My brother Jake used to be envious that I had the top bunk once he outgrew the cot bed in the corner of my room. He'd play 'stormy sea' where he thrashed and rocked while laughing, making the whole bunk bed creak as it shook. I tried to hide my annoyance, telling him that I was a pirate too.

'Don't be silly, Christie, you're too big to pretend,' he said. The only thing I was allowed to pretend to be was a grown-up. After that, I clenched my teeth and gave in to having no control as I waited for the storm to pass.

Now I have a place of my own and nobody else's needs to take care of, so I shouldn't complain. After my breakdown, I had to leave my ex-boyfriend Daniel's home, so Somni arranged for me to move into this central London garden flat. They've never asked me for rent.

I've never asked the true cost of this deal.

I phoned Heidi on the day I moved in, happy to have a different topic to discuss that allowed me to avoid any questions about the last two months of my erratic behaviour.

'You need a new start,' she said, not realising that London had already been my new start. Years before that, I'd tried to wipe the slate clean, knowing all along that you can bury guilt but not extinguish it.

'I'm so stupid, Heidi, I thought "garden flat" meant there'd be an actual garden.' I had visions of nurturing the sights and sounds of a meadow in the city: a haven for wild flowers and nocturnal wildlife to bring a little bit of home to London. 'The *garden* is actually a narrow yard with barely enough room for everybody in the building to dump their rubbish and recycling. The only animals I've seen are slugs.'

'A garden would be a hassle anyway. High maintenance. You could have a window box, grow your own herbs and cook properly instead of eating all that processed rubbish. It's the perfect chance to look forwards now, Christie – that's what you need.'

Heidi was always looking towards a bright future while I couldn't see what lay ahead through the fog. She had firm beliefs in the natural goodness of people and that societies only progress. I longed for the lightness of that disposition, but life had taught me otherwise. There was so much more I wanted to tell her about how unwell I'd been. Questions and concerns that I wanted us to think through together. But by then she'd been promoted to lead researcher. I didn't want to risk putting her in a difficult position. And I felt our outlooks had diverged so far from one another's that we were no longer on the same road at all. There's no point testing an allegiance when you might not like the outcome.

For now, I'm grateful to live by myself. There's safety in solitude – I can't hurt anyone if they don't get too close. I explained that to the slugs. They left me a slithering message of their intentions to remain.

My bedroom window faces onto a front wall below the pavement, with a few inches that permit views of shoes and legs. Maps of damp decorate the walls with strange new continents. Ancient plumbing rattles and bangs half the night: ghosts in the system that are determined to keep me awake. I can't quieten my mind as it jumps between scenes of my past and projections of the future.

Propped up by my pillow, I spell out the word *garden* with my fingers – a trick I learned from a leaflet after my brother Jake's brain injury. While he faced months of rehab in a unit a hundred miles away, I'd wedge myself behind the bedroom door after school and run through the sign language alphabet, the flow of movements hypnotic and soothing. I blocked thoughts and feelings about what led him to be there and my mother's sobs by focusing on the alphabet, over and over.

The word 'garden' elicits a different sense in me now than it used to; a place of binbags and disappointment instead of flowers and freedom. Words are so evocative. They can trigger an image, a sensation, a memory, each of which sets off more mental links, fanning out into a tree of expectation as we build our understanding of how things are connected. This ability to chain makes us capable of so much creativity as a species. But it can also lead to terrible events.

My passion – mine and Heidi's really – is to find ways to undo our patients' unhelpful associative patterns. Trauma takes one horrific experience and translates that into perpetual danger: it shatters assumptions of the world as a safe place. The brain develops an alert system to avoid future calamity. But this can lead to an over-sensitivity that warps smells, sights, touch, taste into a warning to get the hell out before it happens again, even when a person is safe.

One of my first patients during psychotherapy training four years ago was a young man haunted day and night by flashbacks of a car accident. As he drove to a football match with his father, a toddler ran into the road. There had been no chance to brake in time. Every detail of that day became saturated with new meaning: the light wind that blew willow branches nearby, the red shade of the child's clothes, rap music that played as the horrific scene unfolded, the smell of menthol from his father's chewing gum. Callum became triggered every time he left the house: a postman's red bag, the movement of trees along the road, a blast of a beat from oversized headphones on the Tube, a whiff of mint in a café. He stopped leaving the house. But then he couldn't tolerate the sound of his father's voice, as 'do you want a cup of tea?' twisted into 'what the hell, oh God it's a kid'. So, he stayed in his bedroom. In the end he couldn't escape at all: his mind recreated the scene each night in multisensory horror. Past became present.

I squeeze myself tight as if that can stop my own past seeping through. Unspoken confessions clog my throat.

It's nearly four in the morning. In treatment for insomnia, we advise patients to get out of bed if they are not asleep within twenty minutes but I rarely take that advice myself. Perhaps I should try it. I head to the toilet for something to do: a zig-zag route around the slugs who manage to bypass my line of deadly blue pellets no matter where I place them. I've come to accept they'll always be there.

'Trauma is a trick of the mind that turns into a trick of the body. It seems so real, so inescapable,' I say to the fattest slug, who is a metre up the magnolia wall.

I wait for a response, both relieved and disappointed not to get one. This is not a dream then, no Alice-like scene with an argumentative animal. Just another sleepless night.

The small bathroom is tiled in an avocado colour that must have been the envy of the other inhabitants of the building a few decades ago. During my time in the Maximus trial that aimed to maximise work performance – when I was in a kind of 'super-cognition' state – I couldn't be near tiles, patterns, numbers without counting. In the time it took me to have a wee, I'd figured out how many tiles it would take to cover every bathroom in the district. I've always been good at maths with the help of paper, a pen, a calculator, but last year the answers seemed to show up without effort.

I creep back to bed as if there's still somebody nearby to disturb. As much as I try not to focus on the fact there's only three hours sleep opportunity left, I can feel the anxiety gnaw at me, chasing sleep further away as the adrenaline starts to circulate around my system. This is the cruel cycle of insomnia: worry about not sleeping sets off an alarm system that rules out any chance to switch off. I turn from my side to lie flat on my back and tuck the sheets tightly around me in a cocoon, hoping the tight hold will soothe me.

Then it happens again.

An image forces its way through my weakening mental barriers. I'm in a bed. Flat on my back. A feeling of being strapped in, constrained. There's a strong smell of citrus floor cleaner. There's a torn piece of paper on the wall opposite where a map used to hang. Above me is an unusual light fitting with seven sides. I can't move my arms or legs. Paralysed. A man leans over me. It's my boss, Harry. His jaw bulges as he grinds his teeth. However hard I try, I can't get my words out: my mouth won't work, my limbs can't move. He sighs like a disappointed parent.

'Christie, you really do need to stop all this. You're off the trial and should be back to normal.' I stop battling then – there's no point.

The memory melts away and tries to take my certainty with it. Hypnogogic hallucination or dream or memory? A residue of fear lingers. A word lights up behind my eyelids. It's surrounded by red circles with a diagonal line through them. At times I hate this ability to turn thoughts into images so easily. *Danger* flashes in red within a stop sign. DANGER.

Lying on my side, I curl my legs towards my middle and hold them there. Something old and familiar presses down on me, wants to unfurl and expose my failings. Am I in danger or am I the dangerous one? I squeeze tighter to create a shell to protect my soft, slug-like underbelly from being crushed.

4

I sit in the back corner of the boardroom out of my boss's eyeline for this month's team meeting. Dr Harry Curzon is a sleep scientist and CEO of Somni. His white fringe flops forwards as he speaks. If I sketched Harry, I would use all straight lines. He's devoid of curves or softness, as is his accent: clipped and cutting. Harry has secured millions of pounds in grants and international contracts over the years which gave him the standing to take over when the company moved from university-owned to private two years before I arrived.

'What appetising breakfast gifts do you bring us today, Lois?' he asks our caterer. The company has a supposed focus on staff health via smoothies, gluten-free baked goods and superfood salads. All food is provided at team events and there's an expectation to eat and be grateful. There's the possibility that our reactions and eating habits are being logged by team leaders. Lois beams like she's addressing a retired film star. Harry is near-handsome with a charm that means all eyes are on him.

The curly kale brioche makes me feel sick. None of the teas smell like tea. Everything seems defined by what it isn't: wheat-free, caffeine-free, guilt-free. Lois presents each dish to us in turn, chanting a spell of ingredients. Thirty staff members join in a game-show style ooh and ahh as required. Across the room, Ben unwraps his sandwiches with no care for others' judgement. He folds the foil over neatly. If he wasn't so diligent and good at his job, he would have been discarded years ago for not joining in with the Somni Way. Near the head of a long table, Heidi brushes crumbs from her jacket while enthusing over the health benefits of a smoothie the colour and texture of vomit. A semi-circle of male scientists surround her. They nod at every word as they watch her fingers stroke down her lapels.

Harry makes his way around the room as he shakes hands. My colleagues' backs straighten, their smiles ready to please him. He's the kind of man who can make you feel like you're the most important person in the room for sixty seconds before he turns his attentions away and you fade without his light. Julia is an assistant professor at the university who joined the company part-time recently. She almost bows when Harry speaks to her.

Although Harry is affable and encouraging, I'm wary of him. There's a hunger to his speeches that suggests he'd do anything to succeed. When I first joined Somni, his drive was invigorating and well-humoured. Now and then in recent months I've seen his mask slip. He can't switch off. His speech is more pressured, his gestures over the top and he occasionally barks at staff rather than schmoozing them into working harder for him. Not that anyone else seems to notice. In Somni offices, Harry has that status of a president who can do no wrong.

Little white plates with the Somni logo sit in most people's hands or laps. But Harry hasn't taken a bite. Usually, he makes a show of tasting each item like a head chef praising his team. His glass seems to contain only water, not one of the smoothies or juices. It's unlikely that Harry would be on a diet as he's tall and slender with a great love of healthy food. His cheekbones appear a little more prominent than usual with a slight twitch above his right eye. The rest of the staff chat and laugh as if nothing at all is different from usual. I learned to watch carefully long before my therapy training. I never want to miss the signs again – the stakes are too high.

'Settle down, all, and prepare for the PK!' Harry takes his seat at the head of the table to man the video equipment. The Pecha Kucha is a super-speed version of what is basically a PowerPoint presentation with time limits. It's treated with the levity of prayer. A speaker has twenty slides which display for twenty seconds each. One saving grace is it cuts off those who love the sound of their own voice. So far, not only have I managed to avoid getting roped into presenting, I've never actually said the phrase Pecha Kucha out loud as I'm unsure about the correct pronunciation.

We once had a Somni Soup Off where staff brought in bizarre varieties of vegetable soup. I made the mistake of saying I prefer to throw things into a pan than follow a cookbook. Receptionist Anja had laughed to the point of smudging the Egyptian curl of her eyeliner. She led me around the staff telling me to repeat 'cookbook' with my long 'oo' sound from Staffordshire. I laughed with them – louder than them – and allowed myself to be court jester. Then I slipped out to the toilets and heaved up dark purple beetroot and ginger soup, scrubbed my hands without looking in the mirror, and vowed in future to rehearse my words before I let them loose, just as I had to after Jake's injury. I must make myself worthy of London.

I try to follow the presentations but fatigue skews my concentration. Words and speakers merge into one another. As each slide moves to the next, I focus on the Somni logo in the top right-hand corner: a tightly packed bunch of sleep waves called a spindle. These help us to lay down our memories of learning from the day. As each new piece of information is displayed on the screen and a variety of voices drone, I feel grounded by the unchanging nature of that logo.

Julia takes her place to speak. I try to revive my attention. The title of her presentation stirs my guts: Ethics of the Unknown in Sleep Engineering. That phrase – ethics of the unknown – scratches at something long buried and scarred over. I mustn't let it.

I roll my shoulders and stretch my neck one way, then the other, like Jane Fonda in my mum's old workout video that she insisted on watching rather than switching to DVD. We'd eat dinner on our knees in front of the television, counting along to stretches and bends without doing any ourselves. Mum would shout words of encouragement to *keep at it* and *push it, Jane*. Jake and I chewed and gawped as we witnessed the rare energy outbursts from Mum. I'd secretly stretch my toes in time with the aerobics.

'You're not supposed to stretch your neck like that, it's dangerous,' said Mum to the screen, pleased to feel superior to Jane as she sat in her dressing gown at four on a Monday afternoon. She saw the possible danger in everything, except when it mattered. But I could just as easily say that about my younger self.

Applause interrupts my thoughts. Julia has finished the final presentation of the meeting. Time has hopscotched. Did I doze a little? A quick check of my colleagues fails to clarify whether anybody saw my lapse.

'What we must remain vigilant to within our studies,' says Julia, 'is the possibility that altering participants' sleep architecture over a significant period of time may result in unintended – perhaps even undesirable – side effects. We should investigate and remain cautious.' She's spent all her working life in academia. She doesn't yet understand the Somni take: there are no problems, only solutions to be tested out.

I'm in that half-awake state where my body seems to do as it pleases without my instructions. I don't notice that I'm nodding vigorously to Julia's statement until she smiles at me.

'I'd love to hear your thoughts on the matter, forgive me for not knowing your name.' Julia holds out her palm to me in invitation. In my peripheral vision, I can see team members have swivelled in their seats to face me. I want to swallow but there's no saliva left in my mouth.

'Christie, research psychotherapist.' My voice doesn't sound like mine. Or rather, it doesn't sound like my London-voice, my professional cloak. It's the schoolgirl squeak that followed me from primary school into my twenties. At fourteen, a middle-aged man had given each of us a careers questionnaire to complete that had a duplication sheet behind for scoring as if computers hadn't yet been invented. In my one-to-one appointment with him, he glanced down at the sheet with my scores before asking what I wanted to do when I left school. I didn't want to give the wrong answer but couldn't see his notes. Social worker, teacher, nurse. He clicked his pen nib up and down as he awaited my response.

'I'd like to help people,' I said, my voice even softer than usual, slightly higher pitched as my throat tightened. That wasn't quite right. I *needed* to help people, as reparation. But he wouldn't understand that. Nobody would. Because nobody knew why.

'Excellent choice. Plenty of work around these parts for care or shop work and so on. Home economics is one of the options you might consider for GCSE.'

I knew he was the expert, so I slipped out of the room leaving my plans for further study behind on the chair for Suzy Chambers to pick up as she swished past me. Being the quiet girl is so easy that you forget how to be anything else. It facilitates careful control over thoughts and feelings.

Harry coughs and pulls me back into the room, my face thankfully neutral out of habit. Julia needs to forget about my nodding along. There are ethical issues in all research projects, it's my specialist subject in a way. I painstakingly write a section in each research paper we publish to show they were considered, anxious to never make a slip-up around consent again. But there's an unspoken rule at Somni that we only share the positive together: the decaffeinated, allergen-free, organic version of what we do. I catch Ben's eye across the room and crave his certainty. He moves one hand up to his chin as if thinking, then places one finger over his lips as a message to me.

Silence for Somni.

'Nothing in particular. I mean, it was interesting. What you said.' I can tell that I'm on the fifth floor, that I'm dangerously high above the city, waiting to fall. Julia opens her mouth to respond but before she can, Harry calls out from the back of the room.

'Yes certainly, we must hear from you and your important work as a cog in our machine, Christie. Perhaps you could present at our annual conference.' It's not said as a question but as an end to the matter. I exhale a lungful of air.

Chatter fills the room as people disperse back to offices or home to sleep. Harry places his hand on Heidi's shoulder as they leave the room. She has her arms crossed over her body in the same way I do when I want to cover the curve of my stomach, not that she has that problem. Heidi glances at me as they leave the room in discussion and that sick feeling returns.

They're talking about me.

Ben takes a convoluted route towards the exit of the boardroom. By impulse, I join him near the recycling bins away from most staff. He posts items into the correct bins and whispers.

29

'I need to speak with you, away from here, something's not right.'

I fold a blank piece of paper into the yellow bin. 'I have a patient next. Lunchtime?'

Ben is surely tired after a whole night at work but he nods. This must be serious.

'Room at the back of the library, one o'clock.'

Then he slips in-between chairs that are out of place without setting them right and leaves the room: his usual order forfeited for chaos.

5

The solid squareness of firefighter Mike's shoulders allows his strength to show through the distress. He's in his fifties, but I imagine he could pick me up and sling me over his shoulder, charge down five flights of stairs, and not be out of breath. He was surely born to do the job. But tragedy often breeds further tragedy: Mike hasn't been able to work for the last eleven months since a terrible fire that caused multiple fatalities in his crew. I'd trust him to do a good job if he returned to work; I'd trust him to save someone I loved.

Nobody pulled me from our house fire aged twelve, I coughed a way out by myself. Mum's discarded cigarette downstairs had been far away from me in my bedroom giving me time to get out of a window. But a firefighter saved my little brother Jake from his makeshift tent in the living room and my mum from the kitchen chair where she'd slumped to sleep. I never saw Jake's rescuer, didn't even realise he *had* been rescued for a whole day – no one thought to tell me. My whispered prayers for him to still be alive were answered. I had no idea at the time that it wouldn't be the same version of my brother I'd ever see again.

I catch myself travelling back twenty years in my mind and press pause on the virtual time machine of my mind. The air thickens as I struggle to inhale. *Here's Mike, Mike, focus on this moment, don't be selfish.* I press my toes into the carpet to ground myself, then breathe in his stale scent. There's a hint of woodsmoke even though he's not been on active duty. Mike's hands tremble slightly, lips held tightly together as if to stop any unplanned words from seeping out.

'The nightmares are the same,' he says, as he shrugs away their significance. He looks at the wall, occasionally flicking his eyes to meet mine. Mike is respectful, but I can feel the doubt he has about therapy doing him any good. There's a barrier. It's getting stronger. His nightmares spill over into daytime flashbacks: a terrifying reliving that brings back not just the images of what happened but a bodily memory of the physical symptoms. It's ruining his life.

'How did you get on with the breathing exercises to help with panic?' Please say it helped. Let there be some change. As we head towards lunchtime, my energy supply is draining fast.

Mike drops his head down. His body is rigid with tension but he doesn't notice. Or doesn't care. We've spent weeks working on ways to stabilise his anxiety to a level that wouldn't reach panic, but once he leaves the therapy room, he does nothing to change his suffering. I hold back an urge to shake his shoulders. Despite my positive regard for him, I notice my frustration build. His excuses wrapped into reasons come. I've already missed some of what he's saying.

'...and then the pain in my shoulder, I needed to distract myself, and not had the time with doing jobs in the house, the guttering...'

Is it him or is it me? If his therapist was someone with years more experience and training would things be different for him? His doubt turns into my doubt. I don't have the typical trajectory of a therapist. After five years as a research assistant, Somni sponsored my psychotherapy night classes. That gave me the chance to change my job title to include therapist four years ago, but I feel like a fraud. No certificate in the world can change that.

'Mike.' I wait for him to lift his head. If I get him to tap into self-compassion, it could help him to help himself. 'I wonder what would happen if you were kind to yourself in this moment and stated what it is that you need and deserve.'

Why did I say *deserve* this early? I should have stuck with *need*. I daren't hear the wrong answer, so start rambling to fill the space before he says something that neither of us want to hear. 'Maybe your needs are to feel safe in your own body, to feel more in control, so you can think clearly enough to see that none of this was your fault – you did your best but sometimes people can't be rescued, no matter what.' In that last statement, I'm unsure if I'm talking about the fire in which he lost two colleagues and three old people in a care home, or if I'm talking about him and this therapy.

'I don't know,' he says, voice dry and cracked. More blocking. I can't help him if he keeps me out. The sleep therapy in our labs is due to commence shortly after my work-up and could offer him a different future. I want to finish our review on a hopeful note. This session is supposed to be a formality – a final catch-up before the ReStory Sleep Therapy trial begins in earnest with my sleep lab colleagues. Mike has spent several nights in the lab to get used to being wired up for monitoring through the night. The typical timings of his nightmares have been mapped out. At the appropriate time, a series of tones will be played to prompt his dreaming mind to gain control of the nightmare using his newly taught lucid dream skills: dream control for therapeutic purposes.

'The ReStory techniques will help you recreate that day in

your mind, to give it a different ending than the one that happened in real life. Because you'll be in REM sleep, the amygdala in your brain that is linked to feeling fear won't be highly activated like when you remember the event during the day. Rehearsing the different ending without being scared should help those painful memories to be filed away properly to reduce your flashbacks and nightmares.' It's a brilliant new trauma therapy and I'm thankful it means that I don't have to talk about the trauma with Mike myself, only ways for him to try to reduce his distress while awake.

Mike's lips curl downwards in a micro expression, then back to neutral. Was that disgust?

'A happy-ever-after ending in a dream won't bring anyone back.' His voice box is squeezed as the anxiety increases, likely with anger too, at me and my lack of understanding. He won't tell me though, perhaps won't even be aware of his frustration – he's too busy being angry with himself. Self-attack, self-blame, self-sabotage: a trio of destruction.

Mike rubs his thighs in agitation.

'And as for what I deserve...'

Oh God, it's coming, I've messed up here. If he says what I think he's going to say, I'll have to instruct the team to pull him from the ReStory sleep trial for not being ready. His rigid body melts into a slump.

'I deserve all of it, Christie, all the symptoms. I went in the wrong direction at the care home, I didn't save those guys: it was my fault they died.'

I can't make him see that's not true. He couldn't have known the opposite direction held danger for those he wanted to rescue, and I don't know what can help him. I hold my breath and vow not to cry until he leaves the room.

I can breathe easier once I'm out of the building. I take the Golden Jubilee Bridge and gulp the cool air that sweeps across the river. The mild ache in my thighs isn't unpleasant, it helps me feel fully alert. Charing Cross library is one of the few remaining council-run libraries that still seem stuck in a pleasant time warp rather than transformed into a multipurpose glass-and-steel community centre. Two arched windows beneath red brick sit beside the entrance: an invitation to step into a different kind of hush than at Somni that comes from a shared reverence for reading, not a shared fear of repercussions. I emailed Somni reception to say that I had some study to do and would need a longer lunch than usual. That way, Ben and I could meet here – fifteen minutes' walk from work – with little chance of someone from the company being nearby. It's not just the books that I love. Libraries feel like a hub of any community, a place that's genuinely for everyone.

'More than a hand,' is what Jake said in awe, wriggling his fingers when I told him we were allowed to take six books out of the library at a time. He was too young to follow the stories I loved but so excited by each illustration or rhyme in his that I read each evening. I wanted six for myself, every fairy-tale collection I could get my hands on, but Jake didn't have his own library card which needed a parent's signature to be approved. The old-fashioned books were the best: hardback with fancy letters in gold underneath the dust jacket. Stella Markin from my class was chewing gum by the big clock in the children's book department. We sat on bright orange pouffes at a table already too small for my legs to fit under by the Tree of Life tapestry we loved.

'You've got baby books,' she said, pointing down at the pile Jake and I had collected – three each to be fair.

'They're Jake's,' I said, rolling my eyes, not wanting to glance down at my Hans Christian Andersen collection in case my red cheeks gave me away. Jake looked up, puzzled. Then he pulled the top three books one by one and placed them in front of me, leaving the picture books next to him. He smiled, triumphant in his sharing. Stella stretched the chewing gum out in front her, pulled it back into her mouth and made it pop in a bubble. That sound was a like a gunshot to my guts. I grabbed Jake's three books and stumbled to the library counter, pulling his arm so he didn't try to collect mine.

I shake off the memory as I walk towards the rear of the building, wanting to recapture my love of libraries. I let my fingers run over the bumps of book spines along the shelf. I've always liked the feel of hardback editions. I become as solid as their covers in this place rather than feeling like an actress in a film.

It's a few minutes before I'm due to meet Ben. I find myself twiddling the Somni logo badge pinned to my top. I daren't take it off – we're not allowed to remove them during working hours even if we leave the office. It might not be too long before we're expected to wear them at weekends, at home, on our pyjamas. A reminder of who we belong to.

I don't wish to spark suspicion, so dip my head down to a book that contains images of bridges from around the world. As my brain whizzes forwards to an invented future where Ben reveals one terrible thing after another to me, I pull back to focus on each steel triangle that forms part of a robust bridge.

When I started at Somni as a research assistant, I did a run of night shifts to see the sleep labs in action. Ben took the time to teach me, as I was the only one around without a degree. He'd been obsessed with the mechanics of sleep since he was child. While we sat in the staff lab watching the rolling results of various tests and sleep data emerge on the computer, he explained the poetry of both the words and the waves. On the screen in front of us he pointed out changes in wave patterns as a patient moved from one sleep realm to another. It was a language to him, a story of what was unfolding in people's minds. He showed me the long, lazy curves of slow-wave sleep that help memories to be stored. The excitable patterns of rapid-eye-movement sleep showed how busy the mind was creating dreams and processing emotions from the day. I loved the cycling of it, the yin and yang of how we are all programmed to get the right balance of what we need from the night. Until it goes wrong.

Ben arrives precisely on time. He glances around before taking a seat opposite me at the table. Several metres from us sits an elderly gentleman reading the newspaper. A lady with a book trolley returns items to their correct location. We wait a minute until she is out of earshot.

'It's as you said last July, Christie: there are anomalies in the data.' I have absolutely no recall of any concerns I raised last July during the Maximus trial, one month before my breakdown. 'Standard protocols for the sleep laboratories are being changed from above with no consultation. Usually I complete my work based on the short instructions delivered for the week ahead. However, now I've reviewed full data on the system from months before projects I've worked on, I believe that decisions are being made on grounds other than a scientific basis.'

I scan the book titles nearby as if they could prompt me to recall past conversations with Ben. 'It's a company aiming to make a profit. It's not the same as when the labs were owned by the university. For all Harry's failings, his expansion of services probably saved us from going under. But he had to speed trials through to meet demand.' I don't want to admit that I can't remember what I found out last year. 'What do you think I was right about?'

'As Julia pointed out in her presentation – there could be negative consequences to aspects of what we do that aren't acknowledged.'

This feels too close to a two-decade-old secret.

'So, I raised this as a worry nearly a year ago but nobody took it seriously.' Ben flinches. Did I sound judgemental? Damn it.

'I prefer to gather all the facts before I reach a conclusion. What you said was plausible but the evidence wasn't necessarily... reliable.' He struggles to find his words, twisting his body in discomfort. 'It was potentially affected by how you presented at the time.'

He means I was an unreliable witness. By the later stages of Maximus I was sleepless, manic, insatiable for facts and figures. Like a woman deemed hysterical in Victorian times, all faints and accusation as the men tutted.

'Didn't you believe it?'

Didn't he believe *me*?

'I hardly saw you, Christie. And from what was said at the team meeting, you were quite unwell. I should have been more diligent and investigated further. I'm sorry.'

I clutch on to the sides of the wooden chair. They talked about me at team meetings. How could they have not? Seeing me go from that quiet research therapist to a manic worker, demanding the labs bring me more data to process that I needed no calculator for, refusing to leave the office when handover time came because I never felt the need to stop. To sleep. The irony would make it funny if I hadn't ended up so unwell. Was I always destined to tip over the edge in penance or was it directly linked to Maximus?

That eerie feeling that I'm being observed returns. Each

shelf could be a place to hide. Each book a potential source for a microphone. So ridiculous but it sets me on edge.

'What was said about me at the team meeting while I was on sick leave?'

'Harry informed us that you'd experienced a breakdown. That the company knew that it was a risk factor from your screening and family history, but that Somni would continue to support you. We were told that you'd asked for your difficulties to never be spoken of with you. "Discouraged" was the word he used. We were *discouraged* from discussing your health or involvement in any research.'

We both know what that means in Somni-speak.

'I never said that.'

Can I be certain of that?

'Once Julia gave her talk and you reacted so strongly, I realised that your note had truth in it.'

'My note?'

Ben pats his pocket as he nods, as if he could pull out a ten-month-old note right now. I'll never forgive myself for keeping my mouth shut when I shouldn't have, no matter how many years pass. Did I try to speak the truth this time? I don't recall it.

'Don't you remember that you placed it in my hand as you walked past me before you went on sick leave? It said *Maximus: eyes open, mouth shut.*' His confusion at me not recalling makes me feel so stupid. My strength saps. He continues, looking down at the book in front of him as he speaks. 'I took that to mean that you really didn't want to talk about it. But that might not be the reason you wrote it down.'

No. Maybe I was fearful that we would be overheard. I wasn't telling him to keep his mouth shut. I was telling him to open his eyes to what was going on. I found something out that I couldn't share. God knows what, I have no memory of writing a note. But whatever I uncovered was a threat to

Somni. And knowing it became a threat to me. I check my watch.

'I better head back.'

Ben's fingers rest on the open book at one end of a photograph of a tarnished bridge. Mine at the other end. There is a moment of peace as we sit this way before I gather up my belongings and leave for the office.

6

I jump at the ping of an email as it arrives into my inbox. The sender is Julia. Perhaps a copy of her presentation slides that I accidentally showed an interest in. Strangely, it comes from her personal email rather than her work account.

> Dear Christie. Good to briefly meet you at the team meeting. If you ever wish to discuss ethics further, please do feel free to contact me.

The ambiguity of it is unsettling. There's no way she could know anything about my ancient ethical dilemma back home with Mum, she must be referring to Somni. I rummage about in my bag for a chocolate bar, then sink my teeth into the caramel softness. She could mean in general terms for my research reports. Or does she know something about Maximus? Is there a reason that she chose to email from her non-Somni account beyond the fact that she works part-time? It's likely that our messages are monitored by the company. But if so, surely our inbox as well as outbox is vulnerable to be spied on. I delete her message so there's nothing to trace, then again from the deleted items file to be sure. Only after I've removed it do I realise that I never made a note of her personal email address.

An automated reminder pops up on my screen. Lunchtime yoga. God, I'm late. The sessions are mandatory. I missed the latest work night out to practise making 'clean cocktails' while raising money for a children's hospice – a bizarre combination that I couldn't bring myself to join in with. It wouldn't be a good idea to be the only employee not to attend the yoga sessions. I grab my mat and run.

Friday afternoon is not a great time for continuing to give therapy to Mia but the appointment is made to fit her university schedule. It's not that I dread seeing her but it takes a lot of energy that I don't have. I can guess what my clinical supervisor Dr Elizabeth Field would say. 'Interesting that you say it's *not* dread, and yet the word *dread* is the one that came to mind?' Perhaps I do dread seeing her.

Mia's parents pay a lot of money for her to receive therapy. She attends our first trial of sleep therapy to reduce risk-taking in young people by treating insomnia. The theory is that their judgement and risk-assessment skills, which don't fully develop until the mid-twenties, are further impaired by a lack of regulating sleep. We've already covered the basics of sleep hygiene. She had little interest in dealing with the underlying sleep deficit which seems more to do with life choices than insomnia.

I'm not convinced that Mia's motivation to engage in therapy is genuine: her parents have threatened to cut off her lavish funds if she doesn't rein in her impulsive behaviour. This push to attend for someone else's satisfaction bothers me, but I must do my job. Mia appears to enjoy detailing to me her raucous binges of sex, drugs and drink with no urge to change that lifestyle. I'm part of her please-the-parents game. There's little hope for real progress. But she's signed on the dotted line, so I have to offer a service whether I'm expecting good outcomes for her or not.

Mia sits on the chair with her legs bent into shapes that shouldn't be possible. She catches my curiosity at her posture.

'I'm supple,' she says and winks. Her mouth pouts in ruby red that matches her shoes. I bought red heels from a charity shop once although not as ridiculously high as Mia's. My mother threw them out without asking, despite the fact that I was over eighteen by then. I lived at home until I was twenty-one. She told me that I'd get mistaken for a *lady of the night* if I wore those shoes in public so they never left the catwalk of my bedroom. Mum bought me second-hand cherry red Dr Martens to replace them, which she wore herself when I left them in their box in silent protest.

'So, what's today about then?' Mia wraps her dark hair around one finger. There's a streak of purple in her fringe that wasn't there last session. If she scrubbed the pink paste from her skin, let her eyebrows be a normal width, pulled her backcombed hair into a ponytail, she could be a model.

'Mia,' I say, as I ensure my voice comes out kinder than the judgement in my head. 'Remember we discussed that it's up to you what we focus on – not me, not your parents. How about we review one problem area at a time?'

'Here's my problem area!' She rolls up a black strappy top to reveal her flat stomach, then inhales to display her lower ribs. 'I can't get in my size eight jeans anymore. It's all podgy.'

I don't take the bite to contradict her.

I've never looked like Mia. 'Built like a swimmer who can't swim' was how Mum described my frame. She never realised that so many of her phrases hurt me. I'd sweep coloured scarves around my neck whatever the weather to mask my naturally broad shoulders.

Mia pokes at her skin with a fingertip like a butcher before the first cut. Her tiny waist would fit into one leg of my jeans. She lets her T-shirt fall back down, then folds her legs into a lotus position. I shift in my seat, a jolt of pain in my back as I pull my legs under the chair.

'I'm kidding, relax, Christie. God, you need a drink. Might help you let go.'

Let go of what? It wouldn't surprise me if she's carrying alcohol in her furry shoulder bag. I don't know what kids drink these days. I'm supposed to be into elderflower and gin cocktails according to Heidi, but I haven't had a drink in a year. I'm drunk enough with sleep deprivation – straight to hangover with none of the fun.

'What kind of job is this anyway?' She can't help but flutter mascara-heavy eyelashes at me as she pairs insult with flirtation. 'Seems a strange thing to do, to sit here all day long telling people that their lives suck. Does that mean that yours doesn't?'

She looks me up and down. I should address her pattern of degrading me to help her see what function it fulfils. Is this how she boosts herself? But I don't want to enter into anything at a deeper level with her. That's not what she's looking for. And not what I want to open myself up to.

I change tack. 'Do you consider your own drinking to be a problem, Mia?' She rolls her eyes in response. I'm digging deep for a little compassion towards her but all I can find is the urge to tell her parents to ground her. I imagine snipping those credit cards in front of her now, gold and silver shards dropping down as she looks on in horror. 'I'm not sure how I can be helpful to you,' I say. If her parents won't give her boundaries, I will. 'There doesn't seem to be anything for us to work towards.'

There's a relief in saying it at last. The dynamic shifts. A trace of concern passes over Mia's brow before she tightens her face back to selfie mode. I enjoy that more than I should.

'I want to have fun, live my life, but my parents want to control me.' She whinges herself into victim role.

'Well, I don't want to play out that same pattern, Mia. I'm not here to control you or tell you what to do. You're an adult. But did you notice, when we started you asked me what we were doing today? If you want control back then you have to be prepared to take responsibility.'

Mia juts out her chin. A smirk ruins her face. 'You sound like my mother. I bet that's what yours used to say to you.'

She's right. My mum had her own 'three R's' that were nothing to do with learning: Respect, Responsibility and Reap What You Sow. However hard I tried to fulfil the former two as a replacement mother, I failed. I've been living the latter ever since I realised what I'd done.

Mia has pressed my buttons through this whole appointment. I can barely wait for my next supervision session to unpack this and see if there's any way to repair it. Or to get permission from my supervisor to stop seeing Mia completely. I'm not going to book her in for another month, maybe she'll get bored with the game and stop coming.

'Why don't we take a more practical approach, Mia. Do a cost-benefit analysis to work out the price you pay for your choices?' I must keep my cool, stay professional. From the corner of the room, the video camera light glows with judgement.

Mia leans forward. I try to maintain a therapeutic silence, leave the space and time for her to think and decide on what next. My skin prickles. I've stared at her so long to hide my desire to leave the room that her face starts to blur. She has an intensity that makes me uncomfortable in my own skin. My urge to run away from her, Somni, London strengthens. But I'd still be stuck with the cause of all my problems: I can't run from myself.

'We can do that if you want to, make a nice table with a plus and minus sign, but you know what?' She sucks in her bottom lip, then lets it unroll slowly back into place. 'Some things are worth the cost.'

7

There isn't enough work to fill my time as my therapy caseload is still limited, and I've written up all my research reports. I need to prove myself fully fit for work so I can get my complete patient list back and go back to enjoying my job. I head out of the office along the network of corridors, hoping to find purpose along the way. *Useless, they'll get rid of you for being incompetent. Who wants a therapist who can't handle giving therapy?*

Along the first corridor is one room in mid-refurbishment as it changes from a meeting space to a nursery. Somni prides itself on being an employer that nobody ever wishes to leave. This latest development is to provide onsite care for employees' kids from three months to four years. Probably a way to get staff back more quickly from parental leave. No excuses for part-time working when you can pop in to see your baby in a lunch break. Somni's view of staff pregnancy was made clear at our induction. I'd sat with new starters to the research division, Gemma, Helen and Sarah, in the boardroom in our second week. One of the team leaders had called the session 'onboarding' and clarified that there was an expectation that we'd keep our wombs empty for a minimum of five years if we were 'authentic and agile team players'. I didn't have any plans to rush into motherhood, but Sarah spun her wedding ring around and around as we were warned that our choices should be in line with company values.

I push open the door to take a closer look. I have to admit they've done a good job of the décor, all rainbows and jungle animals, exactly how I would have designed a nursery. The toys look expensive, a combination of old-school wooden puzzles and top-of-the-range electronic interactive pads embedded into low table surfaces. I resist the urge to squat on a tiny chair, squeezing play clay between my fingers and sniffing the scent that soothed me back when nursery was a more pleasant place to be than home. A workman in blue overalls with a tool box under his arm pushes past me to get into the room.

'It's not ready yet,' he says, taking the weight of the door to close it once I step back.

I mumble an apology. Once the door is shut, he passes across the room with his tools. I'm on the outside looking in. A pain presses on my chest, tries to move up into a feeling. Not now, I won't let it. I continue along the corridor, humming 'Rock-a-bye Baby' to myself. When Jake was tiny and got up early in the mornings, I'd panic that he'd wake Mum and set off one of her headaches. I sang nursery rhymes and invented ballet moves across the bedroom as a show for him. His podgy hands would clap no matter what I did, a full-throated laugh the faster I twirled. *When the bough breaks, the cradle will fall.* That song used to give me nightmares of Jake falling down, down, down from a tree as Mum slept below. I never guessed that I'd be the cause of the nightmare coming true. I stop humming but can't quite shake off my unease as I continue down the corridor.

Research rooms that are not used for sleep studies have windows. I peer into them as I pass. At the first computer lab, I pause to watch participants press touch screens. There are so many studies that run concurrently I've lost track of what projects Somni are currently focusing on. I've been proud to work on studies to improve sleep for people with chronic pain, to reduce night terrors and to ensure the best types of sleep for healthcare staff who work shift patterns. I must pay more attention to new areas of work that I'm not involved with. If I look hard enough, I might rediscover my love and passion for what we do. I run my finger along the white-tiled walls which are flecked with glitter, the roughness making little scratches in my skin.

In a seat closest to the window, a young guy in a hoodie with his hair tied back frowns in concentration as his finger wavers between yes and no on the screen in front of him. He's too slow. The responses disappear and the screen fills with another red front door, this time with a gold letterbox to the right and a plant on the doorstep. 'Have you seen this image before?' flashes before him. He can't recall. I wonder how long he's been sleep deprived for in this study. How many red doors swirl around his mind from the original learning period a few days earlier? He looks defeated, jabs at 'no', then sits back in the chair and tips his head to the ceiling. There's likely to be the promise of more cash for higher accuracy, otherwise lack of motivation rather than sleep deficit might cloud the results. But with his current craving for rest, perhaps his sense of what is important has changed. In the most challenging of times, only survival matters.

It was a computer lab similar to this in Liverpool where I'd taken the entrance tests to get into Somni at ground level. I'd worked in cafés and the town market in the Staffordshire Moorlands for years after school. It seemed like enough of an escape: meeting different people, using my brain to add up the cost of items or remember large orders. On the bric-a-brac stall, I loved each item with its unspoken history. Mum called it an 'outdoors charity shop, doing nothing for charity' but even she had a fondness for it, I think, appreciating the occasional gifts I laid on her bed wrapped in lavender tissue paper. We sold heavy bracelets, little charms of dogs or hearts that once hung from long-lost chains, jewellery boxes with ballerinas that danced to the 'Sugar Plum Fairy', engagement rings with missing diamonds. Every item was imperfect: tarnished, chipped, unable to fasten. Unique.

My ex-boyfriend Daniel printed details of the job opportunity at Somni and told me I should apply as it could be our ticket to London as a couple. He worked in a specialist branch of finance so all his promotion opportunities were in the capital. I never told him that I didn't want to move to London as it seemed selfish to block his aspirations for the both of us. I didn't have to – surely, I had no chance of passing the tests for such a prestigious firm.

Daniel was naturally serious and striving. He wanted me to better myself.

'Do you really want to spend your life here?' he asked while he helped me to pack boxes into my boss's van at the marketplace one weekend. 'There's nothing here, Christie. I – we – need more than this.'

'I could go for it, I guess, if you think I should.'

'Well, you can think for yourself. It's up to you. It would be crazy not to give it a go, though.'

Mention of 'crazy' stung even though he meant nothing by it. We'd been living together for nearly three years by then. He was looking out for me. I didn't want to upset him after the trouble he'd gone to finding the job advert, so I passed him another box and didn't mention that Saturday market was my favourite. There was a buzz to it that I'd not found elsewhere. Janet's stall next to mine had large plastic tubs of old records with sleeve covers ranging from hilarious to beautiful. She played songs from across the decades on an old record player that made people sway along with their memories. Two blokes opposite collected quirky items with no prices on for the fun of haggling. I'd bought a small, heavy statue from them of a man bent over while clutching his head in his hands and placed it in my bedroom. Daniel thought I was being dramatic and stuck it in the back garden next to withering plants.

'Last thing you need is a reminder of your brother,' he said.

The statue had never made me think of Jake, I simply liked the shape of it. After that, I couldn't look at the statue without imagining my brother wrapped over himself in the bedroom of a unit, his head in his hands as if that might fix his brain and let his speech and body movements flow normally again. It was too late for confession – my mother had died and the chance to set things right had passed. I threw the statue into a neighbour's bin.

The letter with instructions for the Somni testing day in the city caused an unexpected bubble of excitement. Sleep had saved me during my teens: a place to hide away from the world, from Mum, from having to think and feel and carry on. I'd chosen café shifts that ran from mid-afternoon till late closing time so I could sleep the day away. The possibility of working for such an important organisation and playing a small role in sleep research seemed unreal. My chance to do some good, to pay towards my debt of guilt.

The letter stated that incorporated into the tests were questions designed to detect lies. Even though I was well rehearsed in lies by then, the thought of being found out was horrifying, so I decided to answer honestly. This was much easier with a computer screen than with a human face. The questions covered problem-solving, maths, personality and team-working. A little sand-timer in the corner of the screen showed a countdown for each question. I might not be highly educated, articulate, confident but I'm fast at processing information and responding. Well, I used to be fast, before this year. Before it all went wrong and my brain became rice pudding.

It all seemed like a game at the time. An imagined future of a pretend life. I was willing to shake the dice and let them decide my fate, regardless of whether that was a ladder or a snake. On a games board, sometimes a ladder leads up the board as if you're going to win, then takes you straight into the mouth of a snake. I thought I'd escaped. But I'm sliding back down into past-me: incompetent, a disappointment.

The guy at the computer yawns and stretches his arm wide. He's given up on earning extra money for correct responses. He presses 'no' to every question as his chin rests in his hand, going through the motions until he's done what's required of him. When he goes home later and finally makes it into bed, I wonder if he'll fall asleep quickly, or whether he'll be restless, seeing a string of doors in front of his closed eyes, each with a box where the only option is 'no'.

⎯⎯⎯⎯⎯⎯⎯⎯

Back at my desk, a large white envelope sits waiting for me. There's no one around and no envelope on Heidi's desk. Inside is a document headed *Somni Appraisal and Commitment Review*.

Dear Valued Member
    Please complete the Commitment and Loyalty Questionnaire included within this pack and return it to reception within 48 hours. You are reminded that your initial work contract stated that

Somni may terminate your contract with variable notice. Furthermore, please sign this year's data protection agreement to protect all of our interests. We strongly recommend that you use the great resources within Somni to discuss and share information about your work rather than with external organisations and educational establishments, to minimise risk of losing our world-leading status by those who would think nothing of stealing our brave ideas.

As a RESEARCHER, we highly value your commitment to RESEARCH. We believe that GOOD RESEARCHERS PRODUCE AS WELL AS ANALYSE DATA. We are excited to continue to offer you perks such as ACCOMMODATION and CONFIDENTIALITY REGARDING YOUR MENTAL HEALTH STATUS. On departure from the company, any Somni employee is liable to pay back the current market value of perks offered.

Please find enclosed our gifts to you — a new Somni badge and details of an app to be installed on all personal devices, including phones and tablets, to help us keep you connected to the family that is Somni. We reserve the right to audit devices for use and content at any time.

Yours sincerely,
Somni Management Team.

8

FRIDAY, 10 MAY

S upervision is a safe space to reflect on therapy, ensure high standards are being maintained and improve practice. It's most effective when the supervisor is a good match with a therapist. During my part-time training and the four years since I qualified as a therapist, I've had a number of different supervisors. I've learned from each but none has been as insightful and effective as my current one. I'm fortunate to have Dr Elizabeth Field to support my development since I returned to work from sick leave. She's a nationally renowned psychotherapist who specialises in trauma and teaching.

I first heard Elizabeth speak at the local university years ago when I attended night classes towards my therapy qualification. She gave a guest lecture to us called 'Heal thyself: why attending to the therapist-self isn't selfish'. From the back of the auditorium, I could see Elizabeth at the podium but chose instead to watch her face projected onto a huge screen, superhuman. She had the wisdom that comes with age and decades of clinical practice. In the speech, Elizabeth encouraged us to be as aware of our own reactions as those in our patients during therapy.

'Compassionate people make the best therapists but,' she paused for effect, taking us all in as we sat totally absorbed by every word, 'they risk burnout. Separation of self from the other, of past from present, is essential.' I longed for this to work for me.

I scribbled down as much as I could recall at the end of her speech and bought her textbook *Healing Words* which was published the month after I qualified. I'd never dreamed I would get the opportunity to learn from her on a one-to-one basis. But as part of my return-to-work changes, Somni paid for Elizabeth's time as my clinical supervisor at my request.

Today, Elizabeth is dressed in a dark blue velvet dress. She hasn't changed at all since I attended her lecture, the kind of woman who looks her best later in life. Her scarf is decorated with birds in mid-flight. She doesn't dye her white hair or appear to wear make-up. It's hard to judge whether she's twenty or forty years older than me.

'One of the patterns we've been thinking about, Christie, is how much stronger your concerns have been recently about whether you have the skills to help your patients – even sometimes a worry that you could do harm, is that right?'

I wouldn't say it was a worry, just a thought. But Elizabeth can tell that I'm avoiding an issue. I've raced through a summary of recent therapy sessions, glossed over the awkward parts.

'I guess I'm concerned that I might get something wrong and do harm while trying to do good.' The creases in the corners of each of her eyes deepen.

'Can you give me an example so we can unpick that a little?'

But I don't want to do any unpicking. My hem is coming apart already, as if my stuffing could fall right out on the floor between us. I'm not sure I could ever be stitched back together if I undo. There's no way I can tell her what I did, I must focus on my therapy role – separate past from present.

'I was clumsy in my phrasing with Mike. I can't remember exactly what it was.' I rehearsed in bed what I would say to Elizabeth. Now I can't remember what happened in the appointment. 'I wasn't careful enough with my questions and because of that, Mike might not have a place in the sleep treatment for his trauma symptoms.'

Elizabeth waits for me to look at her before she speaks. I do the same with patients myself to keep the connection and wait for them to take the lead. Does it feel this excruciating to them? Do I make them feel this crushed with expectation? I look up to break the silence.

'I wonder what these memory lapses do for you?' she asks. 'What they may protect you from?'

My face heats up. Forgetting as having a purpose is an idea I'm familiar with in my patients. Elizabeth thinks I feign poor memory. Or at least that I'm glad to have gaps rather than remember. She doesn't realise the impact of the last year on me, the extremes of sleep deprivation, the possible side effects of being in the bloody Maximus trial.

'They don't protect me – memory difficulties make everything much harder.'

'It reminds me...' she starts and I don't want to know what it reminds her of. I'm not a patient here – this is supposed to be supervision about my therapy work. 'Of how difficult it has been for you to piece together the period while you were participating in Maximus and then the sick leave you took straight after. By forgetting, you are protected perhaps from painful feelings, but we can't work together to disentangle anything. In the same way, you have a vague sense that something happened with Mike, but we can't figure that out when you block it from your mind.'

'Not on purpose!' I can hear the teenage petulance in my voice but can't pull back.

'Christie, of course not.' She waits. I look at my flat, black shoes. The tips are scuffed. My leggings are no longer jet black but smoky grey. I'm a state. My eyes sting with near-tears. I don't speak until the heat has subsided and I regain control. Then I lift my head and try to repair the rupture between us.

'I'm sorry,' I say, unsure of which part I'm apologising for.

Daniel used to call me Little Miss Sorry. It was so automatic after two decades of keeping the peace at home. Apart from the one time I should have said it.

'There's no need for sorry, Christie. But I wonder what would happen if you stopped pushing so much away: memories, feelings, painful truths.'

'I'm too tired for this. I can't think.' I want to talk about what Ben told me, that something isn't right in the company. But then she'll ask about the concerns I supposedly raised last year and I can't remember what they were. We'll be back to square one of her accusation that I forget on purpose.

'I don't feel like I'm pushing away feelings. Most of the time there just aren't any. It's more like a vacuum.' I don't want her to cure my numbness. What lies underneath could be far worse. The red stop sign comes into my mind, glowing brightly.

'I'd be interested to hear about a time you *did* feel your emotions.' The warmth in Elizabeth's voice is an elixir. I get drunk on it, disinhibited. My reply starts before I'm even aware of the answer.

'The last time that I really experienced strong feelings was during Maximus. From the flashes that come back to me, it was overwhelming. Anger at people for stopping me using my newfound abilities, huge waves of sadness, a yearning to do more, to have the ultimate answer to help every person who suffers. It was as if I'd opened a bubbling bottle with two decades of emotions inside, exploding out. I had to keep away from people, stay at my desk and channel it into learning more and more.'

'What was the most difficult part of that experience for you, Christie?'

I feel a little of the heat in my chest as if the fire never totally went out. That's unacceptable. I must freeze it.

'Being out of control. I never want to be out of control again.'

'Can you recall any other times in your life where you were out of control? Or somebody else was out of control towards you?'

For a moment, I smell the jasmine scent on my mother's blouse as she clutches me, whispering, 'I can't do it, love, it's too hard to be a mum, I've messed up, it's all my fault.' I wrap my fingers over hers and gently pull the razor from her hand before it does any damage. My hand circles her back as it used to when I winded Jake as a baby. He is being cared for by strangers many miles away, a different boy. She sobs onto my pyjama top. I sweep my eyes over the room checking for anything else sharp or poisonous. 'It's not your fault, Mum. It's going to be okay, I promise.' Her torso slackens into me then, wet and warm on the bathroom floor. I could help her by explaining why Jake's injury isn't her fault but I don't.

I glance at Elizabeth. 'No. Nothing in particular comes to mind about anyone being out of control.'

Elizabeth leans forward a little. 'I'm here, Christie. You're not on your own with your pain.'

I imagine my face projected onto a huge screen in front of an audience who boo and hiss at my cowardice. My cheeks are wet before I realise why. The trickle of tears turns to sobs so hard that the back of my throat aches.

I tell the secretary I have a dental appointment and need to leave work early. She takes one look at my puffy face and doesn't doubt my story. The walk home is usually a pleasure, but today I wish I still had use of a car to close out the world. I'm losing control. Tears instead of ice. Pain instead of emptiness.

Mid-afternoon pavements are full of shoppers and tourists who don't look where they're going as they ogle maps on phones. The pavement becomes an assault course. The pleasure of walking London streets entranced by architecture left months ago. I walk faster. My thighs burn.

I'm home more quickly than I've ever made it before. That's when I spot it. It's not the first time that the small blue car has parked near my flat. I can't tell the difference between one model and another but people don't usually sit in their car with a baseball cap pulled low. They don't usually drive away at the exact point at which I arrive at or leave my front door. But this one does.

It started a few months ago when I returned to work full-time. I took it to be someone without a parking permit, waiting to pick up a friend. I felt compelled to peek through the curtains of my bedroom to check out the lower half of the car. It was still parked there but pulled off as I watched. I dropped the curtain down in shame of being caught and thought nothing of it – I had bigger worries at the time. When I arrived back at work after months off sick, nobody asked how I'd been. Clearly everyone had been instructed not to enquire after my wellbeing or ask questions about my period of absence. It was easier that way. Once again, I wasn't in control of what was said about me; not privy to a description of events that on one level I longed for.

The next time I spotted the car must have been winter as it was dark when I arrived home. The car lights were turned off but the engine hummed, perhaps so the heater could blast out its warmth in the chilled air. The streetlamp above provided enough light to see a dark cap and large coat. I continued down the steps to my front door, fighting the urge to run straight to my bedroom window. Instead, I lifted the letter box flap as lights trailed past. It had gone.

Last time I saw it, I tried chanting the number plate over and over. But by the time I'd let myself in, keyed in the alarm, found a pen that worked, the letters and numbers were jumbled. What could I do with them anyway? Report non-harassment to the police? Walk a thousand streets looking for the vehicle?

The blue car's engine purrs. The peak of the driver's cap shows up above the seat. Not today. I can't deal with it today. My fingers tremble as I try to get my key into the lock.

I can't face another night of flailing around in bed so I grab my duvet, take it to the sofa and draw the curtains. I turn up the volume on a white-noise machine I snuck into my bag from work that's used for people with severe tinnitus. It's not sound that I want to block out, it's my thoughts. I listen to the chaos of white noise and let myself drift.

I'm at the bottom of a swimming pool, floating with ease. I hear somebody calling from above but I can't make out the message. A shape at the side of the pool expands as a figure leans over the water. I'm not afraid, but I don't want to leave my calm spot. Along the side of the pool I see numbers that show how deep I am. The number nearest to me says thirty-seven. The figure above holds out an arm. Her arm. Elizabeth dips her hand into the water, offering to pull me out. I push my feet against the wall of the pool and drift further from her. There are other figures swimming behind but they can't quite catch up with me. We swim in unison as a shoal of fish, gliding and swooping in the water: separate but the same. The figures split into tiny silver fish, then again even smaller until there is only me, swimming alone in the glittery water as Elizabeth beckons me back from afar.

9

SATURDAY, 11 MAY

I wake on the sofa with a pulsing head. The curtains shine amber in the daylight. I must have slept continuously for hours for the first time in months. There's no clock in here and I never unpacked my mobile phone from my bag, so it's probably out of charge. Timeless. Contactless. It's so much quieter here at the back of the building, it could be five in the morning or lunchtime. My stomach gurgles its displeasure with me for going straight to sleep with no evening meal.

In the tiny kitchen, I crack eggs into a bowl and whisk them. Such a peculiar foodstuff – how various ways of cooking produce such different outcomes. Only poached eggs are acceptable according to the last conversation I overheard at Somni, but the runny yolk hiding in its white bubble makes me feel nauseous. Better to have an omelette where what you see is what you get. I grind black pepper over the top of the bubbling mixture and notice how much more alert I feel from having slept well.

The cupboards look grimy. Slug trails glisten along the work surface where crumbs of food gather unbrushed. Have I been living like this? I gulp a glass of milk. A peculiar sensation runs along my limbs as if the milk is strengthening my bones. I catch myself at ease, an unfamiliar sensation. Is this how weekends are for normal people? I head back to the sofa and eat off my knee in silence. Each time my mind drifts to past or future, I yank it back to the cool fork against my lips, the peppery softness of the food, the warmth of it as it slides down my throat.

Funny how you get so used to things that have been there a long time, so that you no longer see them. Fully alert, I stare at the sealed cardboard box that sits in the corner of the room. I'd kept certain items separate when I moved out of Daniel's place as they contain personal effects: my notebooks, photographs of us together and items that weren't essential to daily living. Elizabeth quizzed me about my choice to not remember. There could be memory prompts inside that box to explain what happened between Maximus and becoming so unwell, to help me understand why my relationship fell apart at the same time. I have the whole weekend to empty the box and refill my mind.

As I try to recall where I stashed the large scissors to cut open the box, my phone beeps its plea to be charged. I scatter the contents of my work bag onto the carpet and plug the phone in with the intention of switching it off until Monday. A little envelope shows on the screen: a message from Heidi. I could switch off the phone and check the message on Monday. 'Listen to your gut,' Elizabeth would say. The curtains are still shut in the living room so I only feel slightly ridiculous as I sit cross-legged on the carpet, shut my eyes and try to pay attention to what comes up – like the yoga instructor at Somni tells us. Usually, I use the time to follow my thoughts in loops. But right now, I feel calm and aware.

It's not my gut that communicates but my chest. I feel a dull ache, a quiet hint of sadness and longing beneath. I open my eyes and see that sadness reflected in my surroundings. The blandness. No photographs, no ornaments from places I've been to, no piles of notebooks containing scribbled ideas. Even the framed print above the sofa was here when I moved in – a hotel-worthy shot of a Spanish lady with a rose in her hair. My childhood bedroom was set up as a mini-classroom with wall displays of animals that I cut from old calendars, a library of books that I inserted library cards into even though I never got the date stamper I wanted, cushions lined the top of my bed to provide comfort for my favourite toys. In Daniel's flat I had my favourite buys from the market scattered around: a puppy made from coal, a delicate glass swan, a framed photo of wartime ladies dangling their legs from a stone wall. But now, there's nothing in this room that distinguishes it as mine. I've lost myself along the way.

Perhaps the answer isn't in a box of my past but in what I allow into my future. I click on the message and read Heidi's invitation to catch up today. I want to step back into my life. I reply that I'll meet her in a café a few streets away in one hour.

Heidi waves from a booth at the side of the café. She looks younger with her hair in a high ponytail. She could pass for a student although she's in her mid thirties. It's eleven o'clock so the café is not yet filled with lunchtime crowds. I order a black coffee out of habit.

'Have you got actual *make-up* on?' she says in pretend shock. It's only eyeliner and a fingertip sweep of copper powder onto my eyelids, but it makes me look less corpse-like. I've showered and washed my hair. She takes my hands in hers across the table. 'I'm so glad you're looking after yourself, Christie. We've been a bit worried about you.'

Who's 'we'? Heidi and Harry? The whole of Somni? I'm glad when the waitress brings my coffee over and I can put the cup to my lips to prevent any expectation of a response. I miss the days when 'we' meant Heidi and me: our research, our plans, our friendship. Her promotion two years ago has pushed us further from each other.

'I've been having a bit of trouble sleeping, that's all.' Heidi watches as I add another sugar to sweeten the bitter coffee.

'*Is* that all, Christie? Is there anything else?' She searches for the right way to ask as she twirls her engagement ring around from a fiancé who's always away on business. Two workaholics together, perfect for avoiding guilt. 'Do you think you might be unwell again?'

I hesitate. Then picture one foot on a rickety bridge across the river that has widened between us. 'That's the thing, I'm not sure I ever was unwell. I think it might all be related to Maximus.' I can feel my heart bang against my ribcage as I speak. This is the first time I've voiced the possibility outside of my own mind: what if I was *made* ill.

Heidi blanches. She cups her hands around her glass of iced water, the white-tipped fingernails touching each other from each side. When did she give up caffeine? One of many changes in her over the years. We haven't talked about what happened when I was poorly even though she saw me at my worst. I recall her trying to pull me away from the computer at eight o'clock one evening but I couldn't stop. The numbers that streamed down columns in our shared database as I moved my cursor made perfect sense as they formed into clear patterns of cause and effect. I was doing the work of a statistics program with utter ease. She'd tried to persuade me to go home to rest. In the end, I shoved her away so I wasn't interrupted. Had I scared her?

Heidi talks into her glass rather than look up at me. My solidity is disintegrating. This isn't how our catch-up was supposed to go. I accepted her invitation to meet to regain a life outside of work and the flat, not to pull apart our friendship.

'I think you *were* unwell. And you might be now.' Her voice wobbles a little. 'It's not your fault. But it skews your thinking, makes you a bit paranoid.'

The concern in her face triggers a memory of another time she told me I was being paranoid part way through Maximus.

'Look at the numbers, something isn't right, there isn't the right amount of variation in these segments,' I shouted, desperate for her to pay attention and see what I could see on the database from the last research project we worked on.

Heidi shook her head. 'That's what the stats program is for, I can't tell just from looking, it's just a bunch of figures. It's after seven, Christie, time to go.'

'No, no it's here look, the results are too uniform, I think they've been tampered with. And I wanted to show you just a few more things. I think I've made a breakthrough in how we can protect people from getting flashbacks, we can alter sleep waves *before* any trauma happens, like before paramedics start their training or soldiers leave for war zones, or we could start a community-based approach like inoculation.'

'Christie, please stop. Turn the computer off. You're not making sense.'

Heidi reached towards the power switch. I grabbed her wrist. Hard. I couldn't bear the numbers disappearing to throw me back into the slow, blind everyday world.

My behaviour was out of order. Could I be slipping back into confusion?

I lay a hand on my stomach where my breakfast sits uneasily, ready to make a reappearance. Heidi looks worried and it's genuine. I know her, and whatever might be going on between her and Harry, she does really care. I don't want her to be concerned for me. I'm not ill. I'm *probably* not ill. Time to pull it together.

'You're right, I'm sure. I can come out of it by taking care of myself. Look how *hot* I am today!' I smile and she laughs in return, relieved. She fiddles with a pendant on her bracelet and I grit my teeth when I realise she's wearing the Somni logo despite it being the weekend. It's clear that I'm going to have to figure out what role Maximus played in my so-called breakdown by myself. With my mask firmly back in place so Heidi can't say that I'm unwell, we chat about upcoming work projects and what the future could hold for sleep research. But the atmosphere between us has the heaviness of pre-storm skies.

10

MONDAY, 13 MAY

I've tried to make the therapy room less sparse by adding plants but as there are no external windows for natural light, I chose plastic ferns in terracotta pots. They remind me of my intention to grow herbs and cook from scratch once I moved to London, which was never realistic.

The old lady next door to our first house gave Jake and me little packets of seeds from time to time. We mixed them all in an old plant pot and sprinkled them along the edges of the small back garden. More by luck than planning, we created a border that looked like the meadows only ten minutes' walk from our house. Mum said there were too many weeds, but I couldn't figure out why some plants were allowed to be there and some not. Who got to decide?

'Let's go to the jungle,' said Jake. 'Hide and peek.'

I never corrected him on the name of the game. We took it in turns to hide Jake's plastic superhero characters. The game was boring but I loved to bend down low so the plants became forest trees and enter their world. Creating stories and escaping into them was my hobby. The bright red and blue limbs of the toys stuck out obviously in the few square metres of lawn but I'd take my time to find them to give Jake a thrill. He'd whizz around the unkempt lawn shouting 'hotter' and 'colder' depending how close I was to his toy.

'Why don't we let the toys stay out here this time, Jake? It'd be like a camping sleepover for them.'

'But what if they get eated by animals?' He parked chubby thumbs in the pockets of his shorts.

'They've got super-powers, haven't they? Anyway, Spiderman is friends with all the bugs so they won't be mean.'

That satisfied Jake enough to leave his characters behind. I regretted it as soon as I went to bed, fearful that they'd be stolen in the night or rot in the soil, which would be all my fault. While I trotted to and from the curtains to check on the garden, Jake slept soundly. Always in charge, always on the lookout for the next thing that was bound to go wrong, not realising that by trying to escape fate and avoid disaster, I ended up causing it.

Now I've created my own garden in the therapy room, albeit plastic. By seeing patients in an environment that wraps them in colour and comfort, I can signal to them that they matter. Next, I plan to bring a Persian rug and source an abstract painting that can become whatever it needs to represent for each patient.

The corner cupboard unlocks into a video viewing suite ready for me to play back Isobel's home videos. The team has edited the data to show only episodes of sleepwalking for us to review. I should have watched the video already to prepare for this appointment but felt too wiped out.

I was awake until dawn again this morning, followed by a fitful sleep in the knowledge that I needed to leave for work on time. At 1am, I had the sense that I was being observed. Then even my normal behaviours seemed fake, like when my patients forget how to breathe normally when I ask them to focus on their breathing. I didn't want whoever may be watching to see my agitation, to count the number of rolls I made from one side of the bed to the other.

I decided to feign sleep to give my audience no access into my struggles. *Prioritising the other*, Elizabeth would say, as if it were a negative thing to be concerned what others think. Pretending is sometimes enough. Eventually, I pulled the duvet up over my head. Even in the darkness, my eyes refused to close.

Under the covers, the feeling of being watched never left. Somni gave me the flat for free. They could have installed cameras to keep an eye on me. It's a ridiculous idea. And even if they did plant cameras, they surely wouldn't still be spying on me? Unlikely. Paranoid. But not impossible.

What about the hypothesis that I'm unwell? If it were severe enough, then I wouldn't realise it. I'd think things were real that weren't.

I've only assessed one patient whose reality was completely fractured. He saw code hidden in number plates. This young man believed that his friends and family had been replaced by androids that looked just like them and wanted to figure out who was real. He was hospitalised before we had a chance to meet again. If he were sitting opposite me today wondering whether I was real or not, I'd be inclined to wonder with him.

Mum never shared what caused her to cry through the night, to spend months without leaving the house, to sigh rather than speak. The reason Jake and I got nervous about leaving the house when we were young wasn't because we weren't allowed to leave her, but because we didn't know which version of her we would we return to. Would she turn her back to us in days of silence or pull at her hair in terror that we had left her alone as both our fathers had? Maybe it wasn't *us* that she ignored, but voices and images in her mind. Shutting down may have been her only means of survival. What if these sensations of being observed aren't just a result of sleep deprivation or related to the

Maximus trial? Perhaps I've inherited an illness that's going to spiral until I'm completely undone.

Isobel keeps her cream raincoat buttoned up and sits rigidly upright as she fidgets with her buttons. She can't say for sure whether she's sleepwalked, but at least knows she hasn't left the house since an alarm was installed to wake her should she open the front door.

'Have you had a chance to reflect on our last session, Isobel? How the sleepwalking might be linked to stress rather than being a disorder of your sleep?'

'I *have* been stressed.' Her voice and movements are so small, as if to minimise the impact she might have in the world: a whisper personified.

'We'll watch the video footage together and see if we can figure out what the sleepwalking means.' My voice comes out cotton-soft. Despite my revelation last session, she doesn't appear afraid of me. In fact, her doe eyes see me as her rescuer – a role I'm so pulled towards that I need to be careful. There's no easy route for Isobel to become aware of how she's been treated and to change the way she acts in the future; I can't do it for her.

'I didn't mean to walk out in the street,' she says, intertwined fingers white from pressure. 'But sometimes I *do* imagine being somewhere else.' I recognise the flush of guilt and want to tell her how proud I am of her admission but I mustn't interrupt – she's finding her voice. 'I wouldn't do it. I'd never leave my boy. But sometimes...' Tears cover the end of her sentence.

'Isobel, this may sound strange, but it's positive that you're able to accept these normal thoughts and desires. Thinking about an action isn't the same as doing it. It tells us that you need more of a break, that you yearn to have your own life.'

I ignore a tight sensation in my chest, a cord that tries to reach back through the years to a time I've left behind where it belongs. A museum of myself that remains locked.

We can move on to check the video footage. I feel a buzz of hope. Sometimes sleepwalkers enact everyday routines such as teeth brushing or making a sandwich. Isobel indicates that she's ready to turn her seat to face the screen, and I explain that the night-time footage has been condensed using equipment that monitored activity after dark. For a moment, I picture my slugs reporting my night-time actions back to Harry and realise how ridiculous my fears were of being watched at night.

Grainy images display above a date and time at the bottom of the screen. The footage shows Isobel as she walks down the landing and turns at the first door. I feel a fondness watching her swishing hair and tip-toe walk.

'The bathroom,' Isobel explains.

The next clip two nights later shows the same pattern. She jokes about her weak bladder. I'm so pleased to see her relating to me as an equal rather than a little girl speaking with the grown-up.

The video counter shows only thirty seconds more video footage to come.

We watch together as she leaves her room two nights ago at midnight. She walks straight past the bathroom door this time. The camera angle changes as she enters a room with a small bed in it. Isobel doesn't turn her face from the screen, whispers the name 'Riley', I'm unsure whether she is explaining to me or calling out to him. I turn back to the screen as the green-tinged night vision camera captures her standing in the doorway of his room. For a split second, she tilts her head to the camera. Her eyes glow white against her shadowed face. We watch a ghost version of her kneel by her son's bed to stroke his hair. It's a sweet sign of affection, but I feel goosebumps raise on my arms.

Isobel's hand pauses over Riley as if in freeze-frame. I hold my breath. I can't take another. She picks an object up from behind his sleeping head, using one hand to gently lay her son flat on the mattress. She holds the pillow above him. Then places it over his face.

Bubble bath and a lavender scented candle are not sufficient to unknot my muscles after today's therapy session. Isobel almost fell from her chair as she recoiled in horror at what she'd done to her son. Her unconscious desires were stronger than the urge to escape – they were homicidal. It was so unexpected that I was lost for words. As Isobel howled that she was an unfit mother, I broke my code of conduct by holding her tight, needing the contact as much as she did. The boy was safe: he slept through the whole thing, and I was convinced that her mind would never let her actually harm him. She had such love for him. It didn't seem right in that moment to say I'd have to raise the incident as a child safeguarding matter, so I said nothing at all. By four o'clock, I'd calmed myself down enough to report my concerns internally. I felt nauseous as I waited for our child protection lead Nina to answer the internal phone. I gushed out the details of Isobel's appointment, keen to stress that no harm came to her son.

'And you said you are Christie Langdale. From the research department?' asked Nina. 'Okay, thanks for that then.' I'd spoken so quickly I couldn't have given her enough time to write down all the facts to report to social services.

She didn't ask for any details.

'Do you need anything else from me?' I asked, screwing up the paper report I'd written of the session into a ball.

Nina sighed as if I was wasting her time. 'No, I'll make a note you called.'

That was it. I expected to be relieved that I didn't have to fight for Isobel's good name. Instead, I was left with the feeling of being silenced.

I don't know whether Isobel will ever find out I reported behind her back or not – I should have discussed it with her. All I can do is pray she never, ever acts on her murderous impulses. People don't have to intend harm to cause it. Does that mean they are still culpable? I push that familiar question back down.

I close my eyes and blow my breath away to steady it. A welcome numbness returns, spreading through my body like a balm. If I let my feelings emerge, I could release the plug and refill this bath with my tears. That won't help anyone. I can't let Isobel down: I won't give up on her. I know that it's hard to feel resentment towards a vulnerable family member who never meant to make life hard for you. My mother and her fear of everything. My brother who needed me to step in and do what she couldn't. As I lie in the warm water, I feel a pull from my navel upwards: a connection to the dead and the wounded.

11

TUESDAY, 14 MAY

As I nip out to the corner shop for milk, the blue car pulls out and trails me. I'm certain it's the same one. I cross the road into a side street. The car turns. The whirr of the engine seems to vibrate the road beneath my feet. My hands stay jammed in my pockets, unable to obey any sensible plan to video the vehicle with my phone or signal for help. *Keep walking, don't let them know that you've noticed, don't turn around.*

In a strange way I'm not surprised. I've been waiting all my life for the past to catch up with me. Although this must be unrelated, I sense that running away never works in the end. But it's all I know.

Once I'm in the corner shop, I can't concentrate so pick up skimmed milk; thin and unsatisfying. Everything seems more neon and plastic than usual. Tinny music murders a nineties song I used to like. I check for a security camera but can't see one. I dawdle down the two aisles and back, examining soup tins and a pile of mismatched food being sold off as out of date. Nobody enters the store. At the cash desk, rows of cigarettes and booze line up as if they might help me out. But that never works: I've heard enough patients' stories to be certain of that.

The woman behind the counter looks at her phone with one hand held out for cash from an elderly man. Nobody connects anymore. I'm unsure what to say. Two children giggle as they look at magazines with their nan. I could hang around until they leave – create a fake family as we step back out into city life as a unit. There's safety in numbers. The little girl looks over to me. What does she see? A wreck of a woman, wild-eyed with paranoia? I remember what that feels like. The hot shame of being in public with Mum on one of her worst days: I never stopped to think what it was like to be in her shoes. I move away from the family to check out of the window between adverts for buy-one-get-one-free. I can't see the blue car.

I swallow back a whimper and leave the shop. A half-run takes me down three streets back to the flat. Hedgerows seem longer than usual, the pavement surface more cracked with slabs that want to trip me up, the low sun behind me blinds me from checking to see if I'm followed. My chest burns with the exertion.

At my front door, I crane my neck to the road and see no moving cars. I wasn't tracked back.

I know what Mum would have said. One of her favourite lines.

'The Earth doesn't revolve around you, Christie Langdale.'

She missed the point. I never thought it revolved around me – I was more concerned that I was a stray rock flung far into space, ready to crash in and spoil everything.

When I first started at Somni, a lady from human resources sent me a welcome pack that included worksheets for people with low self-esteem and anxiety issues. There was no explanation as to why. I could only guess it related to my entrance tests, and wondered why the hell they'd hired me. I was encouraged to 'consider alternative explanations' when my 'worrying mind' concocted stories that feared the worst. There was a picture of a brain with worried eyebrows to demonstrate how childish they considered anxiety to be. I'm surprised they didn't include a company-stamped pencil to complete the homework.

What are alternative explanations for the blue car? It could be a case of mistaken identity perhaps, as I have one of those faces that everyone vaguely recognises without being able to pin down. But that doesn't fit. When I see the car, I'm certain that someone is watching me and that one day they're not going to be satisfied to stay inside the car.

There is a further alternative. One that scratches at me. Each car may have been different. Blue is a common colour for vehicles. With no one hiding in the shadows. A part of me may be damaged to the point that I don't just feel fear, I imagine things to justify it.

Mum sometimes didn't leave the house for weeks. She'd send me up to the local shop with a ten-pound note, a shopping list, and a plastic bag full of more plastic bags. She saw danger in us reading our magazine horoscopes ('inviting dark forces'), microwaves ('radiation poisoning'), mobile phones ('brain cancer'). She didn't know that in the end, it was me she should have been wary of.

I'm not sure which is worse: to be stalked or to turn out like my mother.

After the Maximus trial, I erased as many trails of myself as I could, as if that would wipe out danger. Facebook, Messenger, Instagram, Twitter. I deleted my personal email account and pulled blog posts on sleep research.

There's no such thing anymore as existing only in the here and now. Versions of ourselves stare from social media pages, tagged by people we no longer speak to. Our friends – or friends of friends, or enemies of friends of acquaintances – can post photographs from twenty years ago of our acne-attacked faces blushing with the first gulp of an alcopop or dizzy drag of a roll-up. Newspaper articles float around the web long after print pages that describe a burnt-out house, a neglectful mother and the tragic impact of smoke-induced hypoxia on the brain of a boy have disintegrated. Databases hold rows of ones and zeros from questionnaires that can be computed into scores that describe an applicant's likelihood of being malleable and silenced.

I wish none of those things existed, wish to warn past-me to be more careful as we leave traces that can't be undone.

During my breakdown last year, I didn't know who I was. In a way, I didn't want to lose who I became during Maximus – that sweet taste of confidence, moments of clarity, even genius. But there came a tipping point. I wrote an email to Jake not knowing who else to turn to as I became suspicious of Somni and estranged from Daniel. It was a long, meandering essay about the changes that happened to me from good to frightening. The sense of excitement when I started to work faster and faster as my memory expanded to fit in so much data I finally felt clever enough. That excitement soon turned to an insatiable hunger: a drive to read, learn, compute that I lost control over. I couldn't stop. Then ideas pouring into my head which made sense in one moment and then didn't the next. But I couldn't lay all that at Jake's door when he had already dealt with so much. So I deleted the whole email and sent a bland version saying that work was extra busy and I hoped he was well.

I crashed so hard that I don't think I've ever recovered.

Pieces of me are scattered and I can't decide which to gather up and which to leave alone. How do you put yourself back together when you don't know what happened to you?

I've saved Elizabeth's website address on my phone. I open her article from several years ago that fits with the lecture I attended about how we as therapists must look after ourselves. Skim reading the familiar text is enough to help me settle a little. I find one of my favourite lines: 'Let your values as a therapist guide you in your own life, like a torch in the night, one step at a time.' It's the way to make amends – do what's right and ethical, and ensure others do too. I'd love to follow her advice but can't access my own torch right now, there's no light to shine. I'll stick with my lifelong method of managing: shut-down mode.

When I have a task to complete that's scary, I pretend that I'm not doing it at all, as if somebody else runs my body while I watch from a distance. It wasn't me that sat with Mum as she wondered whether to keep on living, or who visited my brother in the rehab unit and smiled despite how different he looked, or sat at a computer pressing buttons in a test centre that could give me a new life in London. What if not-me picks up my phone to send an email to Ben that will move me towards answers? I watch my fingers type an invitation to come over to my house to discuss his concerns about Somni more, then add my phone number. No smiley face. No exclamation marks. A grown-up invitation to take a leap forwards and figure out what the hell might be going on – within the company, or within my own mind.

12

WEDNESDAY, 15 MAY

I was prepared for Mike's frustration at his ReStory sleep therapy being delayed because of my concerns that he wasn't ready. In fact, he seems unfazed by the change in plan. Perhaps even relieved. I should have guessed his belief that he doesn't deserve to get any better means this outcome fits with his expectations. It's not that Mike can't make progress, it's that he won't let himself, as a punishment for his imagined guilt. His split-second decision on that fateful night to turn in one direction not the other was one of bad luck not malice. Mike's resignation to living like this causes me to feel worse than if he'd been angry with me.

'I appreciate everything you've tried to help me with, but this is the way things are,' he says, with no judgement in his voice. Mike's shirt is creased with a spattering of stains near the collar. He doesn't look well. His eyes appear more sunken than last time I saw him. The word 'defeated' comes to mind. Some people have intractable post-traumatic stress no matter which therapeutic methods are applied. But that doesn't mean he can't have improved quality of life. I need to change my approach.

'It can be useful to step back and think about the broader

picture of what really matters to you.' I inject as much hope as I can into my voice but worry that I sound like a children's TV presenter.

Mike's voice is slow and gruff in return. 'The things that mattered have gone. Wife, work, colleagues. I get on with it. Still got Roxy, the dog.'

'What about how you spend your time. Outside of work, what did you used to do, or feel passionate about?'

I need to give space for his slowness. The urge to jump in and speed things up could be counterproductive. How many painkillers does he take for his injuries? Enough to take the edge off or so many that it impairs his functioning but provides a hazy relief from reality? I can see the allure of an analgesic fog.

'Well, I'm still doing my pictures. Photography. Sometimes.'

I'm surprised to hear this, to imagine his large hands around a delicate camera, looking for the beauty in detail when I'd presumed that he was blind to it all. I've become dulled to it myself recently, so caught up in my head that I miss the details as the minutes unfold.

'Can you tell me a bit more about that?'

'If anything catches my eye, I snap it. Got a good camera a couple of years ago. Was out in the woods with Roxy the other day. Birds and bluebells everywhere. They don't last long, so I took a few pictures.'

When Mum had episodes where she wouldn't get up all day, Jake and I used to go to what we called the Dingle around the back of our house and set up a cabin with a picnic blanket draped over broken branches. Those few sweet weeks of bluebells were the best. We'd buy sweets and empty them onto squares of kitchen roll in our hidey-hole. I told Jake it was called a midnight feast even though it was the middle of the day because it sounded exciting. He chattered away in those days, when he still could with ease. I told him to shut up because he'd scare the birds away. Nobody bothered to teach us the real names of birds we saw, so we made up our own: brown-beaked boogie-woogie, speckly, rainbowbird.

I'm struggling to concentrate today. I should be happy that Mike has continued with his hobby – that means he's likely to be at lower risk of taking his life as he's not yet given up on everything that makes him who he is. Part of my role is to assess people's risk to themselves. Men with post-traumatic stress disorder are at significantly higher risk of suicide. I must refocus him on those fleeting moments of meaning that are protective if he pays attention to them.

'What have you been doing with the photos?'

'Nothing. I don't look back.' His face shuts down. The animation that showed up as he described his photography is replaced with a deadened expression. He's so afraid of the past that he's closed to it no matter what.

'I wonder if it might be an idea to review your gallery, or even print images out? That would give you a focus, and also celebrate your achievement, to have those prints to show for it.' I want to help him to move both forwards and backwards in time. He's so fearful of where his mind will take him. With trauma, memories are not a cinematic reel of the past, but a virtual reality machine complete with electric shocks.

Mike shakes his head as if I've suggested he run a marathon, not look at photographs of flowers. 'What's the point? Oh, here's a tree, here's Roxy, here's a brown-beaked boogie-woogie.'

A jolt runs right through me. I'm so shocked by his use of our bird name – mine and Jake's – that I feel shaky.

'Sorry, what did you say?'

'Just, what's the point? I see what you're saying, don't get me wrong. But I don't have the energy really and it's not as if I'd get any satisfaction from it.'

It doesn't make any sense – I must have misheard, my tired

brain inventing things. This isn't a safe way to give therapy. I can't shake an awful feeling in the pit of my stomach. It quickly turns to cramps. I need to get out, so I move on to a less threatening topic.

'I could send you handouts to complete to try to increase your activities? That's been shown to improve mood.'

It's a cop out and we both know it. But as Mike says, this is the way things are right now.

He closes his eyes. 'When I first came to this place and sleep therapy was mentioned, I thought I'd be given extra sleep to wipe everything out.'

It's an alluring image: two beds in the therapy room. I wonder what would happen if we both went to sleep instead of this endless cycle of talking. Would he get better outcomes? Would I stay on the right side of sane?

Before I even realise it, my mouth says what's in my head.

'Talking doesn't solve everything.'

Mike nods his understanding, and I feel relief that the burden of expectation that I'll always have the answer is momentarily lifted.

I open two unfinished research reports on my computer and move my cursor up and down with no focus. I scroll, scroll, scroll along numbers on a spreadsheet.

There must be a video of this morning's therapy session that I could try to access to check whether Mike really did say what I thought he said. I enter the therapy video files but can only see those from the previous years. Where's my new data being saved to if not to my file? I don't know where it's saved or who has access to it.

I switch off the computer, defeated. There's no way I can

get to today's video without asking someone to show me where it is, which could raise suspicion that there's something unusual to see. Each query we log with our IT department gets sent to our line manager as explained in one of the mounds of induction paperwork I reread a couple of nights ago. The document that I signed long before I had any worries about Somni gives permission for the company to track every file I open, log my phone calls, 'audit' anything I type including deleted files and emails, and to systematically categorise any internet searches or outgoing messages.

If I'm honest with myself, I'm relieved not to have to face up to what may or may not have happened in the therapy appointment, just as Mike was relieved to not go ahead with the sleep lab therapy. Avoidance is a familiar friend to me.

Rain slashes against the window and the city looks sickly grey below. I love the height of my office. Everything below turns small and insignificant. I place my finger on the top of the London Eye as if I could spin it like a roulette wheel. I walk two fingers along the glass, taking giant steps to the next district. I could pace the streets for weeks, days, years, past hundreds of thousands of people and never see anybody who knows me.

I imagine opening my umbrella so that I could drift down from here to the pavement like Mary Poppins.

13

Thursday, 16 May

The corridors are a hive of worker bees buzzing with excitement about our upcoming research strategy meeting that's been hyped all week. I splash water onto my face in the pristine ladies' toilets to rejuvenate for long enough to appear awake and excited. Harry will be on his way over to perform another act, awaiting the applause and adulation that grows each year: the less staff see of him recently, the more they seem to bow and fawn. A shift in my stomach sends me back into the cubicle. I lock the door and lean my face against the cool wall. The bathroom door slams open.

'He's pushing for more GPs to get on with the next level.' I recognise the senior sleep technician, Marnie. 'Got to be more careful this time, we can't predict the impact. You know what happened with that super-responder girl, she's the kind of GP whose scores were...'

Marnie must have acted something out with her hands. The other lady's dry laugh agrees with her.

'Everything's so rushed all the time. It'll be worth it if we can balance things out for better results this time, I guess.'

An exasperated sigh follows. 'At least it's distracting him from thinking about the inspection. I'll bring up the new ethics committee at today's meeting. We've really got to...'

A cough interrupts the second lady. They've realised I'm in here. I sit tight and wait until I hear the taps run, the hand dryer blast and the creak of the door to know I'm alone again. I'm surprised they dared to talk like that about Harry without first checking who was in the cubicles. That term 'super-responder' plays over in my mind. At least an ethics committee might look into my concerns about Maximus.

A beep over the tannoy tells me it's ten minutes until our meeting starts. This jolts my memory of the alarm that sounded at the end of each session of Maximus to tell us to leave the lab room. It hadn't looked like a lab, of course, more like a decent hotel room apart from the telltale additions: a computer in the corner and a small silver trolley at the foot of the bed. The equipment trolley was where I'd place the discarded cap in the morning. It had sixty-four wires attached to take readings of electrical activity in the brain while I slept. I'd rub the residue of paste on my scalp that was squeezed into each hole in the cap to give a strange tingly sensation.

There was an en-suite shower to help wash away the paste from my hair, but I'd wanted to get back to the map. *Needed* to get back to the map. It was huge, spread across the far wall and covered all the taxi routes that were learned by drivers as part of The Knowledge.

I'd jumped out of bed and tapped at the computer keyboard to try to activate more learning sessions. The screen stayed stubbornly blank. I slammed my hand down on the keys. My palm echoed with pain that spread in neon lines outwards like star.

The overhead lights brightened automatically – a sign that I should have been getting ready to leave the room. There were usually twenty minutes between the second alarm and the signal to leave.

I'd felt as if I was forgetting something important, that it was just out of reach. A pile of papers rested on the small desk. Tiny lettering swam on the page underneath the heading *Maximus*. I signed the bottom of each page as usual, the shape of my signature so far removed from my actual name, a series of curves of lines. The door opened automatically. Time to go.

Each side of the corridor had the same blandness. It was deceptive: both directions looked similar but led to a different future. Instead of going right to exit the building via a staircase as expected, I'd chosen a left turn to my office. Staff in the room next door were likely to be too busy hunched over data to pay much attention to where I was going. I couldn't go home yet, I needed to get to my company laptop. I was certain that answers hid in the data and I was close to them becoming clear.

The beep sounds again and brings me back to the present. I scramble out of the bathroom to the meeting, desperate not to draw attention to myself by being late.

In the boardroom, Harry arrives with a PA who looks school-aged. He goes through assistants faster than toothbrushes. God knows what he does that makes them leave so quickly. It's the daytime staff only here. I heard that Harry already ran this open meeting about new research ideas with the night crew. Has he slept since? As Harry welcomes the staff, his speech is even faster than usual, reminding me of Daniel's cocaine-fuelled banker friends. The corners of his mouth bubble up at points as if he's producing too much saliva. He rubs and squeezes his right arm distractedly.

Harry wasn't always this way. When I first started, I found him inspiring. A former academic, he had been the lead two years earlier in Somni's bid to buy up the old university department which was rumoured to be on the verge of being axed. There was an energy whenever Harry entered a room back then that was positive and invigorating. We always felt on the verge of discovering important findings. Without Harry charming financial backers from around the world with his hype and politician smoothness, we wouldn't have been able to run huge trials into improving sleep for people with severe depression or be the first team in the country to perfect the ReStory technique for post-traumatic stress disorder. He was affable and enjoyed the attention from telling detailed stories of his negotiations and brave ideas for future research. But over the last few years his drive has turned to a kind of mania, and the company has started to feel more like a cult than a business, where to challenge was to be 'against' Somni.

Harry continues with his speech.

'The next phase for Somni is about to begin: we're heading to the brave new world of not only changing the lives of those with disorders via the science of sleep, but changing all of us so we can be the best humans possible.'

I glance at the table. Everyone is enraptured. Or pretending to be.

'We can meld and mould the nature of people's minds; engineer greatness where it does not naturally exist. We are...' He stops, frozen mid-sentence, like he can't find the right word. Nobody takes their eyes off him or makes a sound. 'Pioneers, yes pioneers,' he continues as if the break had been for effect. 'The true plasticity and performance of the brain has been misunderstood until this point. We will no longer need to rely on machines to be the future: mankind will take back the reins of genius. Thank you all for your outstanding work in helping us to rocket ahead. Now we shall turn to you for your ideas of our upcoming project list. Don't hold back. What would you wish to work on if there were no barriers or limits whatsoever?'

That final phrase is a punch to the stomach.

Harry's talk of rewiring brains for better performance sounds like a version of the Maximus trial. If Somni is planning to continue with that research, surely we should discuss the pitfalls and change protocols?

Marnie moves next to him, a small nod to him before she speaks.

'From the start of next month, we will be running our own ethics committee to provide assurances more widely of our robust processes.'

This sounds like the perfect opportunity for Ben and me to have a voice and ensure that the correct ethical processes take place. Above all else, this is what I want to devote my working life to. It's reparation. If it's down to a vote or show of interest, I must step up despite my natural urge to go unnoticed.

'With thanks to those of you who have agreed membership. And thanks to Dr Harry Curzon for his guidance.'

He pats her arm as she looks up to him. It's a done deal. Of course it is. Somni likes its doors closed and its decisions private.

Harry takes back the reins to direct our activities.

'Now for small group discussions and multi-media presentations on next year's research themes. Aim high, my friends, we are the innovators here.'

I float through the next hour, trying to look engaged and part of the pack. But all I can hear on a loop is Harry's phrase: 'no barriers or limits whatsoever'. The barriers and limits are there to protect everyone – they're essential, not a problem to be stomped over, as I know more keenly than anyone here.

We've been divided into groups of four to discuss themes for future sleep interventions. On each table are huge touch screens that can be drawn on with a fingertip to create designs and a small video camera to directly upload recordings of ourselves to the presentation. I dread this type of task; I've never owned good-quality computers, tablets or fancy phones. As my colleagues chatter and laugh, adding images and fonts, and speaking fearlessly into the camera, I wonder why I can't loosen up and be playful like them. I've never been able to let go in that way as if nothing matters.

The red and silver card laid out on our table reminds me of the Kwik Save trolley. Mum was still in bed and Jake found it hard to keep his voice down, too excited by a ladybird that he found in the hallway. It was my job to ensure the house was quiet and to keep Jake occupied. A few days earlier, I'd spotted the trolley at the top of Briar's Bank that led down into the village a mile away.

'Do you fancy a trip, Jakey?'

He stopped dead, wide-eyed. 'On the bus?'

'Even better than that, come on.'

Behind the rows of terraces was a lane that gave a view over the valley. We'd spot butterflies and pick up lost balls like treasure on weekends. This was the last day of May half-term, warm enough for a crop-top and denim shorts cut from old jeans. I was already counting the weeks before the final term finished and the long stretch of summer holidays would leave us restless and bored as Mum retreated further into her own world. Away from heat and noise. Away from us.

'We're going to escape, down the hill. The fastest you've ever been!'

Jake jigged from one foot to the other, ready to do whatever I said, as usual. I put my hands over his eyes and led him around the bend, past the sycamore to the waiting vehicle. He panted with excitement. I stepped back.

'This is our car now, I'll drive, you get in.'

The red handle of the Kwik Save trolley was scratched but intact. It was the deep kind of trolley for a Big Shop. I held it steady as Jake climbed in. He leaned back with his knees bent, hands holding each side. There was a proper road parallel to the path that wound its way down to the village but that would give more chance of being seen so I stuck to the bumpy path. It took effort to push over the uneven surface despite Jake's light frame. At the top of the hill, I paused.

'Go, Christie, go!'

It was just a game. Not real escape, we both knew that. But for those few seconds, we were flying. The trolley rumbled down and was sturdy enough to take my weight as I leaned forward and gripped the sides. Jake whooped as air swished past my face and blew my hair back. But all I could focus on were the stones on the path that could upend the trolley and cause a crash, the possibility of being seen by a neighbour who'd report us to Mum or the supermarket, the fear of how I'd brake at the bottom. Letting go into the thrill of it was too risky. To let go was to tempt fate, to believe everything would work out, then be crushed by disappointment.

The flip chart in front of us is covered in cut-out pictures and bubble writing with phrases like 'community-based prevention' and 'group sleep labs in old people's homes'. There's an air of play as if we're not talking about real people's lives. I know everyone's name and role, but there's nobody I trust that I can break out of good-worker mode to voice my concerns. The Somni badges we all wear seem to pin onto more than our clothes. It's as if the company pierces into our skin, embeds itself into what we think and say. I need to catch up with Ben and Heidi for their opinion. As the meeting draws to a close, I steal away back to my office to dial Ben's number, then realise he's probably asleep so I cut off after the first ring. He calls straight back. I shut the office door and sit at my desk to answer.

'Hello, Christie. I've made notes from last night's meeting with Harry. Tell me what you think.' He was prepared for my phone call.

'He pretty much confirmed that the company does whatever

it wants, regardless of regulations. The ethics committee is a sham.' I can't let my history repeat itself.

'Agreed. I'm concerned at my restricted level of information. My access to data has been reduced.'

'There are more plans that could relate to Maximus.' I want to figure it out to please him, to show him I'm still capable and clever even though I don't feel it.

'What made you think that?'

'I overheard staff talking, they mentioned GPs. I didn't even know we had any GPs on the books. I couldn't help but think they were speaking about me, about Maximus.'

Ben clears his throat. 'Who was talking about GPs?'

'I recognised Marnie's voice, not the other lady though.'

'Marnie used to work in the old university labs when I was there. I've heard her use that initialism before. She doesn't mean General Practitioner if she was referring to you.'

'What does she mean then? And what are my scores?'

'I believe in this context GP stands for guinea pig. That's what you were. I guess it's the same work contract for other research assistants: Gemma, Helen, Marcus, Sarah. There have been so many more over the years. Possibly all the other levels of researchers – the post-docs, team leaders and so on. I think you are all Somni guinea pigs, in ways you didn't ever realise.'

An image pushes its way to the surface: my mother, agitated and restless, my younger self scurrying around the messy house trying to work out how to help her. My feet taking me to the kitchen to find my own way of helping: an experiment without consent. No, no, I must focus on here and now. My colleagues from Somni – what happened to them all? I'm the only one left of our original cohort of trainees. Something slots into place. Click.

'Yes, for the trials that they know we won't get ethical approval for. We have no problem recruiting for our research trials so there must be a reason that staff are used for certain projects like Maximus.' I imagine little rodents whizzing round and round in their wheel. 'Maximus was probably only one of many unethical research projects his so-called guinea pigs have taken part in. We thought we were just adding to the participant numbers and learning about research from the inside out. But I might not be the only one who's been harmed along the way. Harry doesn't care that it could be dangerous! We're expendable. And it doesn't sound as if anyone is planning to stop him.'

Ben exhales. I can almost feel his breath travel down the telephone and reach my cheek. 'It's down to us then, Christie.'

'Yes, come to my place. Friday? I'll be home by half five. Get some sleep.'

I put down the phone. It's down to us, he said. My fingers absent-mindedly spell out 'us'. The 's' letter is formed by linking one little finger over the other in an embrace.

14

FRIDAY, 17 MAY

It seems strange to have Ben in my hallway: two worlds colliding. He drops his rucksack down onto the floor. A ludicrous image flashes in my mind of it containing sleepover gear: pyjamas, toothbrush, teddy. I stifle a giggle that doesn't fit the context: we're here to discuss concerns about Somni. Why do I have the kind of brain that does the opposite of what I want it to? At Mum's funeral, I'd pinched skin on the back of my hands to stop myself laughing at the abysmal organ music that she would have hated almost as much as the hacking cough that preceded her death. Hopefully everyone thought my shoulders shook with the rhythm of grief. What bubbled up was far less healthy and inescapable – guilt, shame, the lost opportunity to reconnect. My laughter was the only way not to scream.

There are two versions of me: the numbed cool façade and the emotional mess. I remember once showing Jake a 'magic' dessert spoon. He gawped at seeing himself so differently on the two surfaces: upside down and enlarged.

'How are you?' asks Ben, interrupting my thoughts as he pulls box files from his bag.

'Like a spoon.' He doesn't appear to react, and I kick myself for using such a silly metaphor when Ben has told me that he sometimes struggles to understand what I mean by them. 'Ignore me, let's sit down and get started.' I lead him into the living room and realise that he's the first visitor I've ever had here. He smells so clean. Shower fresh. I notice bits of crap on the carpet, a dirty milk-stained glass on my bookcase, how smeared my window is. I'm living like Mum used to when I always swore that I'd escape and have a lovely place of my own once I was grown up. It's as if I don't deserve it, stuck in a time warp, tied to a past that I can't rectify.

Since last night, I've been thinking about all the other research assistants there have been over the years, taking place in multiple research trials. I never bothered to keep in touch with any staff who left Somni. Once they left the company it was as if they ceased to exist. I was so caught up in the bubble of my life that I forgot all about them. My familiar pattern of pretending people don't exist is so automatic that I don't notice I'm doing it.

'Do you remember when we were sent an email from HR that warned us about alcohol and said Marcus had been sacked for drink-driving? It was so plausible. His speech had been slurred a couple of times first thing in the morning, he became clumsy like the time he dropped one of the laptops during a team meeting and smashed the screen. We all accepted that he must have become an alcoholic needing booze for breakfast.'

Ben nods. 'Marcus was certainly in a research trial in the months before he left. I recall him waiting outside Carbon lab in the evenings as I arrived for the night. I wasn't involved in the lab work for his research trial – I've only ever been assigned lab duties with members of the public.'

I picture Marcus sitting on the edge of my desk in the first year we worked together. He had relocated from somewhere in Scotland for the job, as excited as me for the chance to work in such a prestigious company. I think he missed his large family and would call them now and then during breaks, laughing like they were his best friends. Did he turn to drink to cope with homesickness?

'Those symptoms could have been the side effects of a trial years before Maximus. If there really was a car accident, maybe it wasn't alcohol to blame at all but the neurological changes from whatever had been done to him. Then Somni had to find a way to get rid of him by attacking his character.'

Side effects. Accident. Those words dance before my eyes, twenty years old. I imagine them written on a piece of old paper and scrunch it tightly into a ball to regain my focus.

Back to Somni. I'd never bothered to make the slightest effort to contact Marcus at the time or afterwards. How easily I discard people, write them off as if they didn't exist rather than face missing them. A good colleague would show concern. But as far as I know, none of us did. We tutted along with HR and took the Silence for Somni route.

What about Gemma, Helen, Sarah? Did they really go to new jobs or countries of their own free will, or did research testing take its toll on them too? I'd kept my distance after our brief joint training had finished. The three women and Marcus would chat in conversations that I didn't feel I could join in with: which conferences they were aiming to submit papers to, who they knew in the field at other companies, what the next steps were in the career ladder at Somni. I'd smile and switch off.

'What about you, Christie, what did you read?' asked Helen in the staffroom one lunchtime in an attempt to bring me in to their conversation. I felt my cheeks heat up.

'This and that, you know.' I didn't know. I had been happy flicking through magazines in the evening or borrowing my mum's thrillers. 'Different books really, whatever was around.'

Nobody spoke. Gemma glanced over at Helen and I knew I'd been rumbled. Was I supposed to name a list of authors? I'd read so much as a child but once I was working and spending time with Daniel, I suppose I got out of the habit of going to the library.

'At university, I mean, what subject did you study?'

I felt like the chair was melting underneath me, pulling me down into the ground with shame. I wanted to explain but I couldn't get my words out. No matter how far I ran, I would be found as different, undeserving. Marcus tried to rescue me by talking about the university of life. I left the room and always ate at my desk following that.

They've all gone now. And the following cohort of research assistants. Come to think of it, the only leaving party we had was for Sarah before she moved to Canada. Other staff seemed to be there one day, gone the next. Then we'd carry on as if they had never been there in the first place because only staff at Somni counted – our second family. Or maybe our first.

I slump in my chair, overwhelmed with what I know and what more we might uncover.

Ben pulls out papers to form neat piles across the coffee table. 'I've separated the information into areas for us to examine.'

I run my fingers through my hair to untangle it. Did I spend the day at work looking this rough? Ben has only one hour until he has to leave for his nightshift. I realise that he's handing over this information with the expectation that I'll be useful, that it will all make sense to me. I don't want it to become my responsibility. A yawn stretches out between us.

I spent so long being the grown-up when I was a child that sometimes I wish I could snatch back missed carefree time of childhood and use it now.

'Measure the moles, Christie, they're growing, I can feel it,' Mum said.

I'd move my finger from one brown spot to the next across her back. She trusted my head for figures and memory.

'No change today, Mum.' I'd join the clusters of skin blemishes into symbols as if they were constellations of stars to read Mum's future. It could be the shape of a torch for hope, or a diamond for upcoming wealth. Or a dagger for death.

Ben hesitates. I haven't been clear that I want to continue. I'm not even sure if I want to. A sharp sensation presses against my ribs. From the inside. Perhaps I'm programmed to push people away.

'Shall I summarise, Christie?'

I nod my agreement. As he starts to point to columns of figures, I can't help but notice the muscles of his arms underneath his grey T-shirt. I wish I could borrow some strength and recharge myself.

'I checked time stamps on the data entries – figures have been altered long after research projects are completed.'

'So they're massaging data for positive results?' I'm annoyed with myself for not noticing anything odd when I wrote up research projects for publication.

'There are multiple copies of research protocols. I have reason to believe that changes have been made after the projects commenced.'

'Well, I guess that's more of the same? Making changes so that the data are positive and publishable?'

'It's even more concerning than that, Christie.' Ben is serious in a different way to how Daniel was. He cares about fairness, doing a great job, about ethics. Daniel cared about getting ahead, following the latest fad diet, diminishing others to make himself feel better. There I go again, wallowing in my own history while

Ben tries to educate me. No, not educate me – he treats me as an equal.

'The changes to research protocols occur after staff have signed up, sometimes part way through data collection. Some of the changes are substantial – blood tests, changes to which elements of sleep are manipulated and for how long, even trialling new techniques that I don't recognise from their acronyms. In the labs, we've only ever been given protocols for the day so I never realised how plans had been altered.'

'In other words, they can do whatever the hell they want to us! Nobody knows what they're signing up to. There's no consent at all. We've been lied to again and again. And not just during Maximus.'

A chill hits me. What Ben is describing is both new and not new. I'd seen reams of data during Maximus. There were irregularities. Hundreds of them. I remember now. I was so excited about catching the data glitches that I lost sight of the bigger picture: the human cost hidden in a game of numbers on spreadsheets. I had my eyes open but kept my mouth shut.

It had happened again. A cycle I can't break no matter how hard I try.

The chill starts with goosebumps but I can't stop it. If I knew during Maximus and did nothing, then I'm part of the cover-up, part of the lie, yet again.

I hadn't planned to lie to social worker Ivy about my mum back then. My mouth did the talking for me, as if I was listening to one fib after another form such a convincing story that after a minute or two it all felt completely real.

'What kind of activities does your mother do with you and your brother?' she asked, a fixed smile on her face that told me I should have one on my face just the same. The pen in her hand hovered over notes, making it clear that she wasn't asking out of polite curiosity.

'We have craft club after school together and make our own puppets to do a show. And Mummy's great at the voices. It's funny.'

Ivy scribbled away as I spoke, sometimes without even glancing down at the page so she didn't have to look away from me. I was happy to continue.

'On Sundays she makes Olympics in the garden. We've even got sticks to jump over and a paddling pool for swimming.' I jump over a stick as imaginary as the one I'm describing to make the story more convincing. 'At night she does story time for Jake and me, we take it in turns to choose a book. And if it's nice out, we do nature trails and draw the animals we spot while we have a picnic on paper plates.'

It was such a wonderful, convincing world that my cheeks rouged with the thrill of it, and Ivy's smile softened. Her pen lowered. The threat of Mum, Jake and me being separated was shrinking.

'Do you help your mummy out still, Christie?'

I'd told them everything the year before, thinking the old social worker would be glad at what a big girl I was. I had no idea how I'd landed Mum in it by listing all the jobs I did. 'Parentified child' was the phrase I sneakily read at the top of a typed letter Mum got before being called to meetings.

'Oh no, she says I'm her baby now and she's the grown-up. I still like to play with Jakey, but Mummy does the boring things like scrubbing him in the bath and making his tea.' It wasn't a complete lie. Now and then Mum did those things. But mostly it was all still down to me. 'She writes menus on little pieces of paper and folds them over so they stand up on the table before we eat.'

Ivy frowned slightly. I was so good at reading faces that I knew I'd pushed the lie too far, maybe this wasn't something normal mummies did.

'I mean we did that for Jake's birthday tea, to make it special.' I placed my hands on my lap, one over the over like I'd seen Miss Beech do at school when we were doing our silent work.

'And what would you do if you were ever worried about your mother or things became difficult at home?'

I didn't pause for breath. It's hard to know the difference between difficult and normal at that age: you only know the kind of life that you've lived.

'I'd tell the teacher the next day because everyone is just there to help.'

But I wouldn't have told anyone because telling tales meant more social workers, more meetings, more chance of being sent to live with strangers who might not want a boy and girl together.

After our conversation, Ivy went into the kitchen to speak with Mum. I didn't dare press my ear against the door but could hear Ivy's tone was warm and melodic, not the serious shrill tone of the year before when Mum was threatened with a register. I hadn't understood at the time why reading her name off a list like happened every morning at school was a bad thing, but she couldn't settle for weeks afterwards. We came so close to being deemed 'at risk'. By the time the evidence seemed to be clear, Jake was already shipped out and I was old enough to look after myself. Hadn't I always been?

As we stood at the door waving Ivy away, I leant my head against Mum's bony arm to complete the picture of a happy family. I felt her muscles tense, then relax at my touch. She pushed the front door shut and muttered something under her breath as she headed out to the garden to smoke. Her hand trailed a thank you along my shoulders. No goodnight story. No hug. But an acknowledgement that I'd succeeding in sending

Ivy out of our lives. I glowed a little inside at my victory. I'd done it. I'd saved our family.

Except I hadn't.

The next deceitful thing I did would be the cause of disaster. I tried so hard to keep me and Jake together, but my actions were the reason that we ended up apart. I can hear my mother pacing and crying in her room. Jake is whiny, needing my attention. I can't split myself in two. I think I know what will help and where to find it. Mum has no idea what I'm doing. She doesn't consent because she doesn't know. Oh God. Make it stop.

My breath becomes trapped in my tightened throat. For the first time in years, a panic attack grips me. I stretch out to Ben for help, I can't breathe, can't breathe. Ben kneels in front of me, holds my head so I face him.

His voice is an anchor. 'Your lungs are opening, the air enters, blood pumps around your body, the breath leaves.' With each word he states with conviction, my body obeys. I place my hands on his shoulders and watch his chest rise and fall until my own breaths slow to the same rate. He doesn't say another word until I'm ready and I'm so grateful for that.

I'm unsure how long has passed but Ben hasn't moved one inch. 'I'm so sorry,' I half whisper, my voice barely able to squeeze past my sore throat and shame.

'Christie, don't apologise. I learned to do that to stop my panic attacks.' He doesn't realise that I truly have things to apologise for.

'What are we going to do?' I ask, even though I'm fit to do nothing but curl up asleep. I'm the last person to do anything when all my efforts seem to make things worse for everyone. Ben needs to get to work but I wish he could stay here and keep watch over me.

He sighs and returns the paperwork and his laptop into his bag.

'We must be careful, find out everything unethical that has occurred and log it. I'll scan these documents on to my home computer.' He stands, then falters. 'Christie, you must sleep. May I fetch your covers?'

May he? What era was this man born in? I don't deserve his compassion. I can't speak, so nod my head in the direction of my bedroom. I lie along the sofa and wait. He returns with a pillow and duvet, lays it over me. *Don't cry, don't cry.*

'Thank you.' I gulp away a sadness.

Then he leaves, closing the door gently behind him. A man so tender that I feel held even without his presence.

15

WEDNESDAY, 22 MAY

I sense that something is wrong the second I walk into my office, although it takes a moment to figure out what's different. The docking station is empty – my laptop has gone. With codes on every door, this is no robbery. I run to my filing cabinets where I keep brief notes of all the therapy patients I've worked with over the years. Attendance and questionnaire scores are shared with the team via electronic files but my detailed therapy notes are confidential. The key to the filing cabinet is kept in my purse. No one else has the right to read these. I pull the drawer. It opens without the key. Empty. All my files have gone. I slam the drawer shut. This is a violation.

My energy returns as one massive fireball which bypasses my warning system. I'm at the admin desk in a flash in front of an open-mouthed PA demanding to speak with Harry immediately. She phones for him without looking away from me. A couple of heads poke out from offices but I don't turn to see who it is or what their expressions are.

'Think you better come down here, doctor. There's a bit of scene.'

Is that what I am, a scene? I don't care. This is outrageous. I think back to the time it took to build trust with my traumatised patients, slowly undoing the hurt that left them sleepless and scared. A middle-aged woman whose neighbour poisoned her with anti-freeze while pretending to care, a retired farmer who lost his grandson in a horrific accident with the blades of machinery, a woman my age whose baby died of cot death as she lay next to him. The notes I took were to ensure that I provided the best care, that I didn't forget details of their stories, and to allow me to track changes as we progressed with our work. It's not light reading for an unethical bastard to flick through like a gossip magazine. I can tolerate being walked all over but I will not stand for my patients to be mistreated.

Harry breezes down the corridor, placatory smile already etched onto his face. I'm not one of his silly little girls he can use his politician-speak with. The level of energy in my body is invigorating: I'm doing this for every single one of my patients.

'You have no right. I want it all back, now. My laptop, my case notes, and a new lock for the cabinet.'

He raises one eyebrow in surprise at this change in me and holds up his hands. My fingers become a fist that I want to slam into his unprotected torso.

'Ahh, Christie, a little misunderstanding here I suspect.' He bends over me as his PA hovers nearby 'We are merely conducting our audit programme, as laid out in the company governance documents. I trust you've read them?'

'What about my laptop. Auditing that are you?' Disapproval streaks his face, then is gone.

'An upgrade for our hardworking staff, isn't that right?'

I ignore the nodding dog beside me.

'I must remind you, Christie, that all our staff have signed confidentiality clauses. Including you.' He pauses for a moment. 'All data belongs to Somni. For the good of the people via our research and development.'

My lips moved in synch with the Somni stock phrases. For the good of the people. But which people and to what end?

The timing of it hits me then. Only last night, Ben and I reviewed documents on the shared drive using his work laptop. All my files – virtual and real – have been seized. They must be aware that we were snooping. I have no chance of getting any further to figure this all out if I'm deemed a threat. I'll be neutralised, one way or another.

I must get control back over myself. With one hand gripped around my identity badge, I exhale my pride to try to become what Harry expects me to be. Weak, compliant, grateful. It's not a huge step to walk back into shoes that I've worn on most days. I let my body bend slightly to make me even smaller.

'I'm so sorry, Dr Curzon. Of course, I appreciate all that Somni has done for me.' *To* me, what they've bloody done *to* me. But I can hold that anger back. There's another way. A stealthy, fox-like approach. 'I was concerned about the management of my patients' records but as you say, the policies are in place for good reason. I think I'm under a little stress. I'll seek supervision, then take a couple of days leave. If that's okay with you?'

The PA trots back to her desk. Harry flicks his hair back as his body relaxes out of threat mode.

'That sounds like an appropriate plan of action. Let's pretend this never happened, shall we?' His smile is as fake as an advert. He's rattled. I walk back to my office as he watches me. Even though this time I'm in the right, acting guilty brings back a familiar feeling. I place my palms over my eyes and twist my desk chair left to right.

By the time I meet with Elizabeth for supervision, I have post-adrenaline shakes. I'm unsure what she expects of me or what I feel ready to share. There's a kindness in her face that makes it hard to keep up my guard. Some people have a parent like this: balanced, thoughtful, demonstrative. I don't know how to hold all the feelings for what I've lost and what I've never had, so instead I let all them go and drift into neutral gear as usual.

Elizabeth unclasps her hands on her lap and gestures towards me. 'What would it be like to tell me what's on your mind, Christie?'

It's a trick. No, rather it's a technique. Instead of asking a patient to tell you a truth that seems impossible to share, you dance around the edges: what gets in the way of saying it, what would happen to your body and breathing if you were to say it. Less pressure, I guess. Safer. I appreciate her taking the time to phrase this as an invitation, not an inquisition.

I stare at the carpet as I reply so that her concerned face doesn't trigger even more emotion in me. What if I let the words out?

'I was thinking about things that I miss. Because they've gone. Or because I never really had them.'

'Thank you for sharing that, Christie. It's a kindness to yourself to share these painful experiences, I understand that this doesn't come easily to you.'

I want her to understand that I'm not being difficult, that I want to please her.

'You asked me last time if I'd be willing to be in touch with my emotions here. But I'm not sure that I can. I'm feeling lots of things but then it always shuts off without me choosing to, and I don't know how to stop it all slipping through my fingers.'

'You don't know how to let feelings emerge, or you're scared to *allow* them to?'

I feel a flash of frustration at Elizabeth, why does everything get turned around as if I'm trying to deceive? As if my one, huge deception of the past dooms me to a life of lies.

'What if they're the same thing! I can't let all this flood out, I'm already spilling over to you, colleagues, my boss in a way I never usually would. I could lose everything I've built for myself in London.'

Elizabeth nods slowly. She takes her time before she responds, as if she doesn't realise how desperate I am for her to lead me out of this recent pattern of letting my feelings spill over.

'Christie, what if this long-standing belief of yours that to keep things in protects you is wrong? What if that's the thing that weakens you?'

I blink my surprise at this. Everything's topsy-turvy.

'You don't understand. You never saw my mum overcome with emotions, each day too much for her because she couldn't switch them off. They harmed her.'

I used to think of Mum's moods as fire and ice. The hot, ragey distress of her fire episodes were much harder to deal with in the moment than her retreat into an ice world. There was only one of those coping mechanisms that I wanted to use myself.

'And what was the impact on you, to see your mother suffer and be so uncontained?'

The incessant focus on me is stifling.

'I was fine, I got on with it. It was awful for *her*, not me.' Memories try to interrupt of just how awful I made it for my mother but I push them away and focus on a brooch pinned to Elizabeth's sweater – a silver ballerina who dances gracefully on her pointe shoes, smiling to hide the pain in her crushed feet from the audience.

'You learned to tell yourself that you were fine. That you had to get on with things. That the only feelings that mattered were other people's and that you would do whatever you could to relieve them of their pain?' She raises her eyebrows as if to invite an answer. I have none. 'So, you ignore your fatigue, you don't take holidays, you constantly worry about your patients, tell yourself you have no time to connect with new friends in London or to have a life outside of work. You do nothing that is for yourself.'

That's not what I said. Elizabeth tries to pour ideas into my ears, words into my mouth. There's a pleasant dizziness now, as if I could swoon to sleep if we stop talking.

She continues. 'Do you think that in fact part of you *wants* to be able to express your internal world? To allow an emotion to emerge without it being pushed away?'

Ben comes to mind. The way he coached me through my panic. The scent of him: shower gel and musk. The emptiness of my flat after he left.

'Everyone leaves me.' My words surprise me.

Fragments of faces hover in my peripheral vision. My dad who I don't remember, he's a stranger in a photograph holding a podgy baby as he smokes and looks away from the camera; my mum's gravestone in a cemetery back home, unvisited; my brother's empty bed after the accident; Daniel leaving my things outside our shared flat and never contacting me again.

'Everyone? Do you see how you maintain a distance from your feelings when you keep your statements so vague, Christie? Could you funnel down and tell me about one particular person who left?'

The chair feels hard underneath me. I wriggle but can't get comfortable without cushions.

'Daniel. My ex. I'm only living down here because of him. He broke up with me when... last year. It all became very challenging for him.' I recall his shocked face at what I'd become. How he had to wrestle the laptop from me. I'd hidden the phone book of local services – Aardvark Lighting, Abacus Tiles, Abdul and Sons Letting Agents: I wanted to memorise numbers. Needed to. I couldn't stop saying the names and numbers over and over, as if my mind had become that phone book. Daniel looked drained. Then one text message from him and that was the end of over a decade together. Bags on a doorstep. That's how awful I was to live with. Or he was waiting for an excuse to get an upgrade.

'Seems to me, Christie, that when you most needed care and stability, your own partner left you and didn't help you through.'

'That's not his fault. I was out of control! I needed more and more information, like an alcoholic looking for hidden booze in the house. It was my fault.' I dig my nails into my thigh. At the height of the Maximus trial, I'd been ravenous for numbers, facts, the certainty of lists. My eyes scrolled so fast that I was barely aware of what I was observing. The data filled a hole in me that had lain empty for so long that it sucked in whatever it could but was never satisfied. It took the place of something, I'm unsure what. But I couldn't stop. I didn't want Daniel anywhere near me. Or I couldn't have him near me – the urge to defend myself and my tasks was so strong that I was terrified I'd rip him to shreds.

'He left you when you were very unwell, Christie. When you needed him.'

I see those bags. Bin liners that contained everything I owned in the world laid outside our door where any stranger could have stolen them, mixed in with bags of rubbish and recycling.

The heat of my response to the image takes me by surprise. It shoots up through my chest and down both arms into my hands. My fists.

'He left my things out like rubbish. He left me out like rubbish.'

'What do you feel about that right now, Christie?'

Searing heat spreading across my body.

'So angry with myself.'

Elizabeth's hands move from where they rested on her lap out towards me, signalling me to continue. 'If you didn't turn that anger onto yourself, where would it belong?'

The heat shoots down my arms, strengthening them. Ready to fight.

'You've not defended yourself, Christie, not had a healthy barrier of assertiveness between yourself and those who've hurt you. You could choose to use your anger wisely.' I look straight into Elizabeth's eyes. I trust her. Believe her. 'And how would you choose to be treated in a relationship?'

My anger drains away. A softness emerges. I can't think of a description of how I want to be treated, only a memory of a phrase that seemed almost ridiculous at the time. I dismissed it. Now I notice the difference of what it means to be treated with care and respect: Ben's offer to meet my needs that started, 'May I.'

16

When I arrive home, my body still feels strengthened and capable. There's no blue car with a driver sitting inside and I'm half disappointed as I feel as if I could march over to demand an explanation. I'd never thought of assertiveness as a *healthy* use of my anger before. My behaviour with Harry this morning scared me. It seems as alien to me as speaking another language.

My patients have changed their patterns over time. Could I?

I drop my belongings in the hallway, then enter my bedroom in hope that hiding underneath the duvet may help me to let go of the tension.

I don't tend to notice small details around me in my usual state of fatigue, but the adrenaline kick alerts me to the air vent straight away. In the corner of my room, the painted vent doesn't look flush against the wall. Does it usually? I climb onto my bedside table. About half a centimetre of the top of the vent sticks out from its rectangular home. I can't recall if it's always been in this position. I don't think so. Someone's been in the flat. Have they put something inside the vent? I pull on the vent cover and it comes out easily. The brickwork behind is bare. I place the grate back on.

I touch the wall around the vent as if that could bring me an answer. The room feels unsafe now. Soiled. Perhaps the aim was never to place something inside but to mess with my mind. I examine the metal slats that become unfamiliar with so much of my attention. There's a screw missing on the top right. Hadn't that been loose already? The weight of the metal cover could have finally pushed the old screw out: no intruder needed.

Real and unreal merge. I need to see Elizabeth again soon, get her professional opinion on what is going on with me. We have no date booked for our next supervision yet. I need the certainty of a countdown to being with her again.

I call Somni and get through to a receptionist with a Welsh lilt to her voice – another temp.

'It's Christie Langdale. Could you put me through to Dr Elizabeth Field, please.'

There's a pause, followed by the sound of typing.

'Sorry I... no, I don't have a number for anyone of that name. Do you mean the lady who does those podcasts?'

'Yes, she's not a Somni employee, we buy in her time. She must be on the system somewhere. I need to speak with her.'

The swoosh of a hand going over the phone receiver as two people talk.

'I'm sorry, she isn't on the list of approved staff you're allowed to contact out of office hours. Restricted access numbers are beyond my permissions.'

I hang up. Restricted access. For everyone or only for me? They clearly don't want me to be in contact with Elizabeth. What they don't realise is that Ben is coming over on Friday and there's nothing they can do to stop him.

Time off work is a treat for most people, a chance to do whatever they want. That only works if you know what you want. If you can *have* what you want. I try not to worry about my cancelled appointments – has Isobel had a visit from a social worker? Is her son safe? Time to myself and the uncertainty of how to use it sends me into a spin. Free time is an invitation for the past to revisit. I don't want to create enough space for my history to slip through to today.

It wasn't always this way. I had friends from school, colleagues from work, a circle of people that Daniel and I had drinks with. We'd eat tapas in the local bar with two other couples or go for tequila-fuelled nights with his friends to plan a different kind of future, far away. But even then, I didn't let people get too close, afraid of what they'd think if they saw the real me or how I may hurt them without meaning to.

In our worst argument – when I had a panic attack as we packed our life in boxes for London – my feelings got the better of me and spilled out right in front of him.

The enormity of leaving everything hit me as I looked at the pile ready to be loaded into Daniel's car. As half the space was needed for him, I saw my life reduced to two suitcases and three shopping bags. I'd ignored the unsettling feeling that argued with me on the way to a local charity shop that week, as we dropped off bin bags of my belongings. I mistrusted my decisions, so took my cue from Daniel.

'Christie, you don't have to look so anxious. It's fun, like when you're on a rollercoaster or watch a horror film.' I never told him how I hated scary rides and films. That I didn't understand why anybody would put their body into threat mode on purpose when it happened so often with no choice. Daniel was the kind of person to scream with his arms in the air as the carriage tipped over the edge to plunge down to earth. I was the kind of person to grip the bar, close my eyes and tell myself that it wasn't happening in order to survive.

As London was our new start, I didn't want to contaminate it with my second-hand clothes, or novels Daniel called trashy that had helped me switch off from bad times. But there were things I couldn't leave behind.

My hair was pulled back, but with no breeze and the heaviness of the suitcases that I lifted into the car my neck was damp with sweat. I didn't want Daniel to see the wet patches spreading under my arms on the cornflower shirt I'd bought for my new London self. As I pushed the last bag into a small space in the corner of the boot, I ran my hands down the soft material of my top to pull it away from my skin and let in air. But the heat just grew and grew until I felt engulfed. I ran back to our flat and crouched in the kitchen, knees up against my chest.

Was London a new start or just another version of not facing up to the truth?

'What are you doing, Christie? We need to leave.' Daniel leaned against the door frame, flushed. I couldn't explain. I clutched my knees as each snatched breath was a struggle. My shirt was plastered against sweat-soaked skin. I was disgusting.

'For God's sake, do you really need to do this?' Daniel yanked my arm and pulled me to standing. I didn't know if I was more scared that he might leave me or that he might stay.

We'd packed all the kitchen items, so I placed my head under the tap to gulp water, then sprayed a little onto my face and neck. I could feel Daniel's anger without turning to him. What a pathetic mess I was.

'Asthma attack,' I mouthed. We both knew I was lying.

'Sort yourself out. We're leaving in ten minutes. I'm not going to be an audience to this little performance, Christie. Your mum's dead and gone, you don't need to pick up her drama.'

All those years when he'd never said I was anything like her despite my fears. I'd done my best to rein all my emotions in, stay calm and neutral. He'd seen the sickness lurking inside me too, my mask cracked under the strain of change. I unlocked the back door and stood in our yard so the sun could dry off my shirt, which I untied and let loose over me. I imagined the heat scorched all the weakness out of me, turning me to stone. I later learned that's called petrification. I was petrified, that's true. Of myself. Of being alone. Of no escape from the weight of guilt that tied me to the past.

I got back into the car fortified by a total shutdown. It was so effective I couldn't feel anything below my knees. Every emotion floated away and left me in a shell of myself that Daniel could love.

'I'm London-me now,' I said, making myself look at Daniel. Look through him. 'Let's leave it all behind.'

'Good girl.' Daniel kissed my cheek. His stubble grated my skin. I ignored the name Judas that floated into my mind as if in jagged red lettering. I wouldn't let anything ruin things for me. As we drove, the hours melted into each other as I watched the sky darken. I felt weightless – I believed I'd been able to leave my past behind.

I strip parcel tape from the box in my living room like ripping a plaster from the wound of my relationship. I pull out photographs of a younger me sitting with Daniel. I'd never noticed how he always took up more space in the photographs, how I seemed to shrink next to him.

There's a battered leather diary with a broken lock I bought from a charity shop. I loved the smell and feel of it. I flick through the pages and see my handwriting change from familiar rounded loops that Daniel called 'school teacher writing' to barely legible scrawl. This is the book I used to make research notes during Maximus. I logged the experience up until I moved out from our shared flat.

I skim through the final pages.

If they would just give me access to all the data I could show them their miscalculations the slowness of everyone is unbearable I must keep absorbing material or the churning overwhelms me why can't they all see what I see and everything will be different from now only zeros and ones.

Despite the jumble of words, I'm certain there was meaning for me that I could decode. The changes that I've described across time in this diary might be the evidence we need to figure out what happened. We. I text Ben to confirm him coming over the day after tomorrow.

17

THURSDAY, 23 MAY

A 'health MOT' the Welsh assistant said when she phoned this morning. New procedures in the company for sick leave. First I'd heard of it. I'm back here at Somni when I really need a break from the place.

Bryony is the Somni nurse who checks out research participants prior to them enrolling on studies. She's proficient, bordering on cold. We worked on a project together looking at how accurately people rate their impaired thinking after a period of sleep deprivation. The results were clear: we are not good at assessing the impact of late nights on our thinking and judgement the next day. I was interested in what the implications for our findings were in terms of improving people's decision-making. Bryony handed the data over with no interest in outcomes, only in getting more data for the next publication with her name on it.

'So, have you expanded to occupational health now?' I ask, keeping my tone as even as my scratchy throat allows.

Bryony shrugs off my question as she tightens the blood pressure monitor around my arm. It's an old-school version that she pumps air into manually rather than the usual electronic version. It's not standard practice. We sit in her research office rather than a formal clinic space. The shelf above my head is filled with box files and thick text books not medical equipment. The shelf opposite is stacked with boxes of medication that I recognise as dementia drugs: a strange place to keep prescription medication. Why would Somni stockpile drugs that aren't linked to sleep problems?

'That's fine,' she says, removing the sleeve without telling me the blood pressure measurement. I shrink into child mode. We don't feel like colleagues today.

'Is that everything then? I could do with getting back.'

Bryony cocks her head to the side.

'Any particular reason for you to go home?' she asks, glancing at her watch.

'For a rest. Bit of telly maybe, you know?' Of course she doesn't know. Daytime television isn't the escape of professionals. *Stupid woman, why didn't you say to read or catch up on emails.* The heat starts in my cheeks and spreads across my chest in red splodges, a map of my shame. Bryony sucks at her teeth.

'Are you experiencing hot flushes? Dizziness? Excessive sweating?' She's tapping into her tablet. I can't see the screen.

'No, not at all. It's a bit warm in here that's all.' She's already taken my temperature and said it was fine.

Bryony swipes something on her tablet. One corner of her mouth lifts slightly.

'It's 18.6 degrees. Under average room temperature. I think we should keep you here for a little while for observation.'

'There's really no need–'

'I'll be the judge of that, Christie – that's my job. Make sure you keep hydrated. Somni smoothies are specifically designed to meet dietary deficiencies. And you should be aiming to lower your BMI, it's just outside the healthy range – we don't want you needing more time off.' Bryony stands, her tablet pressed against her chest. 'I'll come and get you when the observation period is over.' I glance at the door. 'I'll let reception know.'

She'll let reception know that I'm here, or let them know that I'm not to leave? My words won't come out. Before she leaves the room, Bryony fiddles with the computer monitor in front of me, slightly adjusting the angle of the screen even though it's switched off.

Alone in her office I purse my lips and blow the air out as if in a straight line. There's no space to move to so I stay in the plastic chair in front of her desk computer. The small circle of its webcam points straight at me.

18

FRIDAY, 24 MAY

I tell myself it's a spring clean – getting the flat ready for company later today. But it's more than that. I can't get the idea out of my head that I'm being monitored. I need to check the place isn't bugged. Trouble is, I've no idea what that would look like. A tiny black microphone or a mini camera? Can it be smaller and subtler these days, disguised as an everyday object? The metal screw in a drawer, the circular end of the curtain pole, a nut on the radiator? I turn them and inspect for signs of something that doesn't look right. I yank off the flimsy fireguard and feel around in the dust but there's nothing there. I'm flying around so fast that I can hardly keep up with my own thoughts. I imagine people in an office in Somni, laughing as they watch me on a monitor.

I find nothing out of the ordinary.

There's a particular voice my mind uses to mock me. It judges me, at how ridiculous I've been over the last two hours. How self-obsessed and paranoid. It's my voice but with an edge to it. Sometimes I talk to patients about their 'internal bully'. They have no idea that I live with mine every day. We learn how to talk to ourselves by the way we are talked to when we are young. In this way, we never really escape our parents. We create a mini mother or father inside ourselves to tut, attack, mock us long after the real person is gone. On good days, I can ignore it. On tricky days, every criticism from inside my own head feels utterly true.

That voice also makes guesses about other people's intentions. I judge myself through their eyes. My first proper boyfriend was Daniel whose communication style and self-focus fitted with my expectations. It felt wonderful when he paid me attention, understandable when he didn't. But years before we got together, I nearly allowed myself to get close to a friend, Ravi. He worked part-time at the café to fund his studies at university. We'd chat in the lull between lunch and dinner about music, books, politics. Ravi had a low, soft voice that soothed me after a morning at my mum's house. We made up stories about the regulars at the café. His were never unkind but funny and fantastical. A few months before I turned eighteen, he left a card on the counter with my name on it as he finished his shift. I opened it in front of the manager, unprepared for its contents. It was a Valentine's card – two cartoon bees buzzing around a flower. *It's a joke, he's being kind, he feels sorry for you, he doesn't know what you really are.* My cheeks flamed. Lesley the owner said Ravi was utterly in love with me and laughed raucously to see how I'd never noticed. That information changed the way I felt about him. *There must be something wrong with him* was my conclusion, as nothing else made sense. I cooled our friendship – no more stories, no more gossip. When he stopped doing shifts to start his graduate job, I had no contact details for him. Now and then he slips unrequested into my mind. I never told Daniel about Ravi; pretended it didn't matter and didn't hurt. But I kept the Valentine's card, hidden between pages of a notebook.

I collapse onto the sofa. My arms ache from housework. The

room looks pleasant at least: I've pulled out items from drawers and boxes. A candle I had for my thirtieth birthday fills the room with vanilla scent. Wire statues of little figures with water jugs decorate the mantelpiece. A ceramic egg with odd earrings in – in case their lost sibling reappears – sits at the centre of the table. I've rearranged my books from chaos to colour-coded.

There are ways to get more control of our minds but it isn't what people think. Patients say they want to 'get rid of' anxious thoughts or only ever 'think positively'. That's the Somni dream. But what happens then is they get into battle with themselves and invest huge amounts of energy into a fight they can't win. Minds do what minds do: you can't pick and choose which images or words show up. But you can change your relationship with what emerges. You can watch it flow like a river without being sucked into the current.

I know all this. And I believe it. I've seen it be effective for scores of patients. But I haven't tried it on myself. I couldn't get through to Elizabeth today but I can guess what she'd say: 'Isn't it interesting that you don't allow yourself to benefit from that which helps others.' I love the way she speaks. Clever without trying to be. So, what if I purposefully pay attention to what my mind is saying?

What a ridiculous thing to do, don't you have better things to spend your time on? A deluded woman running around. What time is it anyway, how long until Ben comes? You don't seriously think he's coming for anything other than work, do you? Have you looked in the mirror? This is a waste of time.

There it is, a monologue: half me and half Mum. I let it whitter away as I walk to the shower. My judging mind will have plenty to say once I'm in there, naked.

I spot Ben's legs through my bedroom window as he walks over from his car. Before I pull open the front door, I unclamp my teeth and lower my shoulders.

'Hello, Christie. I wasn't sure if this counts as dinner time so I brought cake.' He hands me a tin: it must be home-made. Heidi once said his lopsided face made him look like he'd had a mini-stroke. I should have told her to google a young Harrison Ford.

'Cake is always good, thanks.'

'You should never arrive empty-handed.' Years ago, Ben explained how he has worked hard to learn 'rules' of what to do in different situations. It matters to him to make an effort for me. I wonder who decides what 'right' is? He takes off a thin jacket and hangs it on the coat hook that I've never thought to use. Maybe I'm the one who needs life lessons.

As we enter the living room, Ben looks from one new item to the next. I cringe at the memory of what the flat looked like last time he was here. What *I* looked like, all panicked and passed out on the sofa.

'You've changed it in here.' He leans his bag against the table and pulls out paper and pens.

'Yes, I've had a bit of time off work, it's given me a chance to sort a few things out.' I signal for him to sit on the sofa with me. How do I say what's happened without sounding unhinged? I long for a normal conversation with Ben. 'Tell me about why you work at Somni.'

'I can make sense of sleep, in ways other people can't. Polysomnography maps out far more than we'd ever realised. Cognition, emotional processing, memory consolidation, creativity. Each is linked to specific wave patterns that I can read from the charts.'

I've experienced the dire consequences of one type of sleep being altered too much. In Maximus, my function was initially boosted but eventually became severely impaired: messing with nature has consequences. You can have too much of a supposed 'good thing'. An imbalance of one type of sleep dysregulated my whole system, tipping from attentive and creative into obsessive and paranoid. I don't want to interrupt Ben and make it about me, so I keep these thoughts to myself.

'I'm comfortable in that world.' He doesn't seem comfortable with me here now though, not knowing what to expect from me after last time we met. I notice the fingers of one of his hands move in a pattern: thumb to first finger, then thumb to middle finger and so on, up and down on repetition. I've learnt to read his hands. He follows my gaze and stops his finger movements. 'Christie, you know I'm autistic. Working in a sleep clinic fits for me. There's less pressure on night shifts, fewer people to see. I can get on with my work without worrying when to smile or look at someone or stop talking about sleep. We lower the lights in the sleep lab, it's so quiet that I can think clearly. I love my job and the life I've created. Part of the reason that I'm good at it is that I'm different to you and most others there.'

'I like that you're different! You taught me so much when I arrived. Nobody else saw that I struggled. Or they didn't care.'

'I get things wrong sometimes although I do my best. I don't always understand it when people say the opposite to what they mean. Or they talk for a long time without really saying anything at all.' He turns away from me. 'It can be exhausting.' He has faint freckles across the ridge of his nose. I wonder if he hates them or embraces them. *Different* isn't a dirty word when it's applied to him – it sounds like interesting, special, unique. I wish I felt that way about my own differences.

'Do you know the thing I appreciate the most about you, Ben? I can trust you to tell me the truth.'

He smiles. 'You can. I will.' I get the sense he's figuring out the next truth to tell me. 'When I don't look at you, it's not ignoring, it's so I can pay full attention to what you're saying without the visual information overloading me. But I also *enjoy* looking at you.' He turns to me then and I realise that his eye contact is so rare that when it hits, I hold my breath. I don't have a way to cope with a compliment, scared that my brain will betray me and make me say something stupid in return.

'Let's eat and I'll update you,' I say, scurrying from the room. In the kitchen I notice a slight tremor to my hand. There's something happening between us. I don't know what to expect or how to act. I cut slices of cake and make coffee, then use my old waitressing skills to balance it all along my arm to take into the living room. 'They're onto us.' I bite into the cake – lemon sharpness mixed with sweet icing. 'My laptop's been confiscated and they've pulled all my paper notes. I even thought they'd been in the flat, but I can't find anything they could have planted so that's probably my imagination.'

Ben eats his cake with a spoon that I'd brought in to stir the coffee. I feel ashamed of my sticky fingers and suck them clean.

'Perhaps they weren't leaving anything behind; they may have been looking for an item to take?'

I hadn't thought of that. What is there that they would be interested in? It would have to be linked to Maximus. Removing evidence. My laptop is still here and I don't keep any work notes at home. I kneel in front of the box in the corner of the room and start to remove photos and notebooks.

'Oh God, I had a diary with notes from the research trial. It was definitely here two days ago; I had a quick look through. I should've read it all but I skimmed through. I was waiting...'

Ben leans forward, as if unsure whether to get up or not. But there's nothing left to see.

'What did it look like? It's a very full box.'

I empty out the box one item at a time in case it fell through a space to the bottom.

'It was old, second-hand, real leather. With a broken lock.'

As I describe it, the diary sounds as if it's from a fairy tale: a dusty old diary full of secrets that disappears? Sounds a bit unbelievable. But I saw it, I even read an extract from it, I recall the feel of the soft material of the cover under my fingertips. That was before I got trapped at work under false pretences yesterday. Giving plenty of time for someone to get into the flat that Somni owns. That Somni probably has keys to.

'You said you didn't look at the diary properly as you were waiting. What were you waiting for?'

Ben has shown me years of kindness and respect. Taught me so much when nobody ever took the time before: not at Somni, not at home. I've grown to notice and understand his ways. He craves certainty and safety as much as I do. But he has achieved what perhaps I never can: acceptance of self.

I crawl over to him. He opens his arms and holds me against his chest.

'I was waiting for you.'

19

SATURDAY, 25 MAY

My dining table is covered with scraps of paper: old work schedules, research papers, a timeline of last year that I've tried my best to put together. Ben is coming back shortly to spend the rest of the weekend over here. He's gone home to download his work documents onto an untraceable home laptop.

My notes summarise what I can recall from Maximus. It might help to untangle my memories to write them out in order.

April –
Accept place in research trial while it awaits official
sign off for the public. Study states it aims to improve work-
related performance by boosting non-REM sleep.
May –
Preparation sessions: in sleep lab with monitoring
equipment.
June –
Nightly sessions in sleep lab to change sleep
architecture. Booster sessions in research room. Notice
increased speed at work in daily tasks on computer.

July –
Memory capacity greatly increases, multiple tests for
this including learning London routes. Database work: able
to see patterns in data to inform staff where to focus next
research trial. Urge to learn builds stronger, becomes more
like a need to learn and memorise. Working long days,
difficult to stop even when people tell me to. Frustration
builds.
August –
Hazy. Obsessively learning lists of facts from
Wikipedia. Reduced appetite and thirst. No dreams that
can be recalled. Easily upset and frustrated. Believe people
are against me and not making use of my improved skills.
Shouting, pushing someone?
Lying in a medical bed somewhere at Somni.
Confusion, memory loss, distress. Harry visits. Rehab work
and relaxation training in chair. Discharged.
Dumped by Daniel, moved house. Emotionally flat and
drained. Continued memory and concentration difficulties,
signed off sick from work.

Rereading my list I can see how appalling this is. Why
wasn't I pulled from the trial earlier or debriefed afterwards?
What happened to the other participants? I should have
demanded to find out more and written the results up to warn
other researchers. The only way for science to progress is to
learn from mistakes. The initial results were sensational: there
could be ways to harness the potential without causing harmful
side effects but only if we pool information and make changes to
the next research protocol.

This time away from work appears to have cleared my head
a little. I can think and remember things far better than over the
last few months. But none of my questions are going to be

answered by staying at home. I can't let Somni buy me off with a rent-free flat and the threat of confidentiality clauses. I need to take the risk – get back to work to investigate. But first, I have the rest of today with Ben.

We sit on a wall in my backyard drinking bottled beer. The sunset throws gold shades onto the paving slabs, beautifying a place I usually hate. Earlier this evening, Ben looked through my notes and tried to access files to see what happened to the other people in the trial, but he was blocked from viewing. We both agreed to return to Somni to gather as much data as we could. We already have a working document that proves several studies used different techniques on the staff than the original consent form described. We don't know how widespread the fraud is. I'm unsure we can manage this by ourselves.

'I could ask Heidi for help as her clearance is higher than mine?'

'We have to be careful, Christie. We can't be certain who we can trust.'

'Heidi's my friend.' The beer speaks then, 'Don't you think she's beautiful?'

Ben's nose wrinkles. 'She looks like a shop mannequin.'

There definitely aren't any shop mannequins that resemble me.

Ben places his half-drunk bottle on the wall next to him. 'Do you remember that research trial a few years ago when we had such a high drop-out rate that it was at risk of collapse?' It was a project to help women who'd been sexually abused and suffered with nightmares and sleep phobia to regain their ability to sleep for seven hours. 'We went through the test data again and again to see what we'd missed in terms of motivation, personality, avoidance scales but nobody figured out what was wrong. It took you less than a minute because you asked the right question.'

Sometimes scientists get so trapped by numbers and hypotheses that they forget what it means to step into somebody else's shoes. The question I asked was, what gender are the lab techs working on this project? They were male. All of them. These vulnerable women were expected to feel safe to sleep in a room where a man had attached wires to them, and another man was observing their sleep waves in the room next door.

'It was a different focus, that's all.'

'Exactly. That's what you bring though, Christie. You're so good at getting inside people's heads. That's why I'm certain that you will find a way to understand and persuade Harry to review practices so that they fit an ethical code. If not, then we will have to take action outside of the company. Whatever it takes to get Somni back to the way it was when it was a university research institute.'

'I wish I had as much faith in me as you have!' *He's going to be so let down when he realises what you're really like, no better than Somni.*

'I think you're brave. And clever. And kind.'

Nobody has ever called me brave before. Clever, yes – a curse in high school where doing well made you a target. I soon learned to do worse to fit in. I'm really careful to make sure what I do can be considered kind rather than selfish, ever since I worked out what happened that led to the fire. But 'brave' seems an unusual description when I feel so cowardly most of the time.

Things are changing.

'Let's go inside,' I say, as I take his warm hand and lead him back indoors. It's strange to be the one to decide what we do, to allow myself the vulnerability when I could be rejected.

We sit close together on the sofa. It sinks in and moulds

itself around us. It feels as though everything fades into the background apart from Ben. His hair and freckles have brought the orange night indoors to warm me. His shoulders look made for rugby.

Or for holding burden.

There's so much to find out about his life. I almost cherish the unknown, what we have to learn about one another. Last night I slept for over six hours. My dream dissolved as soon as I woke but I'm certain Ben was part of it. I don't remember the content but I do recall the feeling of safety and contentment.

I squeeze his hand. 'I think I'd sleep better if you were here.' His openness releases mine.

'Research shows that couples gain more quality sleep in separate beds although their verbal reports tend to state they sleep better with their partner.' He catches himself and laughs. 'But it's not all about sleep waves, I suppose.'

Was it his unconscious desire that jumped to speak about couples and partners? Or was that fact triggered by me stating I wanted him to stay here tonight? I crave his touch. Closeness.

I turn my arm over, palm upwards.

'Show me the sleep waves, how they look.' I place his finger so that it rests on the top of my arm. He understands my request and moves it in a dance down to my wrist.

'These are the chaotic brainwaves in waking time. No pattern. So much information at once.' His finger dances an erratic rhythm along my arm to my wrist. I move his arm around my back. He places his hand flat against my skin and pulls me closer. 'This is a sleep spindle.' His finger traces short bursts of activity across my back.

My body responds: an ache of desire.

His hand curves around my middle and I freeze. He stops, looks up to check I'm okay. The world divides into two paths: do I push him away or trust that he won't reject me? I place my hand on top of his to show my consent. Ben sweeps his thumb over my stomach more slowly with a greater rise and fall. 'This is non-REM sleep: slow-wave activity where the peak-to-peak amplitude is high while the wave frequency is low.' My skin there has been untouched and hated for so long, now it melts under his movements. He traces a pattern from left to right across me. 'You're beautiful. All of you.'

I pull him down to lie on the sofa next to me. My head rests on his chest. I hold on to him as if we're the only people left, floating together in a boat on the ocean as the world burns.

20

I've been off work for five days. My head is clear, my mood is buoyant and I feel ten years younger than last week.

I wave to Anja on my way into the building and watch her mouth drop open as I press the button for the lift for the first time since Maximus. Although I have enough energy for the stairs, I don't want to let avoidance run the show anymore: I need to get into small spaces and survive. As I step into the lift, I see a version of myself in the mirror that looks different – resilient. With my shoulders pulled back and spine straight, I'm steadier. The lurch to my stomach as the doors shut isn't enough to knock me. My finger hovers over the buttons for higher up the building – six, seven, eight – before I choose the familiar fifth floor. One step at a time.

Heidi leans on the Somni reception desk as I exit the lift. Not her usual perky self. Her body twists towards me. Did Anja phone up to say I was coming?

'Hey, good to see you, Christie.' She looks me up and down. 'I heard you took time off, you look great!'

'I feel so much better for it. Are you sticking around?'

She nods and we go through to our office. Her eyeliner looks a little smudgy – I can't help but wonder if she's come straight off a night shift but hung around to check up on me. It's unusual for any of the female staff not to look immaculate – sometimes the office corridors are like catwalks.

'What have you been up to then, Miss I-don't-take-holidays?' Her humour falls flat. She could be fishing. Or she's being a caring friend. Ben's suspicion of her has rubbed off on me, but here's my colleague asking after me, isn't that a normal thing?

'Making my pigsty into a palace,' I reply. She rolls her eyes. We are such opposites in most ways. She can't bear that I don't have a section in my handbag for lipsticks. Truth is, I barely have any make-up to put in one. 'Actually, it's really nice to be back.' I realise that it's true. Despite everything, I've missed my office, my colleagues, my patients. I long to be back in my role that tells me who I am. This place isn't forever tainted. I won't let it be.

'Wait a minute, what's that red mark on your neck?' Heidi rushes over and wraps my hair behind my ear. 'Oh my God, you've got a new man! That's why you've been missing in action. Tell me everything.' I sense her relief. What else did she think I was doing?

I want to tell her about Ben. Rekindle our friendship but for some reason, it feels treacherous, as if that would spoil what Ben and I have between us.

'I'll tell you when I'm sure there's anything to tell.'

Heidi squeals and hugs me. She's been good to me over the years. When I passed my psychotherapy course, she seemed even more excited than I was. Than I let myself be. She gave me a gift card for one hundred pounds to spend in the bookshop, knowing that I'd never be so decadent usually to buy books that weren't second-hand. She called me Dr C for the following week despite the fact that my evening class was nowhere near that level of study. I shushed her but it meant the world that someone was proud of me.

'Well, make sure you do. I'm super excited for you. This one better be a good guy.'

A slight frown creates little creases of concern above her nose. Heidi used to be more affectionate to me in the old days, quick to hug and reach out for my hand in excitable conversation. But I rarely reciprocated. It didn't come naturally. Now I miss it. She thinks I don't want or need it. Push, push, push away. I lift my fingers near her right arm as I answer, not quite making contact.

'He really is, I'm sure of it. Unlike any other man I've met. Maybe one day I'll be as happy as you are.' Heidi has a dashing fiancé who still makes her flush to talk about.

Heidi never liked Daniel. She hinted to me that he was controlling but I couldn't see it. I took it as protective that he usually joined me on work nights out and liked to be updated about what I was doing. London was another world compared to home, one full of danger and missing people. One night, Heidi and I were out for unplanned drinks straight after work and Daniel texted to tell me to come home. She took his number from my phone and sent him a message to say she would keep me safe and that he shouldn't smother me. Daniel was furious when I got back in case I put her up to it. To my shame, I let him slate her and went along with his summary that she was a jealous, bitter woman who didn't want me to be in a committed relationship before she was. Guess I wasn't that good at spotting projection when it came to my own boyfriend.

'I'm sorry if I haven't always been a good friend,' I say, now holding Heidi's arm. 'I know you tried to warn me about Daniel.'

Heidi tears up and squeezes me tightly. Instead of this relaxing me, my muscles tense on guard.

'No, no, no. Don't say sorry. You're the best. It's me who's been so busy all the time, then swapped to night shifts – I haven't been around for you. Sometimes it's a little hard to get close to you.'

She's right. My instinct is to keep people at arm's length. I must decide whether that's how I want to live my life. I could lower my forcefield with Heidi, Ben, Jake even, though that feels risky for me and for them.

I need her help. The only way I'm going to get it is to ask directly, regardless of my fears about how she could respond.

'Heidi, you think nothing that happened to me was due to the Maximus trial, but don't you think it's odd that we didn't hear anything about the research trial after that? There was no publication of results or explanation as to why the trial was stopped. In fact, I've never heard anybody speak about Maximus since I've returned to work and nobody seems to be working on a write-up despite some really promising avenues for improving work performance if the methods were amended. I've been wondering – there must be other people who were part of it, I could track them as part of a follow up if you get the names for me.'

Heidi sits on my desk. Her slender legs dangle down from a shift dress like a marionette's. I imagine silver-thread strings hanging from our ceiling tied to her jaw and arms, directing her actions and speech.

'Oh, Christie, we *did* track them. I didn't want to bring it all up so I didn't tell you.' Time slows down as she speaks so that I feel the force of every single word. 'Every other participant was fine. There was mild improvement to work-based tasks in the first couple of days, nothing out of the ordinary really, likely to be a placebo effect. And no one suffered from any side effects.' She fiddles with items on my desk, lines up the stapler, pen box and telephone. I've seen her get more organised when her stress levels peak. 'The study wasn't abandoned because it made you ill, it was stopped because there was so little difference made by the trial, it was deemed ineffective.'

It doesn't make sense. Why would it have only worked for me, then switched to being so disastrous for me with side effects? I can't slow myself down as I garble out my reply.

'But it had a massive impact on me at first. My memory, recalling all those streets. Speeding through the database, remember? I could do the maths so easily, see patterns jumping out.'

Heidi hangs her head down, her cheeks turned even pinker than the generous blusher she wears.

'Christie, I didn't want to have to tell you.'

No, no, no. I don't want to hear it.

'But none of it was real. You were inventing street names. Seeing patterns that weren't there. I tried to explain that but you became so angry. It wasn't Maximus. There weren't any side effects. The truth is, you weren't superhuman, you were sick.'

I grip the chair and stare out over the city feeling as if I'm back in the confines of the lift after someone cut the cords, plummeting.

Nothing is what it seems.

Whatever happens in my personal life, I come to this therapy room for focus. The time here belongs to my patients. Everything else can wait. Heidi tried to steady my nerves ready for therapy this afternoon with a vanilla smoothie and a wholegrain health bar. I told her I'd be fine but neither of us believed it.

It's ten past and Mike still hasn't arrived. This isn't like him at all. I think back to our last session and how I'd felt a seed of hope for him. I take my work phone off silent and check for messages. There's a voicemail.

I'm relieved to hear it's Mike. He's okay at least, although I'm disappointed that he hasn't attended.

'Christie, it's Mike. Sorry I can't come to my appointment today. Hope you're feeling better after a rest.'

That doesn't make sense. How would he know I've been off work? It didn't interfere with his planned appointment. I can only guess that he phoned reception to cancel, then Anja or Harry's PA have spilled details that they shouldn't have. What a mess. The last thing I need is for my patients to worry about me instead of themselves.

But given everything Heidi has revealed this morning, they could be right to worry.

I can't tell what's real from what isn't. I cover my eyes with my palms to try to stop the tears leaking out that would give them more evidence that I'm broken.

21

TUESDAY, 28 MAY

Mia's dressed in a low-cut top and jeans so slim they could be a child's size. Her lips glisten an unnatural shade of pink.

'I've had a wild weekend, no time for sleep.' She stretches cat-like and awaits my questions. Today, I'm determined to remain in control. If she doesn't wish to work on anything with me, then I'm going discharge her regardless of how much her parents bankroll the company.

'It seems to me that choosing not to sleep is very different to having an actual sleep disorder, which is what this clinic is for.' I haven't slept much either. The insomnia is back. I should never have trusted the brief respite I had from it. I don't deserve the relief.

Mia picks at sequins on her top with a long nail. My guess is she will sulk into withdrawal or attack me verbally.

'Well, what if I'm busy every night to cover up my sleep disorder? If I can't sleep then I might as well be having fun, right?' Her mouth turns down a little at the edges.

'Are you saying that your escapades are a way to avoid your

difficulties with getting to sleep? That you wouldn't act that way if you didn't have insomnia?'

She frowns a little. My language was a poor choice. Why did I use the word 'escapade' like a Victorian nanny? Because I'm frustrated with her. She doesn't have any real problems, unlike my other patients. Unlike me.

'I find it hard to sleep in strange places. But I was at a party with Francesca and a drop-dead gorgeous model wanted to be with us both at the same time. Fran was a bit shy, but...'

I don't need to hear this. 'Mia, what you chose to do with your night is your business. It may be a cause of you getting no sleep. That's not clinical insomnia.'

'What is it then,' her teen voice goads me, 'in your *professional* opinion?'

I glance at the clock to see how much longer I have to endure the appointment.

'You're checking the time! I only just got here and you want to get rid of me.' Her whine takes me by surprise. Trouble is, she isn't wrong. 'You're all the same, you want me to shut up and get out of the way. It isn't fair.' The sulk is in full force. I can't tolerate the toddler in front of me. Dizziness starts up as my temples ache.

'Mia, I suggest you take a look at your behaviour to help you figure out why people don't want to be around you.' Her jaw drops. I should stop. I *really* need to stop. But she's attentive at last. 'You have it all. You can go out when you please, with no money worries. You're young and beautiful, under that sludge of make-up anyway. To be honest, it pisses me off that you think you have it hard. Grab your life! See friends, enjoy the world. You could seduce any man around, so why not pick a decent one and stick with him? Why do you throw yourself away into substances that cloud those moments and spend time with people who clearly don't give a damn about you rather than forging great friendships? You have the whole world to travel, so much opportunity to see and do what you want, yet you waste it.'

My breathing is so fast that I have to undo my top button. I feel shaky. Out of control.

'Oh my God, you're jealous of me!' She places both feet on the floor and sits straight. Her arms drop against her sides, the red nail polish chipped at the tips.

'I suppose I am. But not of you as you are. I'm envious of everything you've got that you don't appreciate. That I *would* appreciate.' It's gone way past being professional, I may as well say what I think. I'll probably get the sack after Mummy and Daddy hear about it.

She looks down at her lap. Her lack of argument surprises me. Stops me in my tracks.

'You think this is what I want?' She pulls at her hoop earrings. 'I know what I look like. It does the trick. Gets attention, sex, free drugs.' Her voice sounds different, suddenly a decade older. 'My friends, these men. They wouldn't come near me if I didn't flash my wealth and body. But what else is there? My father lives for his work and is out of the country. My mother always has some crappy event to go to or charity people to impress. They think it's me who's rubbish at communication while their assistants pick out gifts for my birthday. It's always been that way.'

I pay attention now. To what she says, to her eyes glazed with near-tears, to the lonely child in a changing body. A sadness engulfs me: mine and hers combined. In the end we are a resourceful species. If we can't get what we need then we find ways to get the next best thing. She gets adoration on Instagram and her name known on the party circuit. It's not enough but it seems better than nothing.

What do I get from being a therapist that makes it so important to me?

'So, what do you really want?' I ask. The bitter judgement has evaporated. I can work effectively with the scared young woman in front of me. A survivor, doing her best to find a place for herself in a world that doesn't owe her anything.

She shrugs and searches the ceiling for an answer. 'For someone to want to spend time with me for me, not for what I can do for them or pay for. To feel good about myself. What else is there?'

We look at each other for a moment as if looking into a hall of mirrors.

Her words resonate with me. I take my time before replying. Let the words form in front of me.

'I don't think there *is* anything else. All the other behaviours drive towards that: to connect and feel worthwhile.' I shouldn't be talking like this with a patient, as if we are friends, yet it feels the most human thing to do.

We agree to finish the appointment early to reflect on what we've discussed. Mia places her bag onto her shoulder.

'Thanks, Christie. See you next time. Oh, and I think Mike will be back next week.'

I need to get fresh air before my afternoon write-ups. As I stand in the foyer ready to put my glass bottle into the recycling, I spot a little of the smoothie left. I hold the bottle up to the light. Around the glass is a film of white powder. It's the same drink I have every morning that I'm in this section of the building to deliver therapy. I flash back to another drink from a long time ago, the glass heavy in my hand. I force myself back into the here and now, tilting the bottle to figure out if my mind is playing tricks of time. I don't think it's milk residue. Powder. Provided by Somni. In the last two instances, it has been personally handed to me by Heidi.

22

I'm not a gym person. I'd say I'm the opposite of a gym person. But here I am, cycling the agitation out of my legs on an exercise bike while high-tempo music pumps endurance through my headphones. Putting lots of effort into going nowhere.

My thoughts spin along with my legs. Mia's admission that she's in contact with Mike is baffling. They don't attend on the same day so couldn't have met in the waiting room. Has Mia targeted my clients to seduce or play games with? I can't think of a way she would know who I'm working with unless she has a direct line to someone at Somni to gather information about me. If so, I'd have expected her to use it against me in sessions: her version of a power play.

Then there's the powder in my 'health' drink. It could be harmless – a vitamin supplement. Am I confusing past with present? Or getting what I deserve?

I cycle faster.

Pain isn't always an enemy. Not when it has a purpose. I focus on the scream in my thighs and the burn of my lungs as I pant my way through another mile. I can't bear to stay trapped in my head this evening. No matter how I try to piece together the puzzle of what's happened to me and how everything is connected, the parts won't fit. A mirrored wall ahead reflects the ladies pedalling either side of me. One is young, with not so much as one bead of perspiration affecting her perfect make-up. The other is middle-aged, gasping with scarlet cheeks. She's going slowly but doesn't stop. I should have paced myself too. I'm burnt out. As I climb off the machine, my ankles feel as if they could give way and drop me to the floor.

I refill my water bottle and sit on a bench overlooking the main studio. It's a women-only gym. I wonder about the stories of everyone here: how one person's time out can be another person's hell. I don't want to think about Heidi but this is the type of place she belongs in rather than me. The residue on the glass bottle she handed me could have been medication or maybe glucose powder or a crushed vitamin. She'd never harm me. However, she's already shown she can hide things and lie to avoid a difficult conversation. My trust in her is disintegrating. But tampering with my drink seems too extreme. I shouldn't have thrown the bottle away. There's no chance for me to check when my head is clear.

I can't keep fighting my thoughts. What if I run through them instead? I find a treadmill in a corner and set a slow pace. Which each thump of my foot I allow the next name to come up as if in front of me on a screen: Heidi, Harry, Mia, Mike. Then I turn the speed up on the machine and raise my pace until all the words merge into one long stream, too fast to figure anything out.

I close my eyes and run for my life.

I don't leave the gym until after seven o'clock. The Tube ride home felt hypnotic and healing. My body aches in a satisfying way. As I turn into my street, I see the blue car. It's on the opposite side of the road to my flat, facing away from me. Around ten metres. I'm still in gym gear so pull up the hood on my sweatshirt and tuck my hair out of sight. Rather than cross the road where I usually would by the postbox, I stay on the same side of the pavement as the car. I'm unrecognisable. My pulse beats in my jaw.

As I get nearer to the car, I see that it has scratches along one side despite being only last year's number plate. Somebody has been in a rush. The top of the driver's head shows above the back of the seat. As I close the gap and look through the side window, I can make out a mobile phone in one hand emitting light, but not what's on the screen. The driver's head is fixed to the left to watch out for anyone approaching my flat. Definitely watching out for me. There had been times where I argued with myself as to whether I was imagining things or being paranoid. But here's the evidence. I'm in line with the back of the car. I'm alert, awake, alive. I haven't been spotted: I win.

The world slows down then. I knock three times on the window, bending forwards to catch eyes. The figure jumps. Turns to me. Drops the phone in recognition. We stare at each other for a tiny eternity.

Daniel.

My ex found me. It wasn't paranoia; he's been stalking me all this time.

He mouths 'shit,' and I feel bionic. I pull at the door handle as if I could rip it off, drag him out, demand answers while I pin him against the bonnet. It's locked. He grabs for his keys. The car lurches forward as it stalls. He looks up once more, his neck taut, then the car roars away.

I don't move from the spot on the pavement. Although he's

gone, I feel as if Daniel is still here watching me. I swish my glance up and down my neighbours' houses that look no different from any other day and yet feel less familiar. My street, my new home, my new life. All invaded. His desire for control continues. I head home and wonder how he found me, whether he broke into my house from here or the back. Does he have my diary, poring over pages in rage at how I stopped being the malleable, fearful woman that he needed me to be?

Back home, I kick off my trainers in the hallway, then throw myself across the sofa. Getting an answer to who's been following me only creates more questions.

23

WEDNESDAY, 29 MAY

I lean back on the headrest of my office chair. At most, I had three hours of broken sleep last night. Despite the fact I deleted Daniel's number from my phone several months ago, it still lives in my memory. In the early hours, I texted him 'We need to talk, C.' An ache in my face tells me I was grinding my teeth the rest of the night.

Digging around for mints in my bag, I find the early birthday card that arrived this morning. I knew who it was from by the spider-like writing on the envelope. Jake regained a limited amount of dexterity so he can write and get about with assistance. He prefers not to use the telephone as his speech is permanently impaired, but he sends me emails and funny things through the post from time to time. Did I even remember to contact him on his birthday this year? I doubt it. In it, he tells me to switch to anti-wrinkle face cream, wishes me a happy birthday, then says his room and care package at the residential home have been upgraded by a benefactor. He knows I couldn't afford that. It must be Somni. Another way to keep me indebted to them.

Jake used to talk non-stop before the accident, always begging me to play games. We used to play 'would you rather'. His version generally involved snot or toilets, like choosing between eating dog snot or cat poo. Mine were more exploratory.

'Would you rather be as tiny as a woodlouse or as huge as a giant?' Guess I never figured out whether I wanted to be noticed or not. Each had its drawbacks in our household.

'Would you rather live on the moon or under the ground?'

'The moon would be cool, I'd bounce around,' Jake said, springing on skinny legs that would never work properly again after his seventh birthday. He didn't see how the choice was – as ever – no choice at all. Both places were lonely. From one you could see everyone else in the world but not reach them, from the other you couldn't see anything at all.

'You're boring,' was Jake's main accusation to me. I wore my boring like a shield.

'Would you rather have our mum or no mum.' I didn't ask Jake that one. Only myself. Then I felt sick and crept to my mum's room, pressed my ear against her bedroom door to check she was snoring lightly, that her nasty girl hadn't wished her away.

I thrust Jake's card to the bottom of my bag and check my surroundings. I'm relieved to find that Heidi's nowhere to be seen. The office can be a haven today. My laptop is back in place as if it never left. I pull open the filing cabinet to find all the notes where they belong. It's hard to hold on to the fury that I experienced when they went missing. Fatigue takes away my fight. On my desk is a neat pile of books: all of Elizabeth's publications. A gift or a pay off? I instinctively turn to the back cover of the topmost book to see her picture. Elizabeth looks up with a near-smile, her eyes sparkle with questions when all I want is answers.

An email of a video link pings into my in tray. It has been sent to the whole team. Harry has found a new way to invade my space. There's a professional-looking film of my boss with a backdrop that shifts from images of the brain to people asleep. Harry's speech sounds different to in person, the words run into one another like a radio host. When did our research become so commercialised? For the good of the people or the pockets of the shareholders?

'Dear Team. Here we are in the most exciting of times for Somni. Enjoy the journey! We'll be expanding our services and reach to those who don't have sleep problems. Prevention and maximising human proficiency form our new pillars of expertise. Sleep is the future: for work, play and health. I'm delighted you can be part of it.'

I hate the video as a marker of how we now work in a competitive market rather than for an academic institution with knowledge and wellbeing at the core. But Harry's line about work, play and health strikes a chord. It has been an honour to be part of life-changing research projects. In recent years, Somni has had to fill in the gap for so many people who can no longer get the healthcare they need for free. Physical and mental health services are struggling to cope with demand. Somni has expanded year on year the number of different disorders and diagnoses we try to help, mostly through research projects. It's necessary and important, but maybe we've been spreading our expertise too thinly so that nothing is robust and careful. I suspect the main driver for change is him – Harry. There's a tremor down one side of his face. It's definitely new. He's reading from a prompt card rather than his usual approach of creating speeches on the spot. Despite the well-made presentation and visual tricks, he looks older than only a few months ago. Like a president after he's served four years.

Something is going on with him – he's deteriorating before my eyes.

'Somni is a great place to work.' A female voice-over now. 'With opportunities for advancement and a loyalty scheme.'

Loyalty scheme makes it sound like a supermarket reward card, not a threat that you'll never work elsewhere if you leave the company while they still want to get something out of you.

The video ends with a montage of our building and staff that must have been filmed while I was on sick leave. I spot Heidi, a few of the sleep lab technicians including Ben in profile, the lady from the Pecha Kucha presentation. Violins stream over the short videos so I can't tell what they are discussing.

Towards the end, I catch the back of a lady in a patterned dress that looks familiar. The slope of her shoulders, one hand on her hip, her hair pulled upwards in a bun. I'm certain it's the woman I saw in the lift who was also in the Maximus trial. She wasn't only a participant; she was also a member of staff. Another internal guinea pig. Whatever Heidi says, I need to find this woman and hear from her whether the trial really had no impact on her.

I enter the shared drive to try to find an up-to-date staff list and notice how many folders have disappeared: research files, access to test scores, historical data. My security level has been severely restricted. I can't find a staff list to figure out the lady's name through a process of elimination. It's a dead end.

I haven't been cut off from the sleep lab lists. Each sleep lab and research room is named after an element. I check the rooms for bookings. None of them include patient names. But there's an anomaly. The list of rooms is what I expected: we have four sleep labs and seven research rooms on this floor. So, there should be eleven bookable rooms. On the database, there are twelve. That means there's another room used for our research that's not on this floor. I scroll through the familiar lab names: Carbon, Iron, Mercury. There's one room name I don't recognise – Magnesium. I've got to find it. Magnesium lab could hold the answer to whether Harry leaning over me as I lay paralysed was an invention of my mind when unwell, or is in fact a memory.

Anja stares at my lips as I speak as if I'm talking in another language.

'I need to have a copy of the plans for the building with all the fire exits. I'm the designated fire safety officer for our floor.'

She looks unconvinced that she should spend any time helping me.

I lean forward as if sharing a secret.

'I think Harry is trying to build my self-esteem, after my "sick leave" if you know what I mean'. I draw inverted commas in the air and roll my eyes. There's nothing a bitch likes more than gossip about somebody's struggles.

'Hmm, I did hear a few things. Are you... normal now?'

I shrug. 'Well, they did have to call Harry out the other day when I got a little bit mixed up. He says I need something to focus on. It's really important that fire drills occur on an annual basis, I think it's a privilege to be considered for the role.'

Her smirk breaks through. She can't wait to spill that this deluded therapist thinks she's princess of fire regulations.

'So, you'll get me the building plans?'

Her index finger moves in the air as if she's already texting the admin woman upstairs. I run the risk that this will blow up in my face if someone higher up finds out what I've asked for, but I must move forward.

'Great, I'll pick them up from you by Friday morning then.'

If somebody is monitoring my whereabouts, I'll have to think of a decent cover story as to why I'm away from the fifth floor. As I climb back up the stairs for the last hour of work, I notice for the first time the green fire exit signs on the stairway.

There's always a way out.

24

Elizabeth never makes notes during our supervision sessions. One hand rests on top of the other on her lap. Her attention to me is absolute.

'Was there a particular case you wish to discuss?' she asks.

I'd love to be so poised in my therapy sessions.

'I think I had a breakthrough with Mia.'

'How so?'

I don't want to describe my unprofessional outpouring. Ultimately, a supervisor is not only there to provide guidance. If they are concerned that your work is inadequate or inappropriate, they are duty-bound to report it.

'She was able to dig down to what she really craves. It's not drugs, sex, parties and so on. What she wants is to be cared for, to belong.'

Elizabeth nods but doesn't speak.

'I'm not sure what helped her to realise that. I guess I challenged her a little and found some common ground.' I squirm at my minimisation. Can Elizabeth read me to realise that I let my irritation show with Mia, then stepped outside a professional boundary?

'Perhaps the fact that you allowed your basic human needs to show encouraged Mia to experience and express her own?'

What a perfect, positive way to put it.

'Yes, yes! I didn't realise there were parallels between us at the time – but once I did, I felt it for both of us. I didn't experience it as so painful anymore, it felt normal, a relief.'

Elizabeth moves her hand from right across to left, then into the middle as she says, 'So there exists a state – for both you and Mia – that lies between fire and ice.'

I understand what Elizabeth is saying although I can't remember having shared my phrase for mum's mood with her before, I thought I'd been careful never to give specifics about my family. How much has spilled out in the past without my realising?

'Do you think that acknowledging your own healthy longings for intimacy and self-compassion helped her to realise her own?'

She's right. But I never disclosed to Elizabeth that I'd talked about myself. Is that what she's pieced together from talking with me, or is there a way in which my videoed sessions have been shared with her? My laptop is back but I have no clue who has had access to my recorded data. The urge to delete that session in particular overtakes me so that I've failed to respond to Elizabeth's question.

'Christie, where has your mind taken you?'

I don't want to share thoughts that sound so mistrustful. Better to stick to facts.

'At the end of the session, Mia stated that she thought Mike would be back next session.' I can't help my speech racing; I want to tell Elizabeth everything before she interrupts. 'And Mike called to cancel, but he somehow knew I'd been on leave, he said he hoped I felt better. So at least two of my patients know each other, maybe even things about me.'

Elizabeth doesn't show any emotional change, only interest.

'What do you think are possible explanations for what you're telling me, Christie?'

Her question reminds me of that worksheet for anxious minds. Elizabeth doesn't believe me.

'Maybe they met in the sleep labs before they started therapy and got chatting?' That isn't what I think at all but I want to appear to be considering different options. 'Or there could be someone from Somni leaking information about me to my patients?' I try to mirror Elizabeth's neutrality but there's a shakiness to my voice and hands.

'And why might somebody do that?' Her face remains unreadable. The familiar tightening of my chest starts.

'Because they're testing me? I'm still a guinea pig somehow?'

Elizabeth raises an eyebrow.

'A guinea pig?'

My words become jumbled. 'Yes, I mean I know we consent to be in research as staff members but there's something off, we don't know what we're signing up to with each study. Consent that isn't consent for what you think it is. And they're messing with me now somehow.' I'm on the edge of tears with frustration that I can't explain myself clearly. Even saying the word consent hurts, jabbing at an old wound.

'Christie, it could be helpful to take a moment. To breathe. To gather your thoughts. I'm concerned about you.' I try to imagine oxygen coming into my body, through my blood and back out, just as Ben described. I can't get the order right. Instead, the air feels stuck in my throat. 'If you allow yourself to open up, it would help you to understand what's really going on.'

She thinks I'm deceiving her again, that I push away the answers when in reality I'm desperate for the truth. I gasp and clutch my throat as everything turns black and I feel my legs loosen beneath me.

I sit in reception like a schoolgirl waiting to see the headmaster. Harry's PA is surprisingly kind. Her badge reads 'Lacey'. I wonder what Anja has told her about me.

'Is there anyone I can call for you?' She hands me a glass of water. I glance at it to check for any white particles but the liquid looks clear. Of course it's clear, as the health drink from Heidi probably was. I've been losing my grip on what belongs now and what is forcing its way from the past.

I should be brave but I don't feel like I can make it home by myself.

'Ben. Technician Ben.'

'I'll give him a ring. He seems nice.'

He is. Too nice for me? The judging part of my mind is stuck on a loop: *BurdenBurdenBurden*. I shrink the sound down by focusing on an image of Ben's chest as it rose and fell. My own chest releases the tension a little. Tiredness takes over from panic. I rest my head against the wall. Years of numbness are failing me as I can't keep my emotions in any longer. I hate this version of myself.

Lacey kneels next to me and takes the cup from my hand.

'Ben's on his way. And Dr Curzon says you don't have to wait to see our medic – he's signing you off for a week.'

WeekWeekWeek.

WeakWeakWeak.

I'm only half-aware that I'm leaning on Ben as we make our way down to his car. I'm barely here, like sleepwalking.

Ben doesn't do small talk.

'I'm taking you home. You're going to rest.'

As the car rumbles along, I try to describe a type of homesickness to him. He's so quiet that I'm not sure whether I'm actually saying these things aloud or thinking them.

'It's a kind of longing. For a place, but more than a place. For a certain feeling there. It's a familiar place, but not a real one I don't think, because there's nowhere that I want to go back to, even if I could. Like missing someone you've never met.'

Then I'm on my sofa as he places a cover over me. I seize up in fear until he says, 'I'll stay a while,' then I let go.

25

THURSDAY, 30 MAY

I should ask permission before taking Ben's car but that risks him talking me out of going. It wouldn't take much. On top of my note to say that I'll be back tomorrow, I leave my keys to the flat: swapping isn't stealing. He's asleep on the sofa, trying to catch up on what he missed when he came to pick me up. I've thrown his timetable completely out of order but he hasn't complained at all. I fight the urge to peek into the room and watch him at rest – it would be difficult to leave him if I allowed myself that intimacy.

The streetlamps shine halos of light. A tabby cat pads down the pavement towards me, mewing. I stoop to give it a fuss as it purrs against the back of my hand. A passing car startles both of us. The cat scoots away. I feel a sadness, an urge to find it and return home to bed, the contented cat heavy and warm on my chest.

Out of habit, I head to the passenger door of the car. I've been a passenger for a decade. It's time to get back in the driving seat. I set my phone on the dashboard as a satnav. Did I memorise the streets of London last year or did I create my own map of nowhere?

The assured voice giving directions from my phone takes the edge off my nerves. No choices to be made: do as I'm told and figure out the rest when I get there. I'm relieved that my limbs remember how to drive. The stop-start of lights, roundabouts, and changing lanes keeps my attention focused. Everything feels unreal in the dead of night. I become a robot version of myself: no fears or memories, my metal foot to the pedal for the next one hundred and fifty-eight miles.

In the early hours, I pull into the car park of Collingwood and find a space tucked near a hedge at the rear. From here, the Victorian residential care facility looks like a doll's house. In a way, the hand of God or fate has already played with these figures: smashed their spines in crumpled cars, wrecked their mind with prions or potions, switched off half their bodies with one tiny blood clot. This place of past grandeur is a home for those who can't return to their old lives. Each resident has a defining moment after which nothing was ever the same again.

Maybe all of us have one of those.

I wind down my window to breathe in the scent of fir trees that line the curved driveway to the entrance porch. The early morning coolness makes me shiver. Bird calls that don't exist in the city chirrup their welcome to me. I allow myself a sip of the coffee I bought a few miles back as I filled up with petrol. I need to keep alert. There are lights on in the main building – many of the residents have sleep problems, it's a common issue with acquired brain injury. But it's too early to knock on that heavy door.

We spend our lives unaware of how we limit ourselves because of the pull to repetition. A timetable of work, life, sleep with self-imposed limits on where we live, who we speak to, what we say. It feels liberating to break the chain, to do something different. One decision is all it took to get me back to this place: back through time, back to my brother.

I find my phone in the glovebox and realise I didn't bring my charger. A text from Daniel flashes in return to my request for us to meet. It was sent one hour ago. Peculiar that he should finally reply when I'm so close to where we used to live. I open the message, unsurprised to see a single word response: 'Okay'. But my urgency to know why he followed me – in fact, all the issues back in London – has lost its grip on me now I'm back home. I switch my phone off, toss it into the glovebox, then shut it with my foot. With my seat tilted backwards, I rest my eyes and wait until it's an appropriate time to call on Jake. My gut tells me that I'm already long overdue.

It was my fault.

I hadn't kept the house safe. I hadn't kept Jake safe.

He was alive but part of his brain was damaged forever. He never came home to live with us again. Mum blamed herself and I let her. Can I bear to tell him the truth now or will I continue the betrayal?

A tapping sound confuses me until I orient myself to my surroundings. A weather-worn lady in a white tunic taps her ring against the car window again as she blows out smoke from the corner of her mouth. I push my door open and stretch my stiff legs onto gravel.

'I'm here to see my brother, Jake Langdale?' She takes a long drag of her cigarette, sizing me up. 'I travelled in the night, from London.'

'London!' she says, stepping back to make room for me like I'm royalty. 'Jake'll be up already. Bet he'll be chuffed.' She drops the butt onto the floor and squashes it with her boot. 'Are you stopping?' It had never entered my mind that I could have stayed in the area for a while. I brought no travel bag with me, no clothes, no laptop. I shake my head and follow her to the side entrance of Collingwood. We enter a corridor that could be in any of the rehab units Jake lived in when we were kids. Bleach scent, beeping alarms, signs on the walls with regulations, defibrillator equipment.

'Help yourself to a drink in the residents' kitchen. I'll let his key worker know you're here, he's just about finished his shift.'

We walk through a living room area with a television as big as my bedroom window. The kitchen is adapted to meet the needs of wheelchair users. There's a poster above the kettle that breaks down the steps to make a cup of tea. However much my memory feels impaired at times, it's nothing compared to what some of these people must live with. Last time I visited Jake, I discovered that the man next to us in the lounge, who practised writing strings of letters with huge effort, used to be a solicitor. He'd been knocked off his bike on the way to work. His hand wouldn't obey what his mind told it to do. He cried, noiselessly.

A young guy with spiked hair approaches me with his hand out.

'You're here for our Jake? I'm Lucas, his key worker, I'll take you down to him.' I follow him along the corridor, aware that my black trainers squeak with each step. The walls are covered with artwork by the residents. Lucas notices my interest.

'Here's Jake's. More talented than our occupational therapist!'

I stop in front of the painting. It's a version of the Tree of Life wall hanging we used to admire in the kids' section of the library. Jake has painted tiny birds within the branches. I had no idea Jake could paint. Or that he'd gained such good control of his hands. I always had a talent for creating images in my mind but they never translated onto the page, so I avoided art in shame.

'He did part of it with his mouth. Not cos he needs to like

one of our other residents, but he wanted to have a go and prove that he could.' Lucas laughs as he continues down the corridor.

We pause outside room eight. Music pours through the door – I haven't woken Jake up. I notice a slight tremble in my hands that remains from the stress of yesterday.

At times it felt as though I didn't have a brother as we lived apart from when I was in high school. Other times, I ached with a loss deeper than fraternal. Mum struggled so often that I practically raised Jake before his injury, even though I was only a few years older. I knock on the door of my brother, son, friend, stranger.

26

Jake grins as I enter. Slim as ever, dressed in a rock band T-shirt and sitting in his high-tech wheelchair. He's up to no good. As I walk towards him, he hits a button on his laptop that doubles up as his communication device. With each step I take, the machine emits the noise of a stomping large-footed animal. By the time I'm next to him, an elephant sound bellows out.

'Yes, very funny. Actually, I went back to the gym this week.'

'They got a nice café?' His speech takes a bit of getting used to for newcomers but I can usually make out his words.

'Cheeky git. Didn't see you in there.'

He taps on his keyboard. His laptop has a double screen, one faces outwards. It's a clip from Mum's favourite Jane Fonda workout video but he's superimposed his own head onto Jane's body.

'Your birthday present. I was going to email it, seeing as I never see you these days.'

Ouch. The comment isn't barbed but the truth in it hurts none the less.

'I'm such a rubbish sister. Sorry I haven't been up.' I wipe my nose with an old tissue from the bottom of my bag. 'It's been a tough year.'

Is that okay? To tell the guy who lives in a place like this that I've had it bad? He doesn't look depressed. Never did, come to think of it. He adapted to his disability and being away from home far more quickly than Mum and I did. There were tough years in his late teens: anger, booze, hopelessness. But then he created a life for himself, online and in the community. He has more of a life than me.

'Wanna find a GIF for it?' He offers access to the keyboard in front of him. How does he do it, laugh and play when everything's so awful?

'Okay,' I put the tissue in my pocket. 'Find me one with a zombie in it.' I sit on the edge of his bed, let go of the bag that I've been clinging to. He shows me a cartoon zombie girl who rolls her eyes as one by one each of her body parts fall off.

'Something like that. But a zombie who's been dumped, had months off work, might be completely crazy.'

'You're too boring for crazy.' He turns his chair towards me. This electronic one looks so lightweight compared to what I used to push around when he was young.

An urge flutters inside to step out of sister role. To stop telling myself that this intelligent, funny man who has thousands of followers for his comic videos online is a little boy that I must care for. But that's not quite it. That's not what the avoidance has been about. In order to wipe out the past, I've tried to wipe out the people who are part of it. But there's been a cost. Avoiding reminders has stripped me of a family that I needed more than I dared to acknowledge.

'I'm so sleep deprived, and on top of that I've driven through the night, in a car that I think I've accidentally stolen. So I don't have any brakes left. I'm going to talk, and don't interrupt, okay?'

Jake jerks his head to the side. He's wired differently but makes it work.

'Firstly, do you know what feeling came up first when I saw your painting on the wall outside here? I felt a bit sad, even nostalgic, but what came first was a dose of envy. That you're artistic and I'm not, or that you can feel hopeful and make beautiful things out of painful stuff. I was even jealous that the spiky-haired guy clearly liked you and I wanted him to feel positive about me too. That's how messed up I am. And I haven't been up to visit for so long. It always makes me feel so awful. Not when I'm actually here with you, but the lead up to it, and then there's a dark aftermath. You shouldn't be here.'

My voice catches in my throat but I don't want to cry – that would be a way to hide rather than face what I need to say. 'You shouldn't be here and it's my fault for not keeping you safe. I've never actually said that to you or written it in my letters. I can't put it in a GIF or a joke. But it's my fault you're here.'

Jake turns to speak but I hold my hand up so I don't lose my nerve.

'The worst bit – the very worst bit of it all – is that when you left home to go to the unit, I felt guilty, sad, alone. But I also felt relief.' I can't look at him, my head hangs down. 'Mum was less demanding, stayed in her room or was out visiting you. I didn't have to look after you, worry about her so much. I read books and made up stories in my head about being in a boarding school. I could pretend I was a normal kid in a normal family. But we weren't a family once you didn't live with us.'

His hand is on mine. Slender fingers that should have been able to play the piano instead of typing on a specially made keyboard with large lettering.

'Christie, the fire wasn't your fault, just one of those random, bad luck things. You know Mum was told by her own mental health team not to give up smoking, that it helped keep her more stable.'

That's true. Mum was relieved to not be put under pressure to quit smoking. She usually went out into the back garden or smoked in her bedroom to keep the fumes away from us. But not that night. How do I explain it to Jake, destroy what I'm only just repairing with him in this moment?

'You don't remember, I knew you weren't in your room so must be downstairs with Mum, but I just crawled across the landing and climbed out of the window by myself.' Another act of selfishness. I hadn't figured out anything about the fire then, just the urge to get out. I touch my throat automatically at the memory of breathing in air so hot that it hurt.

Jake frowns. 'Don't be daft, climbed out of where?'

I see it now. Our landing. Patterned carpet. Out of my room, past Jake's box room where he wasn't lying in bed. My desperation to find him downstairs. Choking sensation, nausea, dizziness. The rectangular window I can visualise in front of me as a route to freedom is fuzzy as I blink stinging eyes. The window shows a field, long grass swooshing up where we used to run together. As I pay attention to the memory of that field, the scene turns into a painting. Monet. A print from the charity shop in a chipped gold-sprayed frame on our landing wall, two children in a field of grass and flowers.

There never had been a window there for me to escape from. Not in real life, only in my mind: Jake and me running in the grass. I couldn't have climbed out from there. I've avoided the image so much that I haven't questioned it.

'But I got out. I saw the fire engines, the ambulance. I left you.'

'You were looking for me, must have gone towards the fire actually. The smoke's probably what made you pass out on the stairs. Then you were rescued by the crew. We all were. But I was in a worse way, I guess, because I'd gone downstairs to sleep in the den we'd made. Mum hadn't stubbed the cigarette out properly by the sofa before she left to sit in the kitchen where she fell asleep. I was tucked up in the den, oblivious.'

The den. Covers draped from the sofa across to a couple of dining chairs, cushions strewn below to make a bouncy bed. I would have loved to sleep there but was a rule-follower so dutifully went to my bedroom each night.

It's true. I *had* looked for Jake. Through the fear and blackness, I still pushed ahead to find my baby brother because I couldn't trust my mum to do that. By the time I got near the bottom of the stairs, smoke was impenetrable. I slid down onto my stomach, coughing my guts up and retching, dragging myself along as if in a nightmare.

All this time I've told myself a story that I was selfish. That I didn't help Jake or need help myself. But that's not true. I did cause it but I hadn't realised that at the time.

'I didn't mean for it to happen.' My voice chokes me from saying more.

Jake tuts softly.

'We were just kids, Chris. It shouldn't have been your job to police Mum all the time. She was off her face on all those meds, it's a bloody miracle she got out at all. She wouldn't have had a chance if she'd slumped there on the sofa.' He gestures his arm down towards his body and the equipment in front of him. 'All this, it's just what I've got to live with. And I do. Pretty well if I say so myself. This is who I am.'

He's right. Jake runs online sites for people with restricted mobility to share their comedy and art. He's tried to explain to me that his cutting humour, compassion, positivity that life can be rich and rewarding can't be separated out from his experiences as a disabled child and man. I didn't get it. But maybe I'm starting to now.

'I can't remember it clearly. What happened straight after.'

'Me neither.' Jake taps the side of his head. 'Lack of oxygen seriously messed with my memory for a while. But you know, everything I've been through and live with has made me do things I never would have otherwise.' He turns back to the computer and shows me the number of hits on his last vlog. He has more followers across all of social media than the Somni Company.

Jake turns his chair back around to me.

'I know you avoided Mum after it all. But she did her best. You know how much she hated getting buses or trains. Freaked her out being so close to people. Said she felt trapped. But she came to see me loads.' He doesn't understand why I couldn't face Mum afterwards.

But he's right. Mum travelled nearly every weekend after that to visit Jake. She worked on the telephone for a window blind company in the week, rather than staying in bed most of the day, to afford the travel and equipment. I'd cut my ties by then and spent as much time as I could by myself in my room or out. I never gave our relationship a chance to be repaired. Jake's birth father was another man who couldn't stick with Mum for long. A lorry driver who was probably glad to get away. But he did visit Jake in rehab. He tried to offer me a chance to connect, but I'd told myself that I didn't need a dad so never responded to his calls. Then they stopped altogether.

Do I push people away? Do I not see it when I *am* helped, tell myself that I need to sort everything out by myself?

'Yes, I guess you're right. She was doing her best.' I wrap my hands around the back of my neck to release the muscle tension, then sink down a little into the chair. I've missed the chance to explain yet again. I can't do it.

'So were you, sis.'

Jake moves closer to me. We sit in comfortable quiet for a minute like we are back in time sharing a bedroom.

Before the fire, I always focused on Jake and me. What was it like for my mum in the aftermath? She didn't crumble further under the pressure as I expected. Social workers were back on the scene. Fortunately, the incident with the cigarette was put down to exhaustion not neglect but perhaps she never forgave herself. She lost her son to another city and the intimate care of strangers. And she lost her daughter to daydreams, always out of reach from any chance of forging a new family. If my mum could gain strength to push on, then so can I. Forget the past, I will make the future better.

'I need to change my life, Jake. I mean really change it not just run away from things.'

'What the hell's been going on?'

I don't know where to start. All the stressors back in London seem unreal. The coffee hit is wearing off, so the grey fuzz of fatigue descends.

'That's what I'm trying to figure out.'

'Did you really steal a car?'

I shake my head at how unbelievable that must seem. Jake's eyes shine with mischief.

'Yes. Sort of.'

'Well, you must have really needed to. You're not one to break a rule. Always thought you'd make a good nun.' That grin again.

I sit on the edge of Jake's bed. 'I don't need you to sort anything out, I want to tell you everything to help me put things into order. I know you get tired quickly. Me too as it happens.'

It's taken almost an hour to spill details about Daniel, the Maximus trial, the blue car, my current state of health and mind, my guesses and fears about Somni's processes, uncertainty about my supervisor's role in it all. Jake is unshockable. He listens and I notice how good it feels to not monitor his reactions or pain like I do with my patients. I hadn't really noticed before how one way so many of my interactions have been with Heidi, Jake, colleagues. I close myself off, go through the motions of friendship while keeping most of my real self behind a locked door.

Jake looks drained. The intense concentration of interaction can trigger his fatigue. I gather my belongings and hug him. He holds his finger up to show me he's not ready to finish yet.

'So, you said that arsehole Daniel gave you the job advert for Somni? That's weird isn't it, nothing to do with his banking or whatever?'

'He pushed pretty hard for me to apply and attend the screening process. Part of his control, I guess.'

'It's too much of a coincidence. Him sorting the job. Then tracking you now, at the same time that work seem to keep close tabs on you and you're uncovering deceit in the company. He must have links to the company?'

I'd presumed Daniel was stalking me. But what if Jake's right and Daniel's behaviour links back to Somni? I could be in more trouble than I'd realised.

'How could he be linked? It doesn't make sense.'

Jake starts to tap searches into his computer.

'That finance company he worked for in London doesn't have Somni in their portfolio of companies so that can't be the link.'

I piece the timeline together in my mind. 'He encouraged me to apply for the post before he got the job in London, so I guess it wouldn't make sense to be tied to that.'

'What kind of financial work did he do?'

I try to recall conversations but I mostly tuned out when Daniel talked about his work. Virtual money never meant anything to me, I just wanted enough to pay my rent and eat. The finance world was full of boys playing games in which they'd never suffer consequences of any mistakes.

Jake's search brings up a list of acronyms to do with different areas of finance work.

'Any ring a bell?'

Recognition is easier than recollection. One acronym sticks out. PEAF. Professional Ethics in Accounting and Finance.

'PEAF does. Daniel did freelance work related to that, I'm sure.'

'Ethics? Brilliant.' Jake laughs, breezy as if this is a game. No matter what I do, that word drags around my neck like a noose. 'I guess if you have things to hide, the best thing to do is to hire your own staff who pretend to check on the ethics of your business. Like all that shady stuff they do in the police when they investigate their own muck-ups.'

Jake loves a conspiracy theory. It's one possibility: Somni in too much financial and ethical trouble to allow any straight-laced accounting professional in. Daniel would have been happy to sign anything for the right price. To him, money equalled success.

I can see Jake's flagging. My own energy level is near zero. I suddenly feel so far away from my flat, my bed.

'Thank you for listening, for being you. I better head back while I'm still safe to drive.'

I failed: stayed in the safety of silence about why that cigarette wasn't extinguished properly. I need to make it right at Somni, that's all I can do.

'You've wiped me out! Bloody intriguing though. You're a

mastermind, you can blow it all apart. And don't take any crap from anyone.'

I open the door and get one last look at Jake who I vow to visit again soon. Today, I feel like I let myself have my brother back.

'Next I'm going to do a spot of spying, complete with blueprints of a building acquired under false pretences.'

Jake turns to wave me off. 'I never thought my big sis would be a super sleuth. I think it suits you.'

As I leave his room, his computer emits the soundtrack from the *Pink Panther*.

In the driver's seat, I swig the remains of cold coffee and switch my phone back on. I text Ben to say I'm on my way and turn the phone off to use closer to home. I need to leave before the caffeine stops telling lies to my sleep system.

I've missed the morning rush hour traffic so I let myself pay attention to what's around me. Before I get to the slip road to join the motorway, I take a detour on a dual carriageway past the town centre. There's a newsagent still open that I used to visit after school, half my dinner money spent on a sugar rush of cola cubes and liquorice to feel good for a short while. The old pub that Daniel and I occasionally visited has changed hands to a chain. It's the venue where I first tried an alcopop and once had my interlaced fingers stuck together by a hypnotist who threw out suggestions to the crowd to see who'd be suitable for the show. I hid my hands under the table, fearful that Daniel would notice and send me to the front to be humiliated. As I head out of town, I see the edges of the outdoor market and wish I'd planned enough time to visit the old crowd. I could have wandered around the stalls, surprised people. Would I still belong? I wind down my window but can't smell the scent of it or hear the chatter above traffic noise.

I press play on Ben's CD player, unsure what kind of music to expect. My first guess is classical music. But what I hear is a Bollywood soundtrack: upbeat, soaring voices switching between male and female. As I pick up speed on the motorway, a blast of cool air keeps me alert. Each road sign is an invitation to choose. I don't have to head south. I could turn off at the next junction and find my way back to the market. Or take a new direction: head to the coast or countryside.

But I don't want to run away. Not this time.

27

I enter my flat and call out to Ben. There's no reply. His bag is no longer propped against the wall. *What did you expect, that you'd come home to him waiting like a patient husband? He's probably called the police.* I try not to get sucked in by the mean voice of my mind, but my heart rate increases as I double-check that there are no messages on my phone which I used to navigate the final leg of my journey.

I run to the living room. There's no sign that anyone has been in here. No bedding, no breakfast plates, curtains open. The note I left is gone. Doubt creeps up and makes my skin tingle as sleep deprivation hits hard. I grab the edge of the dining table to steady myself. Was he ever here? Was that really his car that I borrowed? Stole? All of it seems unreal. My brother's jokes, my freedom to choose, a twenty-four-hour adventure.

Rather than panic, I realise that I've gone into my old favourite of switch-off mode: my breathing has slowed to be so shallow I feel faint. I take a deep breath to try to regain control and feel grounded to the here and now. It's a technique I use with traumatised patients to pull them back from flashbacks into reality.

Traumatised patients. People who've been through terrifying events, when they believed their life or that of a loved one was at risk. They respond with attempts to escape reminders of the trauma, reliving it in flashbacks and nightmares, hyperalert to signs of danger. Their memories are unprocessed: broken narratives that are carried and replayed in the body.

They, them, patients, others. Could it be the same for me?

Jake said I didn't get out of the fire by myself. The story I'd told of my own escape isn't true. I was in danger myself. I must have been afraid that I'd die, and that Jake and Mum would die if I didn't get to them.

Everything feels whooshy and strange. If I was traumatised, these sensations would be called dissociation: a way to escape overwhelming feelings by cutting off.

I see my reflection in the glass pane of the bookcase. A hunched figure. I press my fingers one by one against the back of the chair, reminded of Ben and the movement in his hands. 'Here I am,' I tell my reflection. I look around the room to find all the white objects as I tell my patients to when they start to drift away from me and their own internal world. The white window frame opposite me, the plug socket below the television, a candle on the mantelpiece. My body starts to feel more my own as I pull myself back into the present. My breathing deepens. I look at my watch and count to sixty, following the second hand around the dial. Back in the present. I imagine Ben leaving the flat to walk home, then track his path out of the room. On the table by the front door is a piece of paper. It's the same piece I'd ripped from my notebook yesterday. I pull it out and read *I'll be back at six o'clock, Ben.*

I collapse onto the sofa grateful that a full night without

sleep means that my mind will let go for a while and allow me to rest.

Since waking from a long nap, it's taken an hour to sort through all my belongings, cupboards and boxes to find items that I no longer want or need. I tie the bin liner in a knot so that I can't see the old photo album, unused kitchen equipment that I bought when Daniel and I moved in together, notebooks from the years that I spent wondering why I had nightmares as I slept next to a man who saw me as weak and insufficient. The last item I'd thrown into the bag was a folder that contained Somni worksheets on how to handle anxiety. I know what I need, and with time I can apply the right therapeutic approaches to myself.

I dump the bin bag in the backyard next to my neighbours' rubbish and lean against the low wall. I hesitate before I re-enter the flat. This home that doesn't feel like a home. I'm certain that someone broke in and stole my notebook. I'm less sure about whether I've been monitored or not via secret recording equipment but it's a risk I'm no longer willing to take. I call Ben.

'Hello, Christie, I have information to bring over, nearly done.' He doesn't sound the least bit annoyed with me. No reprimands or suspicion.

'I'm home. Sorry about the car, I didn't want to wake you. I've put petrol in.' I head back indoors and lock up behind me while I wedge the phone against my shoulder.

'That's fine, I saw the note. A long walk home did me good.'

'Ben, I don't want to stay here.' He's not good at taking hints, I need to spit it out and be as upfront as he is. 'Could I stay at your place for a while?'

He takes a moment to consider my request. Would I disrupt

things too much? I push away the word *burden* and replace it with *inconvenience.*

'I think that would be wise. I've swept for devices, it's clear here.' Ben always takes my concerns seriously.

With my travel bag packed to bursting point, I grab the car keys, glad for one last chance to drive myself before returning Ben's car to him. Back in the driver's seat, I'm about to check my phone for directions to his flat when I stop. Heidi said my memories of learning London routes was false. But a true researcher presumes nothing: experimentation is the key. Instead of typing in Ben's address, I search for New Cross Station. I've never been to it but it's only a few miles away. I follow the soothing tones of the lady's directions south-east until I reach the station: a brick entrance in front of glass that has none of the Victorian wonder left of its origins.

If what I have is memory rather than fiction, then route fourteen of the Knowledge starts here and ends at the National Maritime Museum. I narrow my eyes out of focus until I can imagine the dusky pink line that I memorised is back in view. It glows ahead to lead the way: straight on. At the end of the road, I follow it to the right onto Edward Street and feel a tingle of excitement. It was a fifty–fifty guess, perhaps. I keep going. Just before taking a left, I wind down the window and breathe in the warm scent from a Vietnamese restaurant. I take a sharp right onto the A200 as easily as if this were my daily route home. The road crosses water at Deptford Creek, and I slow down to crane my neck for boats. I take in the shops and shoppers, the daily interactions of locals that I've tuned out for so long. An elderly couple hold hands at the bus stop; a group of young women gather outside the Oxfam bookshop, towers of new purchases cradled in their arms; a street cleaner dances with his brush and is clapped by a toddler. The tall buildings of brown and cream that belong to the local university look like dolls' houses. Up ahead the pink line fades away. I pass the enormous main building of the National Maritime Museum. Two huge anchors sit at each side of the entrance.

So that part at least was true: I was a super-responder in Maximus for learning new facts. Why did Heidi lie to me, telling me it was all in my head? Whatever techniques were used, they clearly have great potential for improving memory. There are chunks of London I rehearsed over and over during that time and can still recall now. It's nowhere near that of actual black-cab drivers but they take years to learn all three hundred and twenty runs.

So, if my memory improvement was part of Maximus despite Heidi's denial, then my crashing mood and confusion could have been too. I need to find out for sure. What did Harry call me? A cog in the system. The fact is that a cog can make small turns that eventually move every other part of the machine.

28

MONDAY, 3 JUNE

At the front desk, Anja searches through a pile of papers for the floor plans she sourced for me. I sneak a look at the list of extension numbers and names pinned on a felt board behind her desk, but there are none that seem unfamiliar that could link to Magnesium room. She passes the large folded blueprint over with nails so long that they curve over, witch-like.

'So, you're back at work,' she says, rather than asking me what she really wants to find out.

'Looks like it. Didn't need a week off after all.' I drop the huge map of the Somni building into a canvas shopping bag. She glances towards the work phone on her desk. I don't move a millimetre.

'Anja, I know it's protocol to tell them when I've arrived.' It's worth a shot. She already thinks I'm deranged. Her eyelids flutter in confusion. Is that because she doesn't know what I'm talking about, or she doesn't know how to respond to being found out? I almost laugh when I realise she might not understand what 'protocol' means. 'Don't worry, it's all part of how Somni takes care of me. I appreciate it. I guess it's a task they trust you with.' Acting isn't hard. It's how I've dealt with the world for as long as I can recall.

Flattery. She likes this reframe which fits with her view of others and herself: I'm weak, she's special. She applies her front-of-house smile. I have my suspicion confirmed but it's clear that she's been told not to make the call until I'm away from her desk, so there's no chance for me to check which internal number she dials.

This new freedom to be brave could be a really bad idea. She could be on the phone to Harry or a board member telling them about my behaviour. I'd be kicked out before I had a chance to fully investigate.

I leave the desk holding a bag that feels loaded with something far heavier than paper: my chance to prove my theory to be fact.

The mind can work in metaphor. My experience of being unable to speak while physically restrained beneath Harry works as much figuratively as logically: an image that matches the feeling I had of being stopped and silenced. Well, no it's far more plausible as a dream or story I've told myself while unwell. And yet. It's compelling as muscle memory, the way it evoked a constricted chest and nausea. The room I recall may exist. And if it does, it will be somewhere in this building and there's no way I wouldn't recognise it.

In the lift, I itch to look at the blueprints but don't want to risk it yet. There are eight floors to this building. Ben gave me a list of the companies that hire space on each floor. The floor above Somni houses a company with the name Zed that neither of us has been able to track information for using web searches. It's registered with Companies House but has no website, marketing information or trail for employment. That's where I intend to investigate today. But there's someone at Somni who expects me to exit this lift and get to work.

The ping of the lift that announces the doors are about to open makes me jump. I step out into the foyer and check to see if Lacey is waiting for me. She faces her computer monitor as she types a hundred words per minute. There's no sign of Harry. Or Heidi. I crouch next to the water fountain and top up my bottle. Laughter spills from an office opposite. A printer churns out data. Lacey continues to type. Nothing here suggests that I'm being observed. I take a swig of the cool liquid so I can raise my head and check out the smoke detectors. Could they contain concealed cameras? I give up and follow the corridor round to my office.

I stash my canvas bag under the desk and lay my coat over it. Too agitated to sit at the computer, I walk over to Heidi's side of the room. She follows the clear desk policy – there's nothing but rows of office supplies. I sit in her chair to imagine what she saw when she worked daytime shifts opposite me. Her desk is at a right angle to mine. Did she see someone who was struggling with side effects of a clinical trial that went wrong? Or someone struggling with their mental health?

The determination I felt last night to figure out what secrets are being kept from me weakens along with my spirit. Everything looks so normal. But clues can be hidden in plain sight.

In junior school, I had a club for a while with Jake called the Double Detectives. We borrowed a library book that gave tips on how to write in invisible ink using lemon juice and contained illustrations of methods for spying with a series of small mirrors. We never had lemon juice or tiny mirrors but took the learning seriously. There was a trick that I didn't need props for.

'Jake, pass me the top bit of paper off Mum's shopping pad.' He watched as I flounced around with my school pencil, then shaded across the page to reveal Mum's original words. I stopped after the first few letters appeared in white beneath the grey pencil shading.

'Whoa. You made it come back,' said Jake, peering over my shoulder in wonder.

Despite the banal contents of 'cereal, marg, toothpaste' it was a magical way to bring the past back to life.

I pull the top Post-it note from Heidi's pile. It's small and pink. I run my finger along it. There are indentations. I turn her recently-sharpened pencil to an angle and rub across the paper until the dents in the page reveal the last thing she wrote: *Shadow files 1986*. Fluke or not, that's the year of my birth. My own shadow shivers along with me.

It shouldn't create suspicion if I leave my desk over lunch. I sometimes take a walk in my lunch break around the local streets from our South Bank offices. Along my route, each building jumps backwards and forwards in style and time. I peer into grand windows with blue plaques on the wall as chandeliers glisten above wood-panelled walls; pass metallic monstrosities that forfeit beauty for profit; drop coins onto blankets where homeless people slouch with their faithful dogs. The city resonates with a hundred sounds, a discordant dance of those who have it all and those who are stripped of everything. It's been weeks – perhaps months – since I paid attention to the city around me. I've been living in the anxiety of my head and heart. As strong as the urge is today to escape into those streets, I need to stay in the building. Today is for a different kind of exploration.

If I stay within a reasonable time frame, I'll be okay. As the lift arrives at ground level, I press my back against the mirror to keep out of view and hope that nobody enters. The doors shut.

Alone, I dare to press the button for level six and pray that no one is watching which direction the lift travels. I rub my sweaty palms against my skirt. I hold a form I printed off the internet for fire safety checks in case anybody asks me why I'm there. It's fine for waving about briefly but wouldn't stand up to any kind of scrutiny.

I grip the handle of my bag as the lift rises to my new destination. At level six, I step out into a hallway that looks the same as ours below but without the Somni logo on the wall. The external windows are raised to reveal a strip of sky. To my left is a solid door. It has a silver pad for security passes to open the lock. *Stupid, stupid, stupid, of course it does.* I feel a drain of energy as I return to being a bag of fat and bones.

There's no way for me to get in.

As I turn around to head back to the office, I notice that the digital counter above the lift is illuminated with an upwards arrow and the number three. The lift is coming towards me. Floor four now. My legs become lead. Floor five. I use all my strength to tear my feet from the quicksand of carpet and through the door that leads to a stairwell. As it closes behind me, I hear the doors chime open. Through the mottled glass I see a single figure in blue. This is a fire door: the only route to escape.

I wait until the blue figure has disappeared into whatever hides behind that locked door. Then, I pull out the floor plan and find the correct location. Floor six is formed of a foyer, one large space to the right that's likely to be an open-plan office, then a corridor that loops around the whole floor with six smaller rooms and one medium-sized one. If there is a lab here, it will be the latter. Even if I get into the foyer by trailing someone, I'd have to pass every office and person to get to the room I want to see.

The urge to give up is strong, but abandoning my plans now means I have no idea what to do next. I don't want to add more regret to the knot in my stomach. What must Jake have gone through to regain his ability to communicate and move? This is doable. Now or never.

I re-enter the small space outside the lift. I need everyone to get out. And I know a way to do it.

I remove a silk scarf that's wrapped around my neck in a double loop, as close to jewellery as I manage. With the ends tied together, I place it over one shoulder so that it drapes diagonally across my torso as a sash. I pull out an elastic band from my pocket that I use to tie back my hair on windy days as I walk home. I scrape my hair into a tight ponytail, the likes of which I'd never wear usually in front of my colleagues or patients as it makes me feel too exposed. With a twirl of my identity badge, I become nameless: a woman with a lanyard shouldn't raise suspicion, a woman with no name is hard to trace.

I stand in front of a little red box that juts out from the wall. *You can't, you won't, you daren't, you shouldn't.* I'm sick of that voice. Elizabeth asked me where the anger would belong if I didn't turn it onto myself. Anger at why I'm here in the first place, anger at how I've been tricked and lied to. I feel the strength surge through me: down into my arm, my fist.

I smash the fire alarm with my knuckles.

The noise shrieks through my muscles. Let it. I chose this. I wedge the fire door open behind my body. Strengthened, I mould myself into a fire warden, into someone who knows exactly what they are doing.

There's little urgency as the men and women exit level six – they clearly presume this is a fire drill. That works for me. I lift my arm and point them down the stairs.

'It's a drill. Make your way to the rear car park. Mind yourself on the stairs.' I skew my voice into southern tones so I don't stand out. Snippets of conversation that could tell me what these people do are too fleeting to catch as they trudge past me. Their badges have no logo on them. I'm half behind the door to reduce the chances of being recognised if these people are asked who led them away from their workplace.

In the event of a fire, secure doors release their magnetic locks to ensure that nobody gets trapped. There's a short amount of time before somebody will come to check this alarm. I need to get into the department. Two stragglers half run out of the office. I spot the spikes of the Somni logo on the tall man's folder that is wedged under his arm: they're not unrelated companies, this confirms it. I'm about to repeat my message about a fire drill when I realise who his colleague is. The grey chignon. Her glasses propped on top of her head rather than around her neck. She's halfway down the first section of staircase.

I wait a few more seconds to check there are no more people due to leave, then run to the secured door which opens easily. I take a right and follow the corridor around past small offices. There isn't time to check what shows up on computer screens or what is pinned to the walls. The alarm is so loud it overwhelms my system which shakes in response. The final room must be the one. There's no sign to indicate that it's Magnesium or any other name or number. A green light pulses on the key-card box. I push the door and prepare for a bed, medical monitor, memories.

Inside the room, there are five chairs in a circle as if for a meeting, a computer desk with the screen put into locked mode, and a window with blinds. Bare walls give no clues as to the room's purpose. But there is no bed. No bleeping machine to monitor a sleeping research participant.

What have I done? I can't stop the sob from emerging: wild and snotty, chest-aching. This is such a mess. I'm a mess. And I can't figure out what to do about it.

I recall crouching in smoky darkness outside my bedroom,

paralysed by fear and disorientation, my body smaller than now. The pain in my chest mirrors the pain from twenty-five years ago. That sense of needing to escape but being too overwhelmed to move.

The fire alarm stops. Rather than silence, my ears continue to ring in a high-pitched scream. The fire wardens have figured out there's no real threat. They must be at the broken fire alarm. I have to get out of here. I swallow down nausea and force my body back under my control to reach the door. As I swing it open, I look up. The light above is unusual: shaped like a twenty-pence piece.

Septagonal.

I remember that unusual word on repeat in my mind as I lay on a bed in a strange place, unable to move.

29

I'm panting by the third floor but desperate to get to the meeting point outside to locate the woman with the bun and give myself an alibi for the alarm being set off. The two men who stood next to the broken alarm on floor six hadn't questioned me as I ran past, shouting, 'It's all clear.' At the fire doors that lead out onto the carpark, a security guard stands with arms folded to block any re-entry until permission is given.

The car park is packed with workers from each area of the building. I roll my scarf into a ball and bundle it into a bin as I weave my way through small groups of people. I spot Anja's white fur coat. She folds her arms across herself and pouts. Next to her, two other admin staff laugh and chatter – their hands take it in turns to dance along with their stories. With my hair released from the elastic band, I let it hang forwards to cover part of my face in case anyone from floor six is nearby. My sleeves are wet from my attempts to dry my face. I approach Anja at an angle to catch her eye, then jerk my head to indicate that I wish to speak only with her. Special her. She sighs and steps towards me.

'This is so scary,' I say, as I look up at her as a child to an adult. 'I was coming back from my walk when I heard it. I didn't help with the evacuation. The alarm made me panic.'

'It's a false alarm. An idiot making toast again, I bet.' She rolls her eyes at the stupidity of everyone else.

'Oh, thank goodness! Please, Anja, don't tell anyone that it's shaken me up so much. I should've done a headcount as everyone from our floor came out, but I had to stay away until the alarm stopped.' She nods curtly, then turns away from me. I may as well have trained a carrier pigeon.

A bald man with a clipboard announces that we can re-enter the building, one floor at a time. There's no fire crew: so many false alarms mean they only attend confirmed fires these days, so there's no chance of seeing Mike's former comrades. Over to my left I recognise several of the Somni workers including Julia – the lady who asked my opinion at the Pecha Kucha. I switch direction to avoid them. As the crowd starts to thin out, I spy the lady with the bun. She stands next to the male Somni colleague who was with her earlier. Although it's not ideal to approach now, I can't risk losing her again.

Harry doesn't appear to be anywhere nearby. He wouldn't want me to speak with her. Hopefully he was out of the office today at an international conference or news interview.

While I try to gather my jumbled thoughts, the lady approaches me. Her waterfall cardigan and handmade earrings have a dishevelled elegance of a caricature counsellor. I'd remembered her as tall but we are the same height.

'I thought it was you! I'm Pippa Jenkins. We met last year in the Maximus research trial?' Her cockney accent surprises me: I presumed she'd have the news-presenter voice of Elizabeth or Heidi. I mustn't let myself sound desperate. Or unhinged.

'Yes, I want to talk to you about it. Actually, it's important that I do.'

'We shouldn't really be talking, I suppose, research rules and all that.' She pushes her glasses up an inch on her head as they slide down, at risk of falling.

Steady, take it steady.

'I was interested to know how it affected you, Pippa?'

'The intervention didn't do much good for me but then I think I had the lower-level dose cos of my test scores. I never did see the algorithm to work out who got what and why.' She beams as if we are talking about the weather.

It makes sense that we didn't all receive the same trial treatment. I presume by test scores she means the answers I gave at the job screening.

'You should be glad it didn't affect you. It was worse than doing me no good.' I reach out to hold her arm. 'It harmed me. Scrambled my brain. They should have pulled me from it. We have to do something!' I hear my voice as if it's somebody else's: a teen struggling with a surge of hormones and boundaries. I clamp my mouth shut before we're overheard.

She looks uncomfortable now, glances over to her colleague. 'I did hear that you had a hard time, sorry it was like that for you. I wasn't in the trial for long as it had no impact at all.' She lowers her voice. 'That's why I offered to give you support. Counselling.' So it wasn't a guess, that's part of her role. She pats my arm twice, a signal that this is the end of the discussion, however compassionate she may feel towards me.

'But why didn't they let you help me?' I call after her. I'm cracking under the weight of disappointment. Pippa starts to walk towards the side entrance to head back to work. I'm going to lose her. I pace after her. 'Please, you clearly thought I needed help. Why didn't they let you be my counsellor?'

Pippa stops mid-stride and pulls me close to her. 'They told me that you're getting professional help. The new research trial? That's why I need to leave now, I don't want to impact your results.' She offers me a turned-down smile of condolence. 'All the best.'

As she walks away, my mind tries to catch up with the new information. My body tingles as if electrified. A second research trial? It's a puzzle piece that fits. There must be a good reason that I'm monitored. It's not a follow-up on how I'm doing after Maximum. It's new research that I'm already taking part in. It's possible to be a lab rat and not even know it. An image of my mum's gravestone pushes its way through my resistance.

The bus rocks me side to side on the way to Ben's place. He'll have left for work before I get there as a new cycle of research starts this evening with a meeting for the night-time lab staff. I left Somni an hour early – more fodder for Anja to share that I'd been shaken up by the fire alarm so no one guesses it was me who set it off. The rumble of the road travels up from my feet through my body.

I place one hand on the bus window. For a lifetime I've had the ability to numb myself when everything gets too much. I imagine turning to glass. The cool path of numbness travels up from my hand along my arm and into my chest. From there, it radiates out as a frozen web until the whole of me becomes ice.

Somni isn't a person doing bad things to me. I must stop thinking of it that way. There's no 'it' plotting against me. Somni is simply a company led by people who aim to make money and earn prestige, and Harry won't let anything stand in its way. For some reason, I became an obstacle to those goals. If I lay things in order – dispassionately – I can figure it out.

Pippa confirmed that participants were hand-picked due to certain characteristics. I met the profile of what they were looking for. There was no intention of harm to me. It was bad luck: unintended consequences as the Pechu Kucha on ethics called it. 'Unintended consequences' sums up a lot of problems through my life. They realised the side effects but chose to ensure that nobody found out. A dark mirror to my past. Somehow that links to my time in a research bed. Harry knows – he was there.

If Pippa is correct, it was obvious that I needed help. There was rehabilitation in the days afterwards, still within that room that I slept in.

I close my eyes. I'm in the room with the septagonal light. The bed has gone. I'm in a chair, so sleepy. A calm voice speaks to me over and over through headphones with whispered instructions that I can't quite hear. I'm unsure if I'm by myself or not. There's a soft band around my eyes. But I don't mind. I feel calm. Then the headphones are removed. There's a real person in the room, rather than a recording. It's a different voice. The urge to push it away comes like I'm trying to stop myself from vomiting. But holding back won't provide any relief. I let the image return.

'Don't fight it, this is going to help, you have such strength inside you,' she says. I loosen the material from my eyes and squint.

At Dr Elizabeth Field.

It mustn't have been my idea to hire her for supervision: Elizabeth was already a part of Somni and involved with Maximus.

I'm pulled forward in time and space as the bus slows to a halt. This is the stop for Ben's flat. I grab my bag and jostle down the aisle, tripping on clumsy feet that have hardly defrosted.

Elizabeth is as wrapped up in all of this as Somni and Heidi. I need to find out how and why.

'Excuse me,' I say as I direct a businessman out of my way. My voice sounds a little more sure of itself than usual. He steps out of my path. I climb down from the step of the bus and feel the pavement solid beneath me. Grounded. Real. Each step is a stomp. This is what it must feel like to be in charge of myself, to head in the right direction.

30

Mike has made it to this rescheduled appointment. Despite my concerns about his lack of suitability for the sleep therapy trial, he reports that he's already started it. I notice a shudder of frustration with the team for ignoring my recommendation that the ReStory input be halted. Yet, perhaps they were right to give him the chance to take part. Today he looks more relaxed in the chair. He's wearing a blue striped shirt over jeans. His hair has been cut and the stubble is gone. He still looks weary but more robust than when we last met.

'I wouldn't have believed it,' he says, palms upturned as if in a confessional. 'That I could really get control over the nightmares. But the buzzer worked. Reminded me I was in a dream. Then the dream seemed to change as I told it to. Not at first, but after a few goes.' He leans back in the chair, shoulders lowered. There's a change in him. A sense of hope.

'Mike, that's such great work. Tell me a bit more about how the story altered with you in charge of it.'

He hesitates. I know he wants to avoid talking about the fire – the real or dreamed version – but it's part of trauma therapy to help him relive those moments until the imagery loses its power over him. I wonder if his experience of getting control over the scene playing out in the lab will mean he can discuss the incident in detail for the first time with me. That would provide good evidence for psychotherapy to run alongside sleep therapy.

Mike closes his eyes. His brow is furrowed as he grasps the arms of the chair.

'I'm in the rear of the building, about to take a right as I did that night. But instead, I make myself turn left to the games room where they all are. I get down low. I see three women: Greta, Annie and Florence. They're holding on to each other. Dave and Wilko from the crew are a couple of metres away from them. The wooden beam above creaks, about to drop. I can't stop it from dropping. But I can pause it, hold it up a bit longer. They all turn to me. Five of them. They all talk at the same time, saying the same thing: "We want you to escape, it's not..."' He stops, digs his face into his hands. I can hear the battle with his breath as he makes himself take two long sucks of air. Then he lifts his head back up. 'They say "it's not your fault". Then I'm pulled back through the air to the other side of the building to complete the job and save the rest of the nursing home from going up.' He opens his eyes and we share a moment that hurts and heals at the same time.

'Thank you, Mike.' I hope he doesn't notice the tremor in my voice. I wasn't sure how the sleep therapy process would work. I presumed he'd imagine saving them all but I guess that wouldn't work as the reality is they've gone. What he needed was forgiveness: from them, from himself.

'It's mad really. I know it's not real. But since the last session, I haven't had any nightmares. No funny turns in the day. I can even watch the TV and not lose track of what's going on. It's not perfect – I'm not myself yet – but I'm really thankful to the team, to you. Honestly didn't think it would work.'

Did I believe it could work? In a way, the sleep therapy has achieved what psychotherapy couldn't: it allowed Mike to help himself. I'm not sure there's any role for me. But there's a question I really need to ask him.

'I'm so pleased for you, Mike, and well done on facing your fears rather than avoiding the sleep therapy. There's an issue I want to check out with you, though, before we finish our review.' My mouth is so dry. 'It appears that you may be in contact with one of my other patients. That's unusual and, to be honest, could be unhelpful.'

Mike shrugs. He doesn't act as if he's been caught out. 'I don't think I need to come anymore, Christie. You've done a great job and I'm thankful you stuck it out with me. There'll be nothing to say to anyone else about our work from now on, so don't worry.'

'We don't have to stop seeing each other. It's early days yet if you want to come back to review things?' Does this sound like a plea? He shakes his head.

'No, I don't think I need it anymore. I'm going to be okay. I can't ever be the same guy I was back before it all, but okay enough to carry on.' I check my urge to argue with him. Do I want him to return for his own good, or so that I can figure out the connections between him and Mia? 'It's going to take time. But I'm okay. And don't worry about us all chatting to each other, Christie. I think it's supposed to be helpful.'

The phrase jolts me: all chatting to each other. This is bigger than Mike and Mia. Are all my new patients in contact with each other? Is their being in touch with each other supposed to be helpful to them?

Or helpful to me?

I feel disorientated.

'I don't understand, Mike. Is this part of Somni's research that you're all part of? Are you actors?' I regret it as soon as it's out of my mouth. He looks utterly shocked.

197

'Christie, this isn't a game. I've suffered. I'm trying to survive. I've tried to bring honesty here even though that's hard for me. The acting bit was probably before, when I was getting on with things like there wasn't guilt eating me up. It's been hard work to let myself focus on the mistake I made, and try to see that I can name it and feel sorry without being cruel to myself, letting go of holding it all as my fault. But I've done it.'

The earth doesn't revolve around you, Christie Langdale. I sink into shame so deep that I may never be able to pull myself out. I long to curl over with my head in my hands and become the statue that I threw away a decade ago.

I'm unsure how long I've been sitting here since Mike left. My neck and back ache. The leather chair that usually feels so comfortable seems hardened under my sensitive skin. Everything whirls out of control. I want it to stop. To feel that steadiness and certainty that I had a brief taste of only one day ago after stepping out of decades of flitting between anxiety and numbness. I recall the GIF that Jake showed me of the zombie girl falling apart, one body part at a time. There's nothing left of value in my life if I'm too disordered to be a therapist.

In the darkness, the autokinetic effect plays out its trick of the mind as the red light of the video camera seems to move. Knowing that in reality it's stationary doesn't change what I see.

The lecture room in the museum is full with standing room only for latecomers like me. It was by chance that I went onto Elizabeth's website on my way to the Tube and thought to check the 'Events' section. I had my phone out to organise the meet-up with Daniel that he seems to be avoiding but I couldn't bring myself to do it. Not yet. Instead, I felt the urge to reach out to the safety of Elizabeth's website, just to see her photos and quotes. I found out about this special exhibition on childhood which will be followed by an interview session with her as the main guest. Elizabeth is already in discussion with a group of women at the top of the room which acts as a stage. Unflattering yellow light from an old lamp ages her, but her rich, steady voice is unmistakeable.

A lady with a lanyard stands up and indicates for the door of the room to be closed.

'Welcome all to The Foundling Museum evening talk. I hope you enjoyed our exhibit and can now turn your attention to our guest for this evening whose research on recovery from trauma for those separated in childhood from their parents fits so well with the Foundling Hospital's history.'

Elizabeth takes the microphone and turns to acknowledge the audience with a smile before she responds. I pull myself up straight to catch her eye.

'It's a pleasure to be here in the home of this country's first children's charity. The struggles and successes of individuals who faced trauma in childhood is a real passion of mine.' I remember her lecture that taught us to understand that the adult in front of us brings their childhood experiences into the room through the way they interpret the world and interact with us in therapy. I guess the same is true of supervision. What am I to her: someone she supervises or someone she studies?

I lean back against the wall and look from one piece of artwork to another: all paintings of young children or sad-looking mothers looking away from babies in their arms. A poster invites children who have been in foster care to attend for a creativity class. Does Elizabeth know about my background: how Jake and I should have been safely in foster care instead of in a fire but I messed up? Is that somehow linked to Maximus in a way I never guessed?

'Tell us a little more now, Dr Field, about the methods you will be applying in your upcoming research.'

Of course she's still involved with research. She could be about to describe the next stages of research at Somni.

'Thank you so much, I'm privileged to have the opportunity to speak with you all about my exciting upcoming project.'

I try to figure out a route between chairs and bodies to get closer to Elizabeth. I want her to know I'm here so she can speak directly to me and everything will become clear. There's no way through without making a nuisance of myself and besides my legs have become heavy as rocks.

'With the support of a charitable grant from the Children's Commission and an upcoming residency as Visiting Professor at Stanford University, I will be taking with me the spirit of this wonderful museum steeped in the rich history of changing lives through creativity.'

She's breaking away from Somni, but there may still be clues in her methods to piece together the puzzle of Maximus and maybe even the new research trial.

'I'll be continuing to explore the journey of recovery for those with a history of trauma in a longitudinal study that employs creative methods such as art and literature.'

Longitudinal. I think back to my crash course in old attachment research and those studies that followed children across time, tracking change as they got older. It's the type of research that follows the same cohort of participants over time, taking measures and comparing them over years.

The interviewer takes back her microphone and walks towards a painting in the corner of the gallery.

'Perhaps we can start with your reflections from a psychotherapist perspective on this piece, Dr Field?'

I can't take in what Elizabeth is saying now about a piece of artwork. Nothing makes sense. She hasn't mentioned Somni and the description of her new research was vague. Elizabeth's imminent departure across the Atlantic hasn't even been hinted at in supervision.

I need to get out of here. I push the heavy door which squeaks as I move it. Elizabeth glances over towards me, then away again, as if I mean nothing to her at all.

31

FRIDAY, 7 JUNE

It's been a month since our last team meeting. Day-shift colleagues gossip as usual but I feel distant from them all with my secrets and concerns that have to be kept to myself. I'm so relieved that nobody has mentioned the fire alarm. There's no sign of Pippa or her companion. Clearly Zed company is linked to Somni but we're not supposed to be aware.

Harry strolls in late without papers or PowerPoint. He positions himself at the head of the table next to three directors of the company, who look more like bankers than research scientists: suits, briefcases, sales charts. The glitzy presence of his media-self is lacking today. He looks like an alcoholic who's missed his morning drink, even though we're told he's teetotal. With one clear of his throat, the room is silenced.

'We're only weeks away from our inspection. This morning I wish to clarify that we here as a group are driven by a common purpose: the greater good. Somni is the foremost team of sleep researchers in the world, of that I've no doubt. And yet, there may be those who doubt. Those who don't belong.' He looks from face to face of each staff member. Marnie to my right solemnly nods her head, lips thinned with concern. The back of my neck becomes moist with sweat. Harry sweeps his pointed finger across the room. 'Are you here to enrich the lives of those people who don't appear to warrant large government grants, deemed unworthy of the human right to a good night's sleep to soothe the cruel diseases that attack their brains, their very minds?' The speech sounds rehearsed and stilted compared to his usual flow.

A few of my colleagues murmur their agreement as we all look to one another for cues. Is each staff member looking to point the finger so they can take the heat off themselves? There's no room for discussion, that would clearly be seen as evidence of disloyalty. I recall a film I watched about witch trials hundreds of years ago, where any outcome was taken as evidence of guilt, a lose–lose situation.

I don't disagree with what Harry is saying about which people we should be aiming to help but something still feels off; a mismatch between what he's saying and the desperation in his eyes as they shift from one staff member to another. There's something personal driving his recent behaviour. I know Harry's father had some form of rare disease which came on at a young age, could that be what propels him, a desire to prevent his father's suffering in others? If only the answer were as simple as sleep therapy.

'We must push forwards, there's no time to spare, we'll work in ways never before imagined. We shall not only cure suffering but prevent it!' He glances at the directors who sit stiffly in their chairs. I imagine the pressure on his lips to spill what he truly wants to say but he's being careful how much he gives away in front of all the financial and management staff. There's no explanation about the increased urgency of our work. What clock is ticking? 'In short, this meeting is an opportunity for each and every one of you to reaffirm your commitment to our progressive approach that will bring such relief to many.'

As uncomfortable as I find Harry's preacher tone, he does have a valid point about us being the last hope for some people. Funding for sleep clinics and research has been slashed within universities and healthcare. The whole system is focused on reacting to crisis rather than helping those with chronic conditions have a better quality of life. Almost half of our patients are seen free of charge as Harry brings in money from companies, consultancy and pharmaceutical giants.

Marnie's chair screeches as she pushes it back from the table. She picks up a batch of papers from her desk, splits the pile in two and shares half with Heidi. It's clear who's closest to Harry and his way of running Somni. I feel further from my friend than I ever have before.

Another form to complete. I skim read the instructions that we are to join together and pledge our loyalty. Is this intended to make us more cohesive or more careful? The wording is so vague that I'm surprised by how quickly and enthusiastically everyone is signing. The form includes one line about collecting our bio-data for research and monitoring purposes with no further information. I'm reminded of my Catholic primary school. Bowed heads of us school children as we chanted along with the priest, more focused on getting the words right in front of the teacher than ever considering their meaning. We lined up for confession in silence trying to conjure up sins to share that were forgivable in three short prayers. The correct words in the correct order was all it took. My jelly-legged fear was that my mind would erase those words once it was my turn, leaving forgiveness forever out of reach.

I know my voice will be shaky before I even speak.

'Could you give us an example, please?'

Harry squints in my direction as if I'm so tiny he can barely see me. I push on regardless of the slight nervous tremor of my left leg under the table.

'I agree in principle with what it states about being committed to getting the best outcomes for underprivileged people, but it's hard to know exactly what you mean. Like, how are we going to? What is it exactly that we're signing up to here?'

I choose not to look at other people's responses. I've seen the sniggers and the pity from them in the past, like when I've turned up in supermarket clothes on a trip to Cheltenham Races or took the phrase 'town hall' literally when it meant a company meeting at our offices as usual. Their reactions are irrelevant. I keep my focus solely on Harry. I recall all those forms I've signed without hesitation across my years working here, including during my time in Maximus. Why did I never stop to question the details? I let myself become part of the machine instead of thinking for myself.

'Excellent point, thank you, Ms Langdale.' He usually addresses me by my first name – now he reminds my colleagues that I don't have the title of doctor like most researchers here. 'In effect we're talking about an ethos, a way of being, the principles that underlie all that we do.'

He waits.

Now is not the time or the place.

'I see,' I reply. And I think I finally do.

At my desk, my agitated legs cross and uncross. The phrase *ants in your pants* comes to mind – what Mum called it when Jake and I didn't keep still as she watched her TV programmes. We'd laugh when she was out of the room at the image of tiny creatures in our underwear. But this feels like an invasion; a crawling mass of bugs under my skin that won't let me settle. Harry had pulled back from giving his full speech but there's more he wants to say, and it might be enough to bring him down if I can get it out of him.

Heidi creaks open the door to the office and loiters near her desk without sitting. It's unusual to see her without bags and files. She wears flat sandals instead of high heels with no jewellery dangling around her delicate neck.

'Hey, Christie! How are you doing?'

I don't have it in me to pretend today, I'm too worn out to place my mask on.

'I'm okay. Lots to get on with.' I switch on my computer and try to hold my nerve.

She chews her bottom lip as if weighing up what to say next.

'I guess you're spending lots of time with your mystery man these days?' She rearranges her keyboard in front of her computer several times as if she can't get it quite straight. She knows I'm not staying in the flat.

They know.

'Heidi, we've been friends for a long time. I hope that if you have anything to say to me that you know you can say it.' My wobbly voice betrays what I intended to sound nonchalant, a genuine invitation.

She straightens up and smiles. But she looks paler than usual without the high-cheeked swishes of blusher.

'Course not, glad you're happy.'

One of the first research trials that Somni let me collect data for involved logging facial changes during task recall. As part of this, I was taught to see the difference between those muscles that move during a legitimate smile compared to a fake one. Involuntary contraction of a cheek muscle occurs in the genuine version called the Duchenne smile. I can't unsee the difference, and it explains why particular photos are more warming than others: genuine happiness glows.

Heidi's smile is fake.

Either she's under threat from Harry or she's just as bad as him. I need to find a way to confront her but I don't know what the consequences of that might be.

32

SUNDAY, 9 JUNE

Ben and I sit on the floor of his apartment to eat. The hummingbird pendant he bought me lies cool against my collarbone. For my birthday meal he's prepared food I don't recognise in small bowls lined up along a ceramic dish. I copy his posture: kneel with my legs pressed together as the tops of my feet rest against the floor.

'This is the polite way to sit in Japan, called *seiza*,' he says as I wriggle a little. 'But you can sit however you wish, I find it comfortable.'

'Sorry, I don't have good posture like you.' I move to the sofa and lumber on tingling legs, then let my body flop onto the foam cushions. The salty noodle dish is so good but I can't seem to eat it without slurping. While Ben concentrates on his food, I rush to wipe my splattered face with my sleeve.

'You apologise for a lot of things that don't require an apology.' He eats with his hands today but somehow it looks elegant and precise. His fingers fan out like bird wings around each morsel.

I swallow down another apology. It's a habit. One way to defuse Mum's terror or rage was to say sorry and stroke her hair.

Sorry that the rain was sent to punish her for finally getting her laundry out despite the pain in her hip. Sorry for ruining her body by growing inside her before she was ready. I thought I wanted her to say sorry to me, for not being who I craved her to be. But the one time she apologised, the week after the fire when it became clear Jake wasn't going to return home, it hurt more than a wound. Mum mumbled sorry over and over as she sat by my bed, staring at the wall. She was saying sorry for the wrong thing. I hugged my duvet and pressed my toes into a point to stop myself from crying. She didn't know how to be any other way. I never wanted her to hate herself as much as she hated the world. And I couldn't risk letting her know that this time it was me who was sorry, in case she also ended up hating me.

Ben's bluntness doesn't hammer me as it would if it were someone else making the statements. There's no judgement. He holds a mirror up to my choices, which gives me the option to change how I act. It wasn't him that moved to create distance between us. I rub the back of my hand against my lips, place my plate on the coffee table next to me and go to sit next to him, cross-legged.

'I do the opposite of what I want so often, it's almost a reflex, as if what I want must be wrong.'

Ben continues with his meal. I know him well enough to guess that his silence doesn't mean rejection, he's thinking. He dips his fingertips in a bowl of water.

'I spent so long being perceived by others as weird. Once I stopped wasting energy being concerned about what other people thought, everything was so much clearer. Since I freed myself to respond to the world as who I am, my life is better.'

I'm unsure what he's trying to tell me. That I should forget all the issues at Somni and enjoy my noodles? He clears the plates to the kitchen, then sits opposite me on the floor. His hands hold my face steady. I lean my head in so that our foreheads touch.

'Focus on the breath,' he says. The pressure of his skin against mine steadies me. My mouth opens a little. The warmth of his exhalation changes the air above my tongue. As I breathe out, I see two colours of air swirling around each other: his blue to my red. We continue – held together in a cycle of breathing for several minutes until the intensity becomes too much. I pull back and lean against the wall.

'I wouldn't get so caught up with all this crap if I could stay here with you.' Despite the fact that I'm staying at his flat currently, we barely see each other because of our opposite shifts. It's frustrating that we are both awake in the early hours of the morning, but he's miles away from me at Somni as I throw my body in and out of covers in his bed. He places his arm around my shoulder.

'You need to take breaks. Be where you are. Even when you're with those people who make you feel confused and afraid. Try to be with them in that moment with all your feelings and questions. That will tell you what to do.' It seems simple when Ben says it.

'You could write memes. I'll put you in touch with my brother. You can zen the world back into order.'

Ben shifts his head to an angle. 'I'm guessing that's a joke.' He strokes my hair, then tips my chin up towards him. 'What do you feel right now?'

The words get caught in the back of my throat. *Don't ruin things, what does he mean, it's a test...*

I cough, place one hand on his chest, the other on my own. Being with him – really being with him, rather than half of my attention floating a foot above my head – is the best birthday gift I could have wished for. Even if I don't deserve it.

'I feel happy.'

His crooked smile answers. 'Is there anything else that is getting between us?'

Happiness doesn't last. You'll get found out. Or maybe you'll find him out...

'No, nothing,' I say, as I grab on to a moment that will soon be only a memory.

33

WEDNESDAY, 12 JUNE

I'm uncertain what to expect from Isobel today. At her last appointment, the revelation that she harboured such dark thoughts towards her son shocked us. I wish I'd reacted differently – given us both the opportunity to step back and consider the night-time behaviour as a message rather than a true desire. She'd allowed herself to acknowledge how hard it was to be a mother: both wonderful and destructive. Her fantasy to escape from single parenthood seems understandable. I have absolute certainty she holds such love for Riley that she would never harm him, even in a fugue of half-sleep. She wanted to destroy her predicament, not a person.

Isobel once showed me a photo of her son that she kept inside her purse. He looked similar to her: oval-eyed with a dimple on his chin. Unlike his mother, Riley had unruly black hair that seemed too big for his face. I never asked details about her abusive ex-partner as she made it clear she did not wish to discuss that part of her life. Did he have hair like his son, as wild and unpredictable as his moods? Did seeing Riley as a younger version of this abusive man sometimes trigger a trauma response?

It's up to patients to choose whether to explore certain areas of their life or not. But distress is complicated. It rarely comes from only one place but is a knot of past, present and predicted future. Isobel's insistence on focusing on the here and now is working well, however, it could just be scratching the surface. We carry the past with us whether we wish to or not. For Isobel, her son is a reminder of all that is good and all that's been painful.

Isobel has come prepared to her therapy session with a notebook filled with charts. She presents them to me like a child showing homework to her favourite teacher. With no mention of social services knocking at her door, I feel a strange mixture of relief and guilt. There's a healthy colour to her cheeks that makes her look less washed-out than at our last session. I'm unsure whether to start with positive feedback or to revisit how difficult our last session was. My urge to delay a focus on what was painful last appointment means that I'm pulled to treat Isobel as if she's a child: fragile and in need of tiptoeing around issues. It's unlikely to help her know her own strength.

'I can see you have useful information for us to look at together, Isobel.' I must encourage her to act like the adult she is by not ignoring the challenging aspects of our work. 'But first I thought we could reflect on our last appointment.'

The rounded tips of her pink shoes touch the new Persian rug that almost fills the room. I could have sworn that at our earlier appointments her legs dangled from the chair as she was so short. The therapy chair remains the same and her legs can't have grown. Why does my mind muddle things this way to distract me from what matters?

'I thought about it all the time for days. Hugged Riley so tight. He didn't know why I cried and said sorry. I nearly blocked my bedroom door, so I couldn't get out and do anything bad.' I can track the muscle tension up her body: she's holding in her stomach, one hand grips the chair, her shoulders are raised. But the anxiety hasn't tipped yet into becoming overwhelming: she's eloquent, almost poised, without obvious numbness.

'So, you considered blocking the door, but chose not to?' I want to highlight her ability to stop, think and choose what to do rather than acting on her fear impulse. This will empower her if she can keep it up in the face of life challenges.

'Yes, I remembered what you said about keeping a log to help figure out patterns. For when I'd been sleepwalking, but also other things in the day. I made charts.' She flicks through page after page to show me. Each box has multiple columns hand-drawn with different coloured inks within each. 'I wrote down how I'd been feeling that day, what I'd been saying to myself in my head, how things had been with Riley, then this last column is what happened in the night as far as I could tell.'

It's common in certain types of therapy to set structured homework tasks. I never expected Isobel to recall my brief description of how to do this when we first met, I hadn't set this as a task yet. I'd overprotected her and luckily, she took it on herself to investigate the factors which influence her distress and sleepwalking.

'That's perfect, Isobel. As you were filling in these sheets, did you notice any patterns that predicted your sleepwalking?'

She nods enthusiastically. 'Yes! At first I noticed more bad sleep when I'd been stressed in the day: Riley playing up when he had an ear infection or when I'd spent ages beating myself up about not looking forward to the weekend with him.' Interesting she uses the phrase 'beating up', a repetition of the violence she's received. Without meaning to, she has continued the pattern by her cruelty to herself. 'So, then I started writing down lists of all sorts of things. I let myself cry or laugh or be greedy or be cross while I did them.'

She shows me her beautifully written lists.

Sad Things and All The People I Miss
Top Ten Brilliant and Awful Parts Of Being a Mummy
People Who Have Hurt Me That I Don't See Anymore
What Makes Me Cross and Angry (But That's Okay)
Shopping List After I Win The Lottery and Who Isn't Getting Any Money Off Me
Things I Wish I'd Done and Still Can One Day

I'm blown away by these wonderful, creative items. Each list has a full page of carefully constructed handwriting. Several have little cartoons drawn next to an entry, such as a picture of a girl hugging a huge dog on 'Things I Wish I'd Done'.

'These are incredible, Isobel! What was the pattern that you said you noticed?'

'Well, it doesn't matter what type of list it is. The happy ones, the sad ones, the ones where I broke my pencil pushing down so hard when I was angry. Every day that I did a list and had big feelings, I didn't have any sleepwalking. Even when Riley acted up and didn't eat his dinner that I'd spent ages on. But all of it helped. When I didn't add anything to a list, I'd wake up in another room or in the morning the camera light would flash to say I'd been recorded in the night.'

The simplicity of it astounds me. Here I am doing a job where I help people to get in touch with their internal worlds to heal their traumas and move forwards, and yet I'm surprised that this is effective. I shouldn't be.

'How does this help you to make sense of the incident with Riley and the pillow?' Isobel sighs in concentration.

'I think it was a build-up cos I didn't let anything out. Felt too bad to say I need a break from this, that sometimes I wish I hadn't had him. I'd be at college maybe; I'd never have to be in contact with his dad again. It was that fed up bit of me that sometimes wants to do a runner. That's the bit that *did* do a runner, down the street at midnight in my nightie!' She smiles in a way that's full of love and sadness all at once. I feel my tears build to tipping point. 'But most of the time, that's not what I want at all. I love Riley and our life together. When he grows up, I'm going to miss him so much it'll hurt.'

A little of that hurt aches in my chest: is that transference of her pain, or does it belong to me? Is it an ache for the people that I miss, no matter how hard things were at times?

Before we finish our appointment, Isobel looks a little shy as she places her paperwork back into a bag. 'I wondered, Christie, if you don't mind me saying it.' Movement in her neck shows her gulp. 'Writing out patterns really helped me figure out what was going on. I wondered if it might be helpful for you, too?'

34

I finish my reports for the afternoon in the quiet of the office. Today's data comes from a study of the most efficient sleep pattern for long-distance lorry drivers. A microsleep can prove fatal as reflexes are not slowed but completely deadened. How many people's lives are impacted by one accident? Five vehicles, eight victims, fifteen injured, several hundred people dealing with the fallout of an accident that involved their friend, neighbour, colleague, parent, spouse, child? One overtired driver unwittingly succumbs to the natural sleep drive and he may as well have pressed a detonator.

With a few clicks on my computer, columns of figures translate into solid evidence. There's beauty in mathematics. The statistics program calculates the most effective way to take naps and reduce risk on the road. I use a presentation package to display the results visually for maximum impact. This is the kind of research that can inform policy and send ripples out into the world that change the future. I send the draft report to the project lead and sit with the satisfaction.

I could take Isobel's advice and look at my own work schedule data. I'm unnerved that she suggested it. Did she have a particular problem in mind for me to review that she's somehow discussed with my other patients? Maybe not; it could have been a general comment because of my reaction to the previous session's video. I'm not even sure that I know which question I need to answer. I can't change what's happened. But I would like to recapture those days when I could think in a straight line.

I print off my electronic calendar for this year, month by month, including weekends. Taking my lead from Isobel, I colour code different aspects of my week using information from my phone diary, memory and work schedule. I use my finger to trace down the days of the month on each sheet to prevent errors. Next, I add in when I've had a day off work, meetings, therapy, overtime or work at home in the evening. I take a guess at the dates of significant events that may have disrupted my emotional system for better or worse: days that I met up with Ben or Heidi, when I saw the blue car, the few times I've been out of the flat into the city to a café or cinema. On my phone, I've kept a log of the nights in which my sleep was most severely affected in case I needed the data to seek treatment for insomnia myself. I transfer the information onto the printed calendar. Sheets spread across the desk are decorated with rainbow codes. Now what?

My phone vibrates on the table. It makes me jump as I realise that I'm staring at the papers in switch-off mode, overwhelmed. I place my hand across my aching temple to try to soothe it with warmth. There's a text from Daniel giving a time and location for us to meet. Tomorrow, I'll be sitting opposite my ex in a bar that must be near Daniel's new place. He's kept our meeting public. I wasn't the docile Christie he remembered when I was ready to rip the door off his car. A sick feeling rises up my gullet at the thought of meeting him but it will be worth it to get some answers. There was no room for distress when I found him in the blue car – I felt in control, powerful. He's already taken the reins back by deciding where and when we meet. I've let him take over as usual.

The diary sheets in front of me contain too much information. I don't have an appropriate algorithm to analyse these data with the statistics program. I squeeze my eyes and the pages turn to a multicoloured haze. Red lines leap out across the months: the days of worst sleep. There's no need for statistics to be clear that terrible sleep correlates with my worst episodes of memory difficulties, confusion and thinking through glue. There's a regularity to the red. And something else. With my eyes still half-closed, the pattern shows clearly. To the left of the red patches there's usually a purple blob. I pull the last two month's records up towards my face and look carefully. Before each episode of severe sleep deprivation and thinking problems there's the purple box of a therapy session. When my therapy day has changed occasionally, my symptoms follow. The more purple days in a row, the longer the red section lasts. When I've been at Somni for non-clinical work such as report writing, there's no such pattern, even when I've been under stress.

Giving therapy is linked to my sleep and thinking problems in a way it never was before the Maximus trial. I can't figure out why that would be. But there's someone who may already know, and I'm meeting her today.

Despite my concerns, it's impossible for me to sit opposite Elizabeth and not feel glad that she's there. I hold back the gush of questions about her leaving for America, her future research, how much she's entwined with Somni. I can ask those things towards the end of supervision today if I feel brave enough. Whatever her role, Elizabeth helps me to think and reflect in a way nobody else can. It's uncomfortable at times; it's not a pleasant process to peel back my mask and look what lies beneath. But I'm certain of her compassion. It's time to turn that excavation away from me and onto our relationship. What's she really being paid for? If I lay out the evidence, she might admit to her part in what's happened to me. I need to know whether I really saw her during my recovery in the Magnesium room.

Elizabeth wears a gold and royal blue headscarf with a little of her white hair peeping out. Silver hearts dangle from her ears. In contrast to my legs that twist over one another, she sits with both feet planted firmly on the floor. Her torso is upright but without tension. I imagine her spine made from an ancient metal sword. She waits for me to start the session.

'I made a diary of the last few months, to see what linked to my fatigue and cognitive symptoms.' She's so still – no nod or surprise. I fan out the diary sheets to show my work. 'The more time I spend here in this room giving therapy, the worse my symptoms.'

'It seems important to you that you explore possible causal connections between activities and symptoms. What do you make of your finding?' She turns it back to me rather than give her own opinion or let slip anything she might already know about.

'I ignored something relevant as paranoia at the time but I think it might be related.' There's a catch in my throat that doesn't want to let more words out. 'I thought I was inventing things but now I'm more certain: I think my Somni health drink has been spiked with a drug.' It's the hardest statement to make. I hope she can't read my mind. There's a slight reaction from Elizabeth, a flicker of her brow. 'I think it's related to why I can't get to sleep on days after I've had the drink and seen my patients.'

Elizabeth acts no differently than if I were talking about a patient. I need her to break out of character, to speak to me as a colleague now that I've figured out part of what's been happening. She remains silent: focused, attentive, but silent.

'My patients know things about me. I told you that before, but it's not just one – I think they're all in touch and part of a bigger picture. I found a woman from the original research trial.' There's so much to this story, I want to tell Elizabeth everything but don't want to run out of time. I must understand her role in it all. 'She says that I'm in a new research trial. Right now. Are you part of it somehow?'

It sounds far-fetched when I say it out loud but that's what all the evidence points to. Elizabeth has been involved at least since Maximus, if not before. Please, please, please let there be an explanation that makes sense. I can't bear for her to be anything other than a good person who tries to do her best for me. I'm shallow-breathing – a habit when I go into freeze mode as if that can stop anything bad happening next. The lack of oxygen starts to make me feel light-headed.

'Christie, I can see you're concerned. Be assured that I wish to remain alongside you in this and help you to understand your situation. Consider this – what if you already know what's going on?'

No, no, no! She's turning it back on me. Not a denial or an explanation but a game. If I knew what was going on, I wouldn't be in this state. She's a fake. A fraud. I should have listened to the part of myself that thought she was too good to be true.

My voice hardens. 'This isn't down to me! I don't want to figure it out, why don't you tell me – you must be wrapped up in all of this. I don't want any of it – I don't consent to participation in another research trial.'

There's a beeping sound that I've not heard before. Elizabeth looks unnerved for the first time ever. She pulls out a pager from her pocket, presses a button, then slips it out of sight again.

'I'm sorry, Christie. I must go, unfortunately, I'm afraid I can't ignore this.' She hesitates for a moment, then shakes her head and gets up to leave.

Everybody leaves.

35

On autopilot, I make my way back to my flat rather than to the bus stop to return to Ben's. Maybe home is where I need to be.

When I was young, I'd avoid stepping on the cracks between pavement slabs because Mum said it was bad luck. We didn't need any more of that. It meant that my head was always down with my focus at least one step ahead. That way of living has stuck. What was intended to protect me has caused me to suffer. I find it so hard to be in the moment. I'm busy trying to figure out what next, what can go wrong? But when it mattered, that didn't work to protect us all. So today, I make my mark all the way back home: feel the thwack of my foot against each crack. I don't move out of the way for anyone. Rather than duck and dart, I forge a straight path and allow my shoulders to barge into strangers' arms and shopping bags. I don't apologise. It's time there was space for me in the world.

A vanilla scent hits me as I enter my hallway, followed by an unexpected dose of emotion that isn't positive or negative but a jumble of everything at once. I'm not ready to contact Ben who will expect to see me before he leaves for work. I need time for myself, however strong the urge to be rescued is. Ben might not be around forever. But I'm stuck with being me.

I lock the bathroom door despite there being no one else here. There's a smudged mirror above the basin. Mum had a triple mirror in her bedroom. When I placed my nose on the outside edge so that only half my face was reflected, the side mirror would create a perfectly symmetrical version of me: recognisable but different. I preferred the version of me that was two copies of my left side with my arched eyebrow, rather than my right, which looked plainer. Through the dirty mirror in front of me, I stare at the version of me that is both. If I stare for long enough, my face will start to warp into not-me.

It seems one part of me feels happy when I'm with Ben and can accept myself as good enough. How can that be the same person that waits for him to reject me?

My patients often do as their minds tell them. When their mind says *no you can't*, then they don't do the thing they wish to. I ask them to repeat 'I can't raise my hand'. Then I tell them to raise their hand as they say that they can't. It's a small experiment, yet it makes a valid point. We don't have to obey what our minds tell us because that voice we hear does not represent everything we know, want, or can be.

I don't want to strip in front of the mirror. But I do it anyway. I let my clothes drop one by one into a pile on the floor as I keep my eyes ahead. What would it be like to not feel disgust, to see myself as Ben sees me, or at least as a stranger might? They wouldn't care about the crease on my side where a small roll of fat rests on one below. Perhaps the greatest judgement of all comes from within.

I turn around and swing my head back to see my bottom which seems to sink into my legs a little. My calves are covered with short, dark stubble, several days after I last shaved them. I catch my jaw tightening, then let it drop down with my teeth and lips slightly apart. *Let go.* I step towards the basin, pushing my face nearer to my reflection. I take one hand in the other and guide it over my cheek. Then down the other side of my face. A teardrop lands on my fingertip. The smallest unlocking. I guide my hand down across breasts that hang lower than those in the adverts, then over my belly. Then I cross my hands over so that each travels around to its opposite side, holding me in a hug with my arms crossed over me. I let my breath slow down, press my hands firmly on my waist to hold myself. The woman in the mirror has stopped crying. She has a faint smile. *I'm okay as I am,* I tell her. I tell myself.

I can't rely on Elizabeth or Ben or Jake or being a therapist to make me feel good enough. I've got to do that for myself. It's up to me to piece together the puzzle of the last year – perhaps even further back than that – to take back control of my life.

I wrap myself in a fleecy blanket on the sofa and eat packet noodles from a cereal bowl. Compared to the dish Ben made for me, they taste like cardboard. Sometimes you don't notice how bad things are until you've experienced how it can be different. I place the half-eaten food on the side table and phone him.

'Christie, I'm about to leave – is everything okay?' The concern in his voice warms me.

'I should have texted; I've come back to my flat to sort things out. I think I'll be here all weekend actually.' I haven't told him about my meeting with Daniel tomorrow. I don't want to have an argument about it. Ben's behaviour has never given me any reason to doubt him but people aren't always what they seem.

'I received notification that Somni are terminating my contract.'

'What? They can't! What bloody grounds? You're the best

technician they've got.' I'm up on my feet even though there's nothing I can do from here.

'The letter states that my service has been appreciated but is no longer required with immediate effect. There will be a large severance pay out according to this summary.'

My shoulders sag with the weight of repercussions. This must be linked to Ben helping me. With huge projects on the way, the team need more qualified professionals, not fewer. I'm bringing trouble to people's door as usual. 'This isn't right. They must have figured out that we're on to them.'

Why are they going through the formality of redundancy rather than relying on smearing or dismissal like with previous staff? Ben remains calm even though his job means the world to him. Too calm for a man who likes predictability? I shake my distrust away.

'I called Harry already to clarify that there are several ongoing projects that can't be completed without me. He agreed to my working two more weeks. I'll gather all the data I can that shows changes made to research plans after people have signed consent forms, then I'll create a spreadsheet to summarise. Next, we could check which research projects had no ethical approval and which were hushed up with no publication.'

'Hang on, let me check the mail here in case I've got a notice of being laid off too.' I run to the front door and flick through junk mail. 'I haven't received anything; I wonder why they haven't tried to get rid of me?'

'There must be a reason that they need you. Shall I come over tomorrow night after I've had some sleep?'

There's a pause before I answer. A little pebble of doubt in my shoe. 'Yes. Bring whatever data or records you can get copies of and let's spend the evening figuring it out. I'm going to talk to Heidi, too. I hate to say it, but I'm sure she's implicated in all this.' There isn't time to explain that somehow my patients and supervisor are also part of the web.

'Don't rush into speaking with Heidi, it could make things worse if she reports back to them. We need a robust plan. I have so little time left at Somni before it will be too late.'

It's down to me to get the evidence. I grab my handbag to take to the local shop. To face meeting Daniel tomorrow, I'm going to need a toothbrush, milk for the morning tea, and the largest bar of chocolate I can find. As I fasten up my cardigan and press my fingers against the ba-boom, ba-boom pulse under my ear until it slows. I need to find the strength in myself, recharge my battery enough to lead the way. I yank the door open and let the low, invisible rays of sun flood my face, drawing in their energy.

36

SATURDAY, 15 JUNE

The Tube carriage is crammed with people who pretend they don't see one another. I keep my Oyster card in my sweaty hand. I rehearsed in my mind the many ways a conversation with Daniel could go until four o'clock this morning. Pointless, but I couldn't stop. There's a route map above my head. I read the name of each station on repeat as a mantra: Oxford Circus, Regent's Park, Baker Street, Marylebone. They don't sound real. A Monopoly board of places that I don't belong in. When I reach my stop at Harlesden perhaps I'll stay glued to the seat. I could shuttle back and forth all day on this line while Daniel sits in a dark pub jabbing at his phone.

We empty out of the carriage, up stone steps and out of the station as a herd but then separate into our individual journeys. Everyone else strides with purpose and certainty. I check the location of the pub for the hundredth time, then turn left along a row of cut-price shops. Ill-tempered beeps from drivers stuck behind temporary lights set me on edge, as if it's me they're frustrated with. I'm unsure why Daniel wants to meet in this run-down area. I suppose this is the kind of place he wouldn't have to worry about his finance contacts accidentally seeing us together.

The Old Brown Jug is tucked down a side street. Outside the door, a handwritten menu swings on a chalkboard, full of traditional food that Daniel wouldn't touch. I drop my handbag off my shoulder and hold it in my right hand so it's unavailable for a handshake, lift it to my chest to block any further contact. He's the type of person that has different settings and you don't know which you're going to get: charming, sneering, flattering, scary. I spent years convinced that the sweet version was the *real* him: the man who turned up at the café with flowers during my afternoon break or who stroked my hair and told me I was pretty as we watched a film. I translated his need for control as love, his disparaging of my friends as protectiveness. But the truth is he's all those things: one doesn't rule out another.

I push the heavy door and try to adjust to low lighting in the middle of the day. The traditional patterned carpet could be older than me. 'Doesn't show the dirt,' my mum said about ours. It was a good job: she didn't often get around to using the hoover unless professionals were due to visit and a performance of being a Normal Family was necessary. A long, wooden bar runs the length of the pub. Every inch of wall is covered with framed photographs that don't seem to follow any theme: rock stars, babies, war-time posters, seascapes. It's not the kind of venue that serves coffee, so I order a full-fat Coke as I check to see if any of the men nearby are Daniel. No sign. No text messages. I'm both relieved and frustrated.

A raised area of the pub has a rounded armchair tucked into the corner. I park myself in this spot that allows me to see everyone that enters. A rickety table lies between me and a low-set leather chair. As Daniel has a height advantage, these seats will even the score. I'm hungry but don't order anything – I was never comfortable eating in front of him: he saw food as a necessity to be endured. Despite my anxiety at the purpose of the meeting, my surroundings settle me a little. I could be anywhere. It's the kind of place that could be back home if weren't for the snippets of southern and international accents around me.

I can tell by the gait of the man who approaches that it's Daniel before I see his face clearly. He doesn't come from the front door that I've been watching, but the bar. There's a pub emblem on his black T-shirt: this is his workplace. I'm so shocked that I speak without thinking.

'You work *here*?'

Daniel's lips tighten. He pulls the chair back and drops down into it.

'I'm the assistant manager.' His nonchalant tone doesn't ring true. No high-flying finance job: something must have gone very wrong. He looks older. Tired. Still handsome. I take a glug of my drink to wake myself up and focus on the reason that I'm here. I mustn't get side-tracked by other matters. He hasn't dived into a rant or explanation as I thought he might. I need to take the lead. I picture him sitting in the blue car, me standing above, strength running into my arms like a superpower.

'Tell me what your connection is to Somni and why you were following me. All of it.'

Daniel scratches at a chipped part of the table until more dark wood cracks off.

'Does anyone know you're meeting me?' He doesn't seem as robust as I recall, hunched over with his elbows on the table between us.

'No. And if you want it to stay that way, then answer me.' I see the twenty-year-old Daniel that I fell for as well as the bully who added to my sense of worthlessness. Daniel's charm had been his quiet way of complimenting that I wanted so much to believe. 'Not bad,' he'd say when I got ready for a night out and

I'd pretend to not care while trying to figure out if I was good enough for him. His protectiveness was something I'd never experienced from a parent: an arm around me in public, glaring at anyone who got too close, carrying my bags or driving me to where I needed to go for training. It was a tolerable kind of closeness. For a long time, I felt that I belonged with him. But maybe it was more that he led me to believe that I belonged *to* him.

It would be easier if I could hate him. But seeing him out of sorts like this is painful. The swagger and self-belief got him far when the odds were stacked against a working-class boy with the wrong background and education for the finance world.

'I know you're linked to the company, and you were before I even applied for the job. Why did they want me? What did you get out of it?'

'I was trying to *help* you,' he says, his voice knife-sharp. I don't argue with his lies. Let him spin his story and I'll pick out the truth. 'There was the chance for freelance work for me – well paid. I was headhunted for it actually.' He leans back in his chair, back into acting mode as if his life hasn't been ripped apart. Headhunted no doubt because someone at Somni had heard Daniel would lie for cash and produce an ethical finance report no matter what he found.

'What has that got to do with my job?' I keep my tone neutral. He doesn't react well to challenge; I've gone in too strong.

'I told them I'd consider moving down and doing more of this specialist kind of work, just the way they wanted it. I asked if there'd be a job for you, not easy with no qualifications. They were looking to expand a couple of research projects and needed participants who wouldn't be too upset about the proper processes not being in place yet. Those things take so long, all a load of red tape really.' I clamp my teeth to stop me from interrupting. 'I knew you'd love a proper job away from the market to improve yourself. So, I asked for the criteria and you were a good fit.' He glances at his watch.

'Daniel.' I wait for him to look up at me to see if I can reconnect in order to get more from him. 'What were the criteria?'

'Oh God, I don't remember! Don't you see I got you that job that you're still in? You'd be standing outside in a market still if it wasn't for me.'

I need to play his game. 'Yes, you're right. And that's partly why I'm here, to acknowledge that however upset I was about you following me, there must have been good reason. It's you who changed my life for the better by getting me into the company.'

Daniel frowns, then relaxes his shoulders a little. 'Yes, well I knew you'd be the right sort. They wanted someone who would be open to their way of running things, who wouldn't make a fuss but just get on with it. They needed someone who respected authority as this was all a bit off the books. But clever – someone with untapped potential. I always said that about you, Christie.'

He sold me off to get me to come down to London and grow his contract with Somni. The pre-interview testing confirmed what Daniel had told them – I was ripe for their research. Did they pay him off to leave me? I can't stop the anger burning up from my chest into my mouth.

'But you never did work for Somni, how come?'

Daniel exhales loudly in frustration. 'God, Christie, you can be pretty thick sometimes. It wasn't the kind of work you're supposed to do from the inside. Neutral or whatever. So they set me up in another company and kept me on the books. I gave them years of work, on and off. They're in the shit without me, serves them right.'

He's making it about himself again.

'You saw what the Maximus research trial did to me. I lost my mind. They never warned me of the side effects. Why did you leave so suddenly, when I was clearly unwell?'

He doesn't respond. I need to sell what's in it for him.

'Daniel, if you explain this to me, you're off the hook with Somni. I have my own fight with them and they'll never link it to you.'

'I got a message – a letter, not email, so it was untraceable. It said that you were a danger to others and that I was at risk if I went near you.' He has the decency at least to break eye contact and stare at the table. 'You were out of control, wouldn't stop repeating lists and adding stuff up, said horrible things to me.'

'Weren't you worried? Why didn't you tell anyone or check on me?'

He laughs, as sour as lime. 'I texted that bitch, Heidi. She confirmed it all. Said you needed recovery time and it was best I never went near you again. They had me, Christie. Said I was in it up to my neck. That they had evidence of fraud even though all I did was exactly what they wanted.' He shakes his head, feeling sorry only for himself, not me. 'I thought it was all over. Got a job in another company. Then all of a sudden, I'm laid off from my new place and get a phone call from Somni that I've got some kind of gagging clause and can't risk working in finance again. Plus, they said to check up on you without you finding out. No explanation given.'

'Did they tell you to break into my flat?'

'Don't be stupid, of course not. Had to track where you went and who you were talking to. I think they were worried you might blab and they needed you for a few more months.'

'A few months? What for?'

Daniel shrugs, disinterested. 'Now I live and work at this shithouse. Word is out that I won't work in the City again.'

'So why don't you go back home? Back to the bank?'

He raises his voice. 'Are you kidding? Go back and say look at me, a failure? I'm the same as you lot, stuck up here going nowhere!' He stands. 'Are we done? I've got work to do.' I nod although there's so much more that I feel I need to ask and understand before we really are done. Daniel struts back to the bar, picks up a tea towel and flicks it at the bottom of a young barmaid. She laughs and smacks him back, then looks over to me in confusion. The last image I have of Daniel is his sneer. That makes it all the easier to leave. I realise how much self-hatred he carries: so much that he'd rather suffer in a job and place he hates than admit he's no more special than any of us.

If what Daniel said was accurate, I'm on a countdown to getting laid off like Ben. They'll want to dispense with me once they have what they want. But what is it that they want? And if it wasn't him who broke in and stole the diary, then who?

There's one person who can give me answers. I turn my back to the bar and call Heidi's number. It goes straight to answerphone. She's probably at her gym classes on Saturday afternoon.

'Hi, Heidi, it's Christie. I need to see you. Today. I didn't tell you, but the person I've been dating is Ben. I've broken up with him. Can we meet for dinner at my place at six?' I add my address, as if she hasn't already been there to steal my diary.

I don't want her on high alert that it's to do with Daniel or Somni or the research. Heidi won't be able to resist coming to discuss my love life. I send a message to Ben to tell him to come over half an hour after Heidi is due to arrive without letting him know she's coming.

Tonight will either give me all the answers I need or blow everything apart.

As I walk back to the Tube station, I send my brother a message: 'About to put on my cape, wish me luck.' He replies with a GIF of Wonder Woman lassoing businessmen into a rubbish truck.

Hunger, the need for answers and homesickness merge into a kind of strength. No longer disconnected from my desires, I know what I need.

37

I run down a corridor that turns into an alley. Someone chases me with a huge spotlight. Whichever way I turn to hide, the spotlight follows. High walls surround me. I can't see a way out. 'Why are you doing this, switch it off!' I hold my hand up to block the glare.

'So you can see your shadows,' replies the person behind the light.

I turn to the wall. My shadow follows, slightly out of time. There's another shadow on the ground, and a smaller one on the opposite wall. They all move at once, reaching out to grab me. I'm scared. The shadow hands reach my feet, my legs, my waist. I stop wrestling against them, exhausted, allowing them to hold me.

I wake with a jolt, fully dressed on the sofa. My right arm is numb from being trapped under me as I slept. I wiggle fingers that don't feel like mine. Remnants of a dream leave me disorientated. Feeling comes back into my arm so that it throbs.

A couple of years ago I saw a patient with hypersomnia.

Marcus lost his wife to multiple sclerosis at the age of forty-six. Since then, he slept for up to eighteen hours a day. When he was awake, he described a complete lack of emotion. As he tried to do any tasks to settle his wife's estate, he'd fall into a catatonic state. We kept our sessions short. If I pressed too hard to find out more about his love and loss, he would drift into sleep. It took months for him to build the resolve that he wanted his life back.

'I need to be awake long enough to do things. See my parents, cook a roast dinner, sort the garden out.'

As he started to spend more hours awake, more hours feeling what it is to be alive, he noticed how much emotional pain arose. In the end it was a choice between a life of numbness and sleep, or a life rich with a kaleidoscope of feelings. Marcus chose life with the pain of grief rather than a living death. A few months after we finished working together, he sent me a box of vegetables that he'd grown in his garden.

I must get ready to face what's coming. Heidi confirmed she'll be over shortly, what information I'll manage to gain from her is uncertain. I have my work laptop booted up: she has greater access to documents on the protected drive. I'm going to watch my recent therapy videos. Then delete the lot. Whatever it is that Elizabeth says I already know, I need to allow to emerge.

Heidi arrives at my flat with a bottle of iced tea and a carrot cake, managing to make a tunic top and leggings look sophisticated. She hugs me as soon as I open the front door. I'm unsure if she notices my rigid body that doesn't know how to respond, as if the familiar has become unfamiliar.

'I can't believe you didn't let on that it was Ben you were dating!' She passes me and takes her gifts straight to the kitchen.

'He's a little odd, don't you think? Well I guess you do, who'd break up with you?'

I never said it was him that broke up with me. This presumption gives away her view of me. She pours us a glass each that we take through to the living room.

Heidi sits at the table rather than the sofa. It seems suitably formal for what I need to say. My stomach churns. I open my notebook where I scribbled down questions in case nerves scrambled my thinking.

'Have you done *ratings* of him?' she asks, peering at my page. There's something off with her humour – the strain shows through her smile. I want to laugh with her, rewind two years and make this a gossipy catch-up. She notices that I'm struggling.

'Christie, I'm teasing, I'm sorry. You're upset. It's going to be okay.'

She reaches over and rubs the back of my hand. My tears fall as if it has nothing to do with me. Real crying that comes from the heart, flows in waves that build stronger and stronger into sobs. When my patients 'weep' rather than sob, then it's usually a defence against the real feeling that they disallow: anger.

I'm angry. I'm furious. She's lied, let me down, hidden so much from me. There's something else too, an anger towards myself, but all I can focus on is Heidi.

'Actually, it's *you* that I'm upset with.' She pulls her hand back in surprise. 'I need to hear the truth from you. You're supposed to be my friend.'

'I am your friend! Oh God, Christie.' With her elbows balanced on the table, she covers her mouth with her hands.

'I know that you're a part of it all. You tried to throw me off the scent about Maximus, make out that I was confused and none of the changes in my abilities were real. But I tested it out. I did learn the taxi routes, in fact, I still know them.'

'It wasn't like that, I promise. I've been the one to stand up for you.'

'Why lie to me though?'

Her face shows the calculations she's making as to what or how to explain to me. I've been there, I've behaved with as much duplicity.

'Nobody knew the research trial would end up the way it did, Christie. You were in the super-responder category: your work-based skills went through the roof. We were excited at first. We didn't know what would happen next.'

Super-responder. That's what I overheard in the work toilets – the senior research staff know the techniques can go wrong for people who are highly affected like me. It wasn't in my imagination that I could process information so fast with increased memory skills. Could it be that they didn't want me snooping in their data because they were scared that I'd see all the anomalies from their unethical practices?

Heidi continues, fast-paced and flushed. 'But then, it was as if you couldn't switch off. Those skills that were incredible like your memory improvements, speed reading, pattern recognition? They went into overdrive as if you couldn't stop trying to piece every chunk of information together even when it no longer made sense. Then your mood crashed and you became paranoid, frustrated, even aggressive. We stopped the trial but the effects continued for a couple of weeks. That's why we had to bring you in – like a detox.'

'That makes it sound like a break in a spa! Stop covering for what really went down. I couldn't move or speak.' I barely can now; each word hurts.

'We did our best to look after you and keep you safe while we waited for the side effects to subside. It really was for your

239

own good – you were agitated, obsessive.' She speaks to her shoes. That's what was happening when I felt abandoned in Magnesium. I was in withdrawal from the effects of Maximus that I craved.

Heidi's not telling me anything new, but it's good to hear it confirmed at least. They made me unwell, then kept me at Somni. Against my will. Her reasons don't explain the cover-up.

'You could have told me all about this once I was better. The last year would have been so different if I'd understood what had happened to me and why. Where's the apology, the debrief, the research write-up to warn other sleep scientists about the side effects?'

Heidi squirms. I can imagine how Harry has treated her through all of this, but I still need to understand why my friend let me down.

'I couldn't, Christie. We didn't have ethical approval. The trial didn't affect the other participants in such an extreme way, the best results were for you, but then the side effects were too severe to continue.' She dabs her eyes with her thumbs. 'Harry said it would be the end of Somni if it ever came out. I was scared for all of us. He said we could end up in jail. I couldn't survive that. And our patients need us.'

I gulp ice tea to clear my head. The 'greater good' that Harry was speaking about at the team meeting seems to have sucked Heidi in to believe that it's better to continue to deceive than risk the company.

'That wasn't the end of it though, was it? It's not only Maximus. I've been monitored at work, followed, even had a break-in at home.'

I still haven't figured that out: why risk a break-in to fetch my diary?

'You're right, but there's so much more to it, I've been desperate to tell you but I don't know how to get you to understand. I was waiting until you were well enough and ready. I'm so sorry.' She runs around the table to kneel by my side. 'Please believe me, I've wanted to be transparent with you. I tried to figure a way out, to make it up to you. It's not all as bad as it seems. You're doing so well despite everything. In fact, I'd say you're doing better than ever.'

'How can you say that?' I'm shocked that she's still defending her lies. I nudge away the sickening feeling that she's only doing what I have for a very long time.

'I tried to find another way to help you, so I proposed that you were moved to our next project. Everything that's happened recently is linked to that, for your own good. I couldn't explain to you or get you to sign up at the time, you were a mess and it could have affected the results.'

There *is* a second research trial, the one that the counsellor told me about. I'm in it right now. Is this conversation part of it?

'You don't have the right to experiment on me without involving me or giving me choice.' That's the important thing, the mistake I learnt from. It's not intention, it's outcome that matters. Heidi looks lost for words. 'Am I supposed to feel good about myself for figuring out what's going on through clues like I'm in a warped treasure hunt?'

My eyes flit around for evidence that I'm being recorded. Even now, here, I can't shake the sense that this is all a show.

Heidi shakes her head, gets off her knees and moves to the sofa. I don't move to join her.

'I appreciate that it's hard for you to trust me, Christie. But there's such thing as implicit consent, isn't there? You wouldn't continue with anything that you didn't want to. It could undo the benefits if you pull out now, that would be such a shame after getting so far.' She's stalling – her loyalty lies with Somni.

'I don't want my therapy patients to be involved in all this.' They seem to already be involved but did they have free choice?

Did getting therapy depend on their being part of some bigger study on me? 'I want all the data to be wiped. Today. I know you have access.'

Heidi's jaw tenses. This will be a test of whether she can put my needs and my patients' rights over her research project. 'Log in and get me into the video bank.' I carry the laptop over and place it next to her, then return to my chair.

'Christie, you need to let me explain about the Shadow project first. You might not be so upset when you see how much good it can do you, how much good it's *already* doing you.'

Shadow. Her Post-it note was related to the new research.

'Elizabeth Field is in on it too, I suppose. She's not just my clinical supervisor, is she?'

Heidi pauses, her brow drawn into a frown. 'No, she isn't, although her supervisory role is important too. Don't you think it's been helpful to meet with her? She wants the best outcomes for you, I'm certain of that.'

My heart aches as if someone has it in their hand, tightening their grip with each revelation.

'Open the files, please. Now. That video data belongs to me and my patients. Once it's gone, I expect a full explanation.' Heidi whizzes through folders on the laptop until a file appears. 'And don't think this ends here, I'm going to take my concerns as high as I need to so this can't happen again to anyone.'

Heidi freezes. 'You can't. We can't. I need to explain about Harry. It would put Somni at risk if you rattle him now. There's too much to lose, please don't speak to anyone until I've had a chance to explain.'

She seems so desperate, so willing to save Somni at all costs.

'Did you break into my flat?'

Heidi shrugs. 'You know technically it's not your flat. But yes, just to get the data that could be useful. I would've asked you directly if you hadn't been so peculiar recently. There's still so much to learn from Maximus but you're still sensitive about it. I mean, understandably so.'

My temples beat in time with my pulse.

'And you drugged my health drink, didn't you? I noticed the powder but then doubted myself. Why would you need to do that to help me?'

Heidi's speech increases pace with excitement rather than shame. 'It's been so successful though, Christie! It's an Alzheimer's medication: acetylcholinesterase inhibitors. Harry managed to get a huge batch for another study but this innovation uses it in a completely different way for people without dementia.'

God, she's proud of it instead of steeped in as much shame as I am! What the hell would be useful about dosing me up with dementia drugs over the last few months? I've been having more memory problems not fewer. It doesn't make sense.

The doorbell rings. Ben. I'm unsure how he's going to take my deception – he was clear in his concerns about involving Heidi. This was a mistake. I should have postponed his visit until I had all the information I needed. The doorbell rings again, three short bursts this time. I'm glad to escape the room and the person who I can no longer call my friend.

I wrench open the front door to Ben, who stands with a cactus in one hand, a bottle of Lucozade in the other. He'd remembered I said I'd kill any house plant that couldn't survive in the desert. I'd mentioned off-hand that Lucozade was the only fizzy drink we had when we were kids, reserved for days of illness to get us back to school. Such a thoughtful man with attention to detail. I could shoo him out and slink back to his flat with him. Before I get a chance to make a decision on whether to flee, Heidi joins us in the hallway.

'Ben! So you two really were together? *Are* together?'

Ben stands statue-still in the doorway. Time to be upfront. I've made it this far.

'I invited Heidi over to get answers. She's about to give me access to the files that we've been barred from. Please come in.' Ben doesn't move. It was thoughtless of me to embroil him without explanation 'or choice. 'I should have told you. I'm sorry.'

Heidi's next to me, fluttering about as she puts on her jacket like it's the end of a lovely dinner party. Her act is almost convincing. She kisses my cheek, touches Ben's arm. I have an urge to grab her and make her stay to face the music. I press my hands to my sides to stop myself – I need some time to think.

'I'll let you lovebirds figure it out between you. Christie, you'll see how I tried to make things right. You're a strong, fantastic person. Call me tomorrow. I want us to work together to sort this out in any way we can.' She's close to tears. 'You don't realise it, but you're the cleverest person at Somni. You'll figure out how we manage it from now. Please don't do anything without talking to me, this is bigger than you and me.' I mumble a noncommittal reply as she heads out of the door leaving so many questions unanswered.

Ben becomes a stranger in front of me. I've hurt him. I want him to hold me while we look through the Somni files together, but he remains outside on the front step.

'I didn't know Heidi was coming,' he says to the wall behind me. The crushing sensation starts. But if I fall into a panic, he'll feel obliged to stay. To rescue me. I need to let him go if he wants to. I inhale through my mouth as I imagine wide-open passageways that welcome the air and draw it down into my lungs.

'This is on me, Ben. My error. I should have been upfront with you. I need to delete those files. Then – if you want to – we can figure out what to do next?' He pauses, then steps over the doorway and breaks the barrier between us. I hold him as tight as he holds me. 'Will you stay?'

'Yes,' he says into my neck. I let his warm breath sink into my skin before I let go. 'I'll make us food.'

Heidi has logged into her work profile on my laptop and left the cursor on the file that contains all my therapy videos. Older recorded sessions are saved according to year. I open a file from three years ago. It contains a list of sessions that are saved only under anonymised numbers. With one click on a random number, I open a video file of me sitting in therapy with an older lady called Joan who'd spent five years afraid to go to bed as that's where a burglar had pinned her down and threatened her with a knife. This appointment must have been close to when we completed the work. I play a small section to hear her voice.

'It's mine now. He can't take it away from me,' she says, shining with pride that she has reclaimed her bedroom to be a place of safety and sleep. The therapy room looked bare back then without any furnishings other than our chairs. Therapists are not supposed to have favourites, but Joan was a wonderful woman and it felt so good to be able to help her make meaningful change in the later stages of life.

There are no files saved in the same format for this year. The videos of therapy that took place after Maximus aren't collated according to year but now I know the new project's name, I quickly locate a file called Shadowtrial. In this folder there are three different numbers that must represent my current clients. I select the first. The video file won't load: there's a passcode. I could delete the whole folder immediately but I have a strong desire to watch a clip of each of my current patients. Heidi thinks that I don't have access since higher restrictions were implemented, but she doesn't know about my juvenile detective skills. I tap in the 1986 my pencil revealed on her Post-it note. It's not only my year of birth, it's Heidi's too.

The video focuses on me as I sit in my usual chair waiting for my patient: will it be Isobel, Mike or Mia? There are times that I go to the therapy room early for thinking space before anyone is due to arrive. I forward on twenty minutes. Nothing. It could have been a day that a patient didn't turn up. I choose a different number with a little dread. I need to see what happened in the session that I lost control with Mia. I choose one of the more recent files according to the date beneath its reference number. The high camera angle makes it hard to see my face but I catch the rainbow sheen of my hummingbird necklace from Ben. It's recent. I fast-forward to halfway through the session.

Nothing. No one else but me.

This can't be right. It's a trick, part of the elaborate hoax that I've been involved with.

I turn the volume up and hear the ticking clock that has been in my therapy room since I came back from sick leave. The video is definitely recording.

The therapy chair opposite me is empty. My outfits and hair change across time but each video is the same: I'm sitting by myself, very still.

So still that I could be asleep.

38

Ben enters the living room, flushed from the heat of the kitchen and with no sign of hurt left on his face. I beckon him in, unaware of how long he's been out of the room.

'I'm in a research trial now, I have been since I finished Maximus. I'm trying to piece together what I can about it, despite never choosing to be in it. It's called Shadow.' I turn the laptop screen towards him so that he can see me sitting in the therapy chair, alone. 'There's hours of this footage. It's just me. Asleep in my therapy room.'

'Asleep?' Ben sits on his knees in front of the screen. He reaches out one finger to the screen as if he could reach back in time and touch me through it.

'I checked and checked, one video after another. It's not a freeze-frame: there's sound, and micro movements.'

'So, what was really going on?'

'I can't believe I'm saying this. But I think that in therapy, none of my patients were real. Isobel, Mike, Mia: I dreamed them somehow. I can't quite work it out but it's part of the second trial that Heidi confirmed. It must have been using the same lucid dreaming techniques as in the ReStory therapy for trauma. I learned to create these characters and have therapy sessions with them.' Even as I explain this to Ben, I realise that it must be true, despite how real they all seemed. How different to one another with rich, full reactions and experiences.

I scroll on my phone. 'Look, the Alzheimer's medication that Heidi slipped into my drink. It says here that a possible side effect of acetylcholinesterase inhibitors is the promotion of lucid dreams, the drug makes it far more likely that you can take control of your dreams if you've been trained to.'

'What's the purpose of the trial?' Ben still stares at the laptop screen. 'Does the name mean anything to you?'

I've been thinking about what Shadow could mean and how I think it links to one of the hopes that Heidi and I had as a way forward for our patients.

'If it's what I think it is, then yes. In fact, it's brilliant. In Jungian psychology, shadow means the aspects of personality that someone isn't aware of. It doesn't necessarily mean the darker aspects, but anything out of conscious awareness. We don't have a single, continuous self but different parts of ourselves.' Ben stares at the screen and I'm unsure how to explain myself, the words fly out as much a revelation to me as to him. 'We all have aspects of ourselves that we bury as if we're not allowed them.'

'So, they've found a way to make you interact with these parts through dreams.'

'It must be! I can't describe to you how genuine it all felt. It didn't seem as if I was arguing with myself but real people who stopped me in my tracks with what they said or did. But it was all parts of my own mind communicating with me.'

'How does that work?'

It's always easier to give advice to others than use it on yourself. Was this a way I was becoming my own therapist?

'A long time ago, Heidi and I discussed the possibility of

using a dream-like, creative state with our patients so we could interact with the different parts of them for therapeutic value. What we never considered was what if the patient herself is a therapist: could she heal herself?'

'They primed you to control your own dreams as in the ReStory therapy. I'm not sure how though?'

'I was the perfect candidate! Hypnotisable for a start, I must have mentioned my experience of how suggestible I am to Heidi – she's right, this wouldn't have worked without my implicit consent, part of me wanted to do this. They knew I had good visualisation skills, I'm compliant, with a strong urge to help others. When I was in rehab with Somni on the sixth floor, they trained me to sleep in my therapist chair, made suggestions through the headphones via recorded messages I listened to. I was taught how to lucid dream to certain cues, and prompted to create these characters based on my internal world. When I came back to work, they used the same chair in my therapy room, the drugged drink to increase my chances of lucid dreaming, and my mind did the rest.'

Ben leans towards the laptop, then turns the sound up. 'What's that noise?'

'The clock; I always listened closely to it. Do you think that's relevant?'

Ben nods. 'It's too slow to be a clock, listen.' I pay attention: there's more than one Mississippi between each tick. Ben continues, 'It's part of the priming, a signal that you are in a dream state and ready to take control through lucid dreaming.'

'That's one reason why I've had such poor sleep! I've been in REM sleep during the day at work when I've had patients, so I don't have the sleep pressure to get to sleep at night. Then the anxiety about not sleeping keeps me pumping adrenaline into my system. And they want me to be tired and foggy-headed so I don't question what's happening.'

I realise how much I've missed. I never collected anyone from the waiting room or had them brought to me. I've no memory of a patient leaving the room. Each dream sequence started part way through a session. There were no GP referrals, no old medical notes, and no letters for me to write. How did I not pick up any of this? Maybe I didn't want to know the truth – just as Elizabeth said. On some level, I knew all along that I was talking with myself.

I follow Ben as he goes into the kitchen, flicks on the kettle and lines up two cups. It's soothing to watch him prepare coffee and dish out pasta as if this is an ordinary day. I need the boost of caffeine and carbs.

'The past doesn't dictate the future: that's what I tell my patients. This whole mess has helped me to see that's true for me, too.'

There's so much to reflect on that I'm at risk of going into my shutdown mode. I can't allow that to happen. It's fear driven: a way to avoid the truth in case it overwhelms me. But now I'm hungry for it. I swivel on a high stool at the kitchen counter. Today, I've learned that a significant part of my life in the last few months has been a dream and not reality, yet here I am watching my boyfriend make my dinner as if I'm finally allowed to live a normal life.

'I need to see Elizabeth to help me figure out the meaning of all my therapy sessions. She's been part of this all along. I think she's on the research team and was instrumental in helping me to create the characters who became my patients while I was in recovery from Maximus. She has hinted several times but left it for me to figure out when I was ready.' I sip my drink. 'I'm going to be straight with her – although I appreciate that she thought she was part of a legitimate research trial, I think Somni have gone about it in the wrong way. Harry treats us like actual guinea pigs: caged animals that can be tested on without their consent. Hopefully she'll help me to plan how to stop him from doing it again, it's too risky.'

I think there's something I need to reveal to Elizabeth too, if she doesn't already know it.

'What if her allegiance is to Somni? It could be dangerous to tell her you're going to act if that forewarns them.'

'She's a good person. I'm certain of it. She's compassionate and reflective – the opposite of Harry. She has only ever wanted the best for me, even if I disagree with the methods she's used.' Elizabeth helps me to feel acceptable, worthy of her time, someone who can learn and grow. She's provided me with a role model. I push away my disquiet that Elizabeth is due to fly across the Atlantic in a few weeks and hasn't discussed any break in supervision with me.

It's late by the time I call Heidi but this can't wait any longer. I showered to try to clear my head but one memory after another interrupted me with no time to make sense of it all: Isobel walking along her hallway in the middle of the night overcome with the desire to escape; Mike's lack of self-worth as he dismissed the idea of being worthy of relief from guilt; Mia's outrageous behaviour and taunts that overlay a fragile need for love. All of it came from me. Was me. *Is* me.

Heidi answers within one ring.

'Christie! I was thinking about you, us, everything. It's such a mess but we can sort it. Did you delete the files?'

'There wasn't really much point seeing as there were no patients.' The splintered nature of my memories of therapy clarify that these were dream snippets rather than full sessions. Heidi is quiet for a moment. 'I've got you on speakerphone, Heidi. Ben's here.'

'I haven't been able to ask you anything about the therapy sessions but I've watched you change for the better. Please forgive me for unforeseen outcomes of Maximus, I wanted to try to make things right this time.'

My fire has reduced down to glowing embers. I believe her. 'I understand you had good intentions but doing things *to* people rather than *with* them isn't the answer. It's wrong. I've got to explain that to Harry. And if he won't listen, I will take action to stop him. I still don't really know what happened to me in Maximus or what has gone on before with other staff members.'

Heidi sighs – I get the sense she wishes I hadn't found out about Shadow trial so it could reach its conclusion. She can't see how she's been manipulated by a narcissist.

Ben interjects, 'There'll be no future for me or Christie in the field if we don't bring Harry down: he's aware of our insight and will get rid of us with gagging clauses too.'

'He's right, Heidi. We can't just let this go. I'm taking you off speakerphone.' Ben looks confused as I leave him on the sofa and take the phone into my bedroom, shutting the door behind me.

Harry has changed so much recently: his behaviour, speech, even the way he walks. I think Heidi must know more than she's letting on.

'You've spent so much time with Harry over the last couple of years. He's changed. That could be part of Somni moving to more extreme ways of working. Has he been on drugs?'

'No. But there is something I'm going to tell you. Please don't judge me though, Christie.'

I gulp. 'No, I appreciate your honesty, please go on.'

'The truth is we've both been using sleep techniques on ourselves to see if we could boost our own productivity. All off the record. I think there's been benefit. But the more I track back, the more I realise how bizarre and erratic his behaviour has been. He's been doing it much more than me.' Her voice cracks into a cry.

I feel a shiver. An almost not-wanting-to-know barrier. I push through it.

'It's okay, Heidi, please tell me.'

'We've been in the sleep labs some nights, used parts of the new techniques on ourselves. It works really well, like I can just figure things out more clearly.'

I know what that sounds like.

'You're repeating Maximus on yourselves? Are you mad after what happened to me?'

'Yes, it's the same technique – boosting spindle activity has great effects.'

That's why the Somni logo on the slides caught my eye so much. I must have been told that Maximus was aimed at increasing the fast spindles – those bunches of sleep waves that are linked to improved thinking performance when enhanced. I recall Ben telling me that the spindles are like the shuttle bus of memory, helping information to move between short- and long-term storage. Like the taxi routes I learned not only while awake, but strengthened in my brain during sleep as a recording of the directions played as my fast spindles were activated.

'I already know that method improves memory. But why is Harry starting to lose the plot?' I guess it must be for the same reason why I was badly affected.

Heidi clears her throat just as mine tightens.

'I'm worried about him. It's the voltage. We're not allowed to go over nine volts on the brain stimulator, the TES machine, in research. Not officially.'

My hand jumps up to my temple where one of the two stimulator patches was placed before I slept during Maximus.

'He's been using a higher voltage than we know is safe?' I

don't add that I now understand that's what they did to me in Maximus.

'Exactly. I haven't gone much over the research limit but he's cranking it higher each time. At best, it's hyperactivating his system.'

I need to know. 'And at worst?'

'At worst, unregulated voltage could cause brain damage.'

I want to be sick. Heidi is so caught up in her beloved boss that she doesn't realise what she's explaining to me: the risks they took with my health on the Maximus trial. It feels like karma.

'Heidi, how does this fit with what Julia was concerned about, that messing with one area of sleep has knock-on effects on other parts?'

She sighs. 'I think it's the lack of REM sleep too, because he's having more than he should of slow-wave sleep the balance is all wrong. It's basically turning him into an emotional teenager. The worse it gets, the poorer decisions he could make while volatile and disinhibited.'

That's it. A combination of my brain being fried with too many volts and a lack of the regulating dream sleep I needed turned me into an unrecognisable version of myself. That's how Maximus caused my breakdown. I'm not going to let Harry do this to anyone else again, including himself.

'Ben might be able to help us to–'

'No, you mustn't discuss anything with him. I thought that there would be a log of computer recordings of the techniques used on Harry that I could use as leverage to get him to slow down. Then I could hand over some of the decisions back to the Somni board.'

'That's a great idea, we'd have evidence that he's taking things too far and breaking research standards.'

'I've already tried, I don't have access to the data. The

tracking has been wiped from the nights Harry used the lab so there's no evidence left to find. But the records do show which sleep technician was logged in, so I know who sat in the room next door allowing dangerously high voltage through to Harry's brain.'

I hold my breath.

'Please tell me it wasn't him, Heidi.'

'If you'd told me who you were dating, I would have told you straight away. I checked the last date that Harry was in the Carbon Room. It was all set up by Ben. He was the technician who helped us to use untested, unregulated techniques on ourselves, only slightly amended from those you took part in for the Maximus trial. I think he knew all along what was done to you. And maybe it was even him that did it.'

The back of my throat stings with bile. *Stupid, gullible girl.* He's part of it. Daniel said I was hard to love. My father never stuck around. Ben must have been faking his feelings for me the whole time. I fell for it because I wanted to.

'What do we do next? It's such a mess. I can't think straight.'

'You mustn't say anything. I'll sort out a meeting with Harry. If you clarify that you aren't going to tell anyone then he might listen to reason about keeping himself well. Give me a day to sort it.'

Ben's shoes patter along the hallway towards me.

'I've got to go, Heidi. I need thinking space. I'll let you know how it goes with Harry.'

My whole body aches as if the tiredness has finally caught up with me over the last few hours and settled into each muscle. I don't know how to confront Ben, or if that's even safe. No wonder he has a direct line to Harry. He's not being laid off at all.

I re-enter the living room and hear my own voice as if it's

projected from far below me. 'Heidi feels bad about what's happened but it's best if we all try to move on from this.'

'Is that what you want to do, Christie?'

How much of his behaviour is an act? I should have known. Other than my brother who's tied to me by blood, I can't trust a man. They leave like both men left Mum, they bully and demean like Daniel, and now this. The chivalry. Seemingly at peace with himself. All an act. I need to change the focus of our conversation and buy myself some time to make a plan.

'Do you think I've done the right thing? That it's important that I find out about these different parts of myself that have been hidden all this time?'

'What were they like, the patients?'

I numb myself enough to continue, changing my focus back to my patients. Isobel with such determination and love for her son despite everything, Mike who cared so deeply for others that he blamed himself for their loss, Mia who did her best to survive and be cared for.

'They were doing their best.' So real, they seemed so real. 'But something amazing happened through therapy. They changed. *I* changed.' I sit up, energised by the realisation despite the circumstances. 'I did it, didn't I?! By helping them, I helped myself.'

Those parts of me aren't damaged or dangerous: they're essential to me treating myself differently. I'm going to need to use all those parts of myself to outsmart Somni.

39

MONDAY, 17 JUNE

Thoughts whizz too fast for me to slip into sleep. I need help but don't know who to trust. Without a reliable mother to turn to, I've been so used to getting on with things that I don't know how to get some backup.

I must have been only four when Jake had terrible croup. Even at that age, I spent a lot of time checking on him in case Mum was having a bad day. I didn't know what to do. His hacking cough distressed Mum so much it increased her sense that she couldn't cope with the world.

I knelt beside his small bed with my oldest, tatty bear.

'Hey, Mister Ted, what does Jakey need?' I made the bear's head turn towards me as if he was listening, which mesmerised my brother, then lowered my voice.

'Run the bath hot and let him play next to it, Christie, remember how that makes chests all better?'

Who do I turn to now there's no magic left?

I must speak openly with Elizabeth to help me figure this all out, even though she's as implicated as my so-called friends.

Elizabeth is late. She's never usually late, and I'm fearful that Harry has already been updated by Heidi and cancelled my supervision because I know about the Shadow trial. Or Elizabeth has decided not to come because everything has changed. She did try to tell me but I didn't realise: *What if you already know what's going on?* she asked.

I've barely been able to sleep. After sending Ben home supposedly to let me get some rest late on Saturday, I flopped into bed. But each time I closed my eyes I recalled another scene from my therapy dream. It continued all of Sunday as I lounged in unmatching pyjamas on the sofa. Mia's red shoes like mine so long ago. Mike and the brown-beaked boogie-woogie. Isobel's advice to keep a diary to look for patterns, her legs that appeared to lengthen as she became more grounded and robust. What was my resistance to realising who they were and what they represented? Just like Mike, perhaps I was too scared to face the truth, as if I didn't deserve help. Just like Mike because his story is my story – except I haven't faced the music of my guilt like he has. Unintended consequences and a lifetime of self-punishment.

I lean back in the comfort of the therapy room's leather chair. I doubt that I'll be back in this room; I could be out of a job by the end of the week. Even if I say all the right things, now I know about Shadow I can't continue to 'see' my patients. If I'm not helping Somni to gather data for the Shadow trial then I'm nothing but a liability to them. Will they pay me off or just threaten me? They have enough evidence from my so-called breakdown to sack me on grounds that I'm unfit to practice, plus whatever information Ben has been handing them. I can imagine how unbelievable it would sound to the authorities if I claim to have been put into an effective sleep therapy against my will.

'Christie?'

The slam of the door startles me: I zoom back into my body. Elizabeth looks like she may have been crying; her eyes glossy and slightly reddened. I hold back from wrapping my arms around her.

'Heidi has updated me on the situation. I very much hope that you feel strengthened with self-knowledge by your discovery.' Her eyes flicker towards the door as if she's concerned that we may be disturbed at any moment. I recall her pager being activated last session – we may not be allowed much time together. 'What would it be helpful to focus on in the time we have left together?'

Although I need clarity from her about her involvement in Somni, I've already decided to focus first on the Shadow trial. It's only fair to use what little time I have with her to learn and grow. I'm going to need all the self-knowledge I can gain before I take on Harry and the company.

'Help me to understand what each patient represents, how I learn from each part to support me in the future.' I keep my voice low. From now, I have only myself to rely on.

She nods. 'It's wonderful to hear you so future orientated, Christie. You have the freedom of so many choices.' Her voice isn't quite as soothing today, there's a rasp to it as if her throat hurts.

'Isobel – I've been thinking about her for half the night. I understand that I've had an urge to escape for most of my life, while feeling guilty about it. I think her son represents my brother when he was little. All that responsibility fell on my shoulders, it was too much at times. I resented it – him – but never wanted to harm him.'

'But Isobel didn't harm her son, did she? She had to acknowledge the level of grief and rage at being trapped before she could accept that in the end, she loved him and wouldn't want it any other way.'

259

That's true. Isobel's healing came from accepting that both things can be true: to resent somebody's demands as well as want them in your life. Being in touch with her feelings was the key that unlocked her strange behaviours.

'Yes. She taught me that being in touch with feelings reduces symptoms, even though it's painful to face. I knew it on a thinking level, but not on a feeling level.'

I think I said those very words to her. She made progress – that is to say *I* made progress – once she admitted and allowed mixed feelings towards someone she loved. I loved and still love Jake despite how much I wanted to be free of the guilt and responsibility. And I loved my mum although I hated caring for her at times, too. Nobody chooses to struggle so much: she never intended any neglect. Jake was right, she did her best, but it wasn't good enough.

'Mia, I'm not so sure about. I recognised what we had in common – our longing to be loved and accepted. But her behaviours of sleeping about, boozing, being so disrespectful, that isn't me at all, and not what I'd ever want in my life.'

'What *did* you want for your life when you were her age?' Elizabeth's hand remains on her pocket where the pager sits in wait.

It feels like a lifetime ago. 'I wanted to move out from my mum's house to escape her moods and demands. I wished I had more in common with the other girls my age: their ease in social interactions, utter body confidence, attending parties without any burden of responsibility.' Oh God, yes. It's what I *thought* I wanted when I was her age: to be desired by men, drink or drug myself into leaving my cares behind, to rail against my mother. 'I thought I wanted to be like Mia. But that wouldn't have made me happy – it was a mask to cover my deeper longings.'

The sound of vibration is just audible above the music. Elizabeth clamps her hand on her pocket. Her pager. She's turned it on to silent mode. 'Go on,' she urges, distracted. But the tendons in her neck betray her anxiety. We must speed up before Harry sends security to boot us out.

'Mike, that's the one I've been thinking about the most. He blamed himself for a choice he made during a terrible fire. It was the wrong choice to turn one way and not the other, it meant he didn't get a chance to save his comrades or the elderly residents. But that wasn't what he intended. At first, he resisted the chance of help as if he wasn't worthy of it. I think that gave me the push to go and see my brother. I held all that guilt for my choice and what the consequences were for him. But pulling away from Jake was the wrong thing to do. Just as Mike was able to retell the story and forgive himself, I started to be able to reconnect with my brother.'

It has to be now. I've waited so long. It's too late to say it to my mother but I can tell Elizabeth right now, be as brave as the Mike part of myself wants me to be.

'It was my fault, the fire. I didn't figure out the repercussions of what I did. Mum was struggling so much. She'd come off her medications and was distressed all the time. It was impossible to soothe her and Jake needed so much looking after too. I thought it would help.'

Elizabeth nods for me to continue. 'Tell me what you see.'

'I'm in the kitchen, stretching up to the cupboard. Mum's pills. She said she didn't want them anymore, said nothing helped but I could tell the difference they made. They gave her a little peace. And to be honest, gave me some too. The tumbler is heavy – thick glass with etching on the side. I lay out two of Mum's tablets and crush them with the back of a soup spoon, wiping the powder from the chopping board into the glass. The dandelion and burdock fizzes on top, its strong scent masking the contents. I stir the mixture and hold it up to the window to check there is nothing to give the game away.'

My body feels like it could collapse with fatigue. A strange sense of a weight lifted despite how much it hurts to admit.

'I didn't realise how sedating the medication was. And Mum didn't know what she'd taken. I thought it was good that she sat downstairs near Jake that night. As her body started to relax, she must have lit a cigarette. But the tiredness maybe took over, she couldn't even make it up to bed, only as far as the kitchen table. All the while, the cigarette stub was burning through the sofa. I could have told someone after the fire, once I pieced it together. The nurse, my mother, a social worker. But I never dared to say a word.'

Elizabeth shows no judgement. 'What do you think you learnt about this from the Mike part of your mind?'

My eyes prick with tears. 'I needed to name it, to acknowledge what I've done, that I didn't tell the truth and let my mother believe it was her fault. I'll have to explain it to Jake too instead of staying vague. But also, to be compassionate to myself that it wasn't intentional harm. I don't have to hold that against myself anymore, to punish myself and ruin my own life.'

Is that possible? A way to free myself from my mistake?

Elizabeth gently blinks her eyes in agreement like a cat kiss. I wish we could stay this way, pretend that nothing has changed. But the time for pretending is over. I need the next part of our conversation to remain confidential so I don't jeopardise Elizabeth's career if Somni try to use our discussion against her. I take off my cardigan, climb on the small table in the corner of the room that houses a plastic plant and a box of tissues, then drape it over the video camera. That won't stop them being able to hear. I select some meditation music on my phone and lay it on the arm of my chair to cover our conversation.

Elizabeth's pager goes off again, she takes it from her pocket this time and reads the message. I turn the volume up on my music and stand to get nearer to her.

'I know this might be the last time we meet and you're leaving Somni to go off to America soon, but I need your help. Please let me know your role in Somni, and what I should do next. Their internal research programme is unethical, it could be dangerous. I have no power here, it will be easy for them to silence me. What should I do?'

Elizabeth clasps my hands. The pager is on her lap now, its vibrations tingle my fingers through hers.

'Take some time to think. Don't doubt yourself.' She squeezes my hands a little. 'Things are not always black and white, Christie, you must step back to see the shades of grey in between. I'm not entirely sure what will happen next with regards to my role in Somni. Now I must leave, but whatever happens, I'm proud of you.' Her words reach into me and melt away what was left of my icy numbness. 'Find a way to see me once more before I leave, it's time to get things out in the open between us if that's what you wish. Make it soon though,' she says. Her finger tap, tap, taps the top of the pager as if it's a ticking clock.

Before Elizabeth reaches the door, she turns back towards me.

'Be careful. You need to understand Harry's motivations. Speak to someone who has both an insider and outsider perspective.'

40

I press the buzzer on the wall of the sleek, silver building and hope to God that academics work long days at the office. This can't wait another week. Julia works at the university on Mondays. She hasn't been subjected to the years of influence that Harry has held over us: the slow descent into near-cult complicity. I must have faith in my reading of her as someone with a genuine love for research in which ethics are paramount.

There's no answer, so I grab my phone out of my bag to see if I can find her through the switchboard of the university. I notice the Somni app on my phone before I get to a search engine. We all did as we were told and downloaded it but didn't ask why. I go into my settings like Jake taught me to reduce how much information different companies could mine from me for marketing purposes. Under permissions, I see that the Somni app automatically gives access to my current location. They can track us all. I switch the permission to no and see that I also need to disable the app's access to my messages, address book, even a fitness tracker. Then I stop. How powerful the brainwashing is! I press my finger down on the app until it shakes, then send it to the bin. Everything must change.

'Dr Julia Winnow,' comes a response through the intercom. She's there!

'It's Christie from Somni. Could we talk?'

'Of course, come through. Third room on your left.' She buzzes me in. The corridor is a little more grubby than I expected: more high school than high tech. Julia is at her office door. She beckons me inside.

'Coffee?' she asks, as if this were a planned meeting. 'I really need coffee.'

I nod my agreement and take in the chaos of her office as she makes our drinks. Books pile on her desk and across the floor with papers scattered around.

'I must inform you before we speak, Christie, that I have terminated my secondment with Somni early.' She peers over her coffee cup, gauging my reaction as much as I am hers.

The gulp of caffeine on top of adrenaline kickstarts my mouth, which doesn't have the educated eloquence of Julia.

'Is it because of all the dodgy crap?'

She laughs. 'Yes, you could say that: the dodgy crap. My whistle-blowing attempts have fallen on deaf ears, and I don't have hard evidence to take elsewhere. They were careful what was shared with me other than verbally. And to be quite frank, I'm not sure that's what I wish to do anyway.'

'There's so much I want to talk to you about, Julia. Your presentation about the ethics of sleep engineering was spot on. But there isn't time, I may be pushed out of Somni soon. I need your help to find a way to get Harry to change the way he works or to get him out.'

'I've done everything I can to persuade him to follow protocols, but my hands are tied with the company being a commercial rather than academic institution. How can I help?'

I haven't planned what to say but I trust Elizabeth's advice that Julia knows something of value to me.

'Do you know which staff are on board with running projects with no valid consent and data massaging? I need to figure out if the problems would still exist if we find a way to get Harry out of Somni. Would me and my colleagues be at risk from anyone else in the company?'

Julia takes a bite from a biscuit, dropping crumbs onto her lap.

'From what I can surmise, the company functions almost as two separate entities. There's the main Somni presence which continues the work started by past academics prior to the takeover, then there's the section that Harry spearheads which the Board seem happy to leave in his hands. It's less than rigorous, shall we say. Many of the former academics took early retirement when the institute was sold off so there are few people of high standing to check standards.'

The new company on the floor above could be part of splitting off some elements of work away from the eyes of the Board.

'Harry is a liability; you've seen how he is lately.' I'm frustrated at Julia's lack of action about Somni processes. 'He's been using the Maximus techniques on himself without being careful about what damage he could do to his brain with the amount of electricity he's zapping into it. And self-medicating with dementia drugs.'

Julia pulls an e-cigarette from her drawer despite the fact they're surely banned in the building. I have a quiver of doubt about her care for rules.

'Hmm, I did suspect as much. I think his over use of sleep engineering on himself has altered his performance somewhat significantly. Sad, really. He was a great scientist back in the day when we worked together at the university. I recall he was greatly distressed watching his father deteriorate through early-onset dementia, a decorated soldier of some sort. Harry always wanted to be the best and brightest. But it seems his unorthodox methods to keep his brain as youthful as possible may have backfired.'

I hadn't considered the impact on Harry of living in the genetic shadow of a rare dementia. It makes sense that he's fearful of inheriting the condition. Not so different from my own worries of following in my mum's footsteps. Our ways of trying to escape our inheritance couldn't be more dissimilar. Whatever his personal concerns are, they don't justify his behaviours.

But they might just give me a way forward with him.

I've been so busy being scared and angry with Harry that I forgot to apply my basic training to help me understand the Somni way. We have to understand ourselves and see that there are viable alternatives before we can change.

'Thank you, Julia. I must stop him from continuing with these practices, on staff and on himself. From what you're saying, these unethical issues are not Somni-wide, there are a handful of workers in on it. If my plan works, I'll be in touch. If it doesn't, you need to find a way to report him to the authorities.'

She sighs. 'Yes, he's already threatened me with legal action, concocted garbage that I've falsified data. But if I have to, I will fight him in court.'

'He's been weird recently. Do you think it could be the same illness his dad had? He's agitated, off his food, seems to have some kind of muscle cramps in his arm, his walking is unusual and extra saliva bubbles in the corner of his mouth. Could they be the early signs of dementia as they don't fit with the side effects of brain stimulation?'

Julia crunches another biscuit and speaks with her mouth full. 'Hmm, not really other than agitation. But gait disturbance, hypersalivation, nausea and muscle cramps can be side effects of the medication used for dementia.'

The shelves full of anti-dementia drugs in the room I had my health check in come to mind, plus the fact I was tricked into taking them in my health drink.

'You mean acetylcholinesterase inhibitors?'

Julia nods. 'Precisely.'

Harry is self-medicating as well as using sleep techniques on himself. It all links back to his dad's dementia, I'm sure of it. Is he trying to stave off illness or is it too late and he's masking his decline?

I head back to the Underground to get the train to Ben's flat while he's at work. As I return my key, I can check out if there's any evidence at his place that would help me to blackmail both of them if it comes to it. I text my brother as I walk to say I'm going to need his help.

I start to jog so that I can tell myself that the ache in my chest comes from exertion.

***

I let myself in to Ben's flat with the spare key that seemed such a gift only a few days ago. Unsure where to start, I head to his study to investigate what may be in his desk drawers.

'Christie, I wasn't expecting you.'

I can barely breathe. Ben is in his dressing gown, hair wet from the shower.

'I wasn't expecting you either.' I can't move from the spot I stand in. Do I stay? Go? Confront? Lie?

Ben walks towards me. My chance to run to the door is now. Now. But I don't. He wraps his arms around me and I wish the world was different.

'I've tried my best to keep it together but I'm finding it very hard,' he says, as he rests his head on top of mine. 'They're saying that I'm being sacked on grounds of incompetency and data breaching. I can't let them smear me, Christie. I'm going to fight it.'

I pull back, confused.

'What do you mean?'

'I wanted to be strong and calm, for you. But I couldn't handle the dismissal at all. I challenged Harry on the fact that the company stated they need fewer lab techs, I can't stand back and let them take it all away from me. Now I've had a letter to state that my contract has been terminated with immediate effect. One of the reasons they give is that I've lost a sensitive piece of equipment. It's a lie, Christie – you know how careful I am.'

My legs loosen beneath me. 'What does it say you've lost?'

'My identity card. It went missing a couple of weeks ago from the lab computer, I've been using a temporary replacement. There's no way that I would have left it there overnight by mistake, my wallet feels empty without it.'

Is he covering his tracks because I'm onto him or telling the truth? I don't trust my radar on this anymore.

'I've got to go.' I bite down on an apology. 'There's a meeting tomorrow where this should all be sorted out.'

I retreat to the door and don't look back at Ben before I leave.

41

TUESDAY, 18 JUNE

'I need your help,' says Harry, throwing me off the opening speech that I've rehearsed for half the night. 'Whatever your concerns, let's discuss them but we mustn't put Somni and our patients' opportunity to thrive at risk.' His curved leather chair faces me as I perch on the edge of a velvet sofa. I've never been into Harry's office before. I can't trust this extended hand as it's likely to be self-serving.

'With respect, the issue is bigger than that. It's about every staff member that you've mistreated by lying about research they were in. It's about the reputation of this company that you claim is focused on what's best for disadvantaged people. And it's about the way you try to intimidate and lie to people who've dedicated their working lives to Somni and all its patients.'

'The last thing I'd ever want is to make people feel that way. Especially you, Christie. Heidi has championed you all along and I sanctioned all of her efforts to make life better for you.' His charm lacks the warmth of sincerity.

'The flat? Paying my brother's fees? That's not to make life easy, that's to buy my silence.'

My heart is thumping. Harry shakes his head.

'It's unfortunate that you can't accept we would want to support you, particularly given your shortcomings. At Somni, we're careful to put back the profits into our staff – it was Heidi's suggestion to upgrade your brother's accommodation and the board ratified it.' He pushes some papers on the table between us. They look like minutes from a board meeting. He's prepared well for my visit. I can't help but wonder what the other papers behind it are.

'It's the same pattern as happened with the Maximus trial, my guess is with plenty of other trials before that used staff as guinea pigs, and now Shadow. You don't have the right to make choices on other people's behalf. You should have asked me.' I'd walked into a repeating pattern of my past but that wasn't my fault or what I deserved.

Harry shrugs. 'Heidi informed us that you wouldn't have accepted the offer.'

What can seem the right thing at one time can seem so wrong at another. Who knows what the outcome would have been if I'd told Ivy the social worker just how much Mum struggled? Would she have got help and turned things around, my brother uninjured in a foster placement as a fire took hold miles away? Or could things have been even worse: Mum drowning her sorrows in a sea of sleeping pills, Jake and I sent to an abusive children's home? I could have tried to persuade Mum to take her medication rather than secretly give it to her without her consent. But if she'd stuck to her refusal, could her mood have deteriorated so much that she may have used those razor blades to tragic effect one night while I wasn't watching over her?

My head spins a little as my certainty starts to disintegrate. Black, white, grey.

'I need to know how Ben was part of this.'

Harry raises his hands. One shakes a little.

'Ahh, Benjamin was potentially problematic for the company with his inquisitive mind and penchant for the truth, so I took matters into my own hands for the greater good.' Harry pulls a leather wallet from his pocket and extracts a card. It's Ben's identification for logging on to the computers. 'That is my guiding principle.'

It wasn't Ben who used his card in the lab recently. He was set up. I doubted that wonderful man; I took stories of how men have treated me in the past and threw them into my future. It nearly wrecked us.

My inner tuning fork that I've developed as a therapist knows that Harry's explanation doesn't ring true. There's got to be more of a personal explanation for his drive that tramples over other people's needs and rights.

'Christie, I owe you an apology for the distress caused. But that is no reason to put our great work in jeopardy. You must surely wish us to continue to offer the expert help to those in need?'

I feel prickles on the back of my neck – Heidi has never been able to see what a threat Harry is. He strides over to the glass door behind his desk and pulls it open onto a small balcony. He looks out over the city as he speaks and gestures for me to join him.

I hover on the opposite side of the balcony aware that there would be no surviving a fall from this height.

'You must consider the bigger picture, Ms Langdale. Let me give you an example. It wasn't really dementia that killed my father, in the grand scale of things. It was red tape. It was lack of investment in drugs that won't make a profit for greedy pharmaceutical companies, and because a rare disease is of little interest to them. It was the length of time it takes trials to get the green light of approval. It was the excruciatingly small odds of gaining grants for research into those areas not placed upon a predetermined list by secretive men in rooms full of power. Do you understand? I changed all that at Somni.'

He turns to me. Tiny red capillaries feather across his face. There's no bluster or charm. I can visualise a diagram of what he's saying, arrows tracking back from his father's illness, further and wider to show all the influences that resulted in his suffering and death.

What random events, choices and other people's decisions got me here to this point? What led my mother to become the type of person she was? Each causal arrow tracks back into more and more arrows of influence, smaller and smaller.

He's trying to blame external factors for his father's death but the only sentence where I felt the truth of his words was the first – that it wasn't really dementia that killed him.

'What killed your father, Harry, if it wasn't his illness?'

Harry leans his weight on to the metal bar that separates him from the sky.

'You weren't listening to a word I said about the impact of rigid systems. Have you any idea what it must be like to lose your language? For your limbs to not fully obey your commands? To know that the road ahead will leave you no longer in charge of your own actions?'

I don't. He's talking about his father, but also himself. His tremors, emotional outbursts, weak legs. He thinks he's following in his father's footsteps. Or doing everything he can not to.

'What *actually* killed your father?' I ask, as gently as I can, moving to stand next to him. He doesn't realise the unconscious drive that led him to bring me out on to the balcony at just this moment. Harry dips his head down. We both stare at the ground so far below us, as if there were something – or someone – to look down at on the pavement. 'Did he take his own life?'

Harry's knuckles whiten as he grips the rail harder.

'Not directly. But he may as well have done. There was a document that he'd signed in the early months in which he declined any experimental procedures – no neurosurgery, no medication trials, no stimulation techniques. Despite my greatest efforts, experience and connections to the most innovative researchers, we were not permitted to act in his best interests.' Harry turns to me. 'Sometimes people don't know what's best for them. We must be proactive, push forward, prevent as much harm as possible. Passivity is as destructive as negligence.'

Harry sees himself as taking control because other people don't make the right decisions for themselves. People like me. Heidi has tried to tell me that I'm hard to help. If she'd offered to sign me up to Shadow, I doubt that I would have agreed to it. Even if I had, maybe I couldn't have created Isobel, Mike and Mia deliberately. Then where would I be now? What version of me would be walking around today, thinking of herself as a burden, frozen in guilt? I shake off the fact that I'm grateful for the impact of Shadow. That doesn't change the lack of consent.

Harry can't bring his dad back or change the course of what he went through with his illness.

'And now you're trying to take control over your own health in an experimental way.' Harry doesn't respond. I need to be clear about his motivations, even if he isn't. 'I know you use the Maximus techniques on yourself. And that you're taking ACE-inhibitors. What you think is the solution could actually be the problem.'

Harry is trying to escape what he fears is written in his genes: dementia. The irony is that in trying so hard to avoid losing his thinking abilities, he's actually causing himself the damage he wants to avoid. We sometimes act in ways that bring about the very thing we fear. I wanted to keep myself small and safe but my silence has pushed me further towards the risk of harm.

Harry faces me now but his eyes appear foggy with fatigue. 'You were a super-responder in Maximus because the fourteen hertz stimulation was a perfect fit for your own sleep spindles: matching internal and external properties heightens the effect. Sadly, I'm naturally at twelve hertz.'

He's losing me with technical talk.

'You went above the recommended maximum voltage with brain stimulation on me. I know you've done the same on yourself. Whatever your good intentions are, you can't cut corners and do whatever you want, it's dangerous. It must stop. Now.'

Harry takes a step forward to lean on the balcony rail. It would take some effort for him to climb over but it's not impossible. His unpredictability worries me as his voice becomes more emotional.

'I had no intention of causing overstimulation in you. Once I realised the effects, we pulled the trial. I'm using myself as a test for a slower approach to increasing voltage. My memory for data played during sleep is extremely high. It's working. I'm certain of that.' But he sounds anything other than certain. 'This form of intervention could become the norm to improve human minds, rather like the acceptable use of caffeine is today. I need this right now. And when it's perfected, everyone will want it.'

'At what cost, though? You look unwell. I've seen your health and clarity worsen. Don't you think your current difficulties are better explained as side effects of the treatments you've prescribed for yourself rather than the start of an illness?'

It makes no difference. Harry doesn't hear me – he's too stuck in what he believes. As a way to cope with the uncertainty of the future, he's trying to control his own health as well as ours. He's dragged staff along with him on a journey that has shut down their reasoning and critical skills, worsened by his lack of REM sleep which has affected his emotions and stability. Like the behaviour of some animal rights extremists, his initial values have warped into something darker and desperate. Although Harry tries to make his actions seem noble, we've become nothing but data to him.

'Why don't we sit down indoors,' I say, leading him by the elbow as if he's older than his years, closing the glass doors as he shuffles to his seat. It's time to get back some control.

What's the cost if I follow the rules and report Harry's behaviours and Somni's deceits to the inspectors? I see arrows heading to a future that impacts on all my colleagues, all the patients in treatment, all those people we could help in the future who have nowhere else to turn.

Back in his chair, Harry appears to regain some of his composure. He flicks through the paperwork in front of him.

'Of course, it would be most unfortunate if it came to light that you were responsible for the disability in your own brother. The transcripts here from your time with us in recovery contain full information.'

Hot shame and anger heat up my body in a second. I must have already admitted my role in the fire while I was out of my sleep-deprived mind. He's trying to use my self-judgement to silence me. I have to focus on why, what's driving this behaviour. Not cruelty, not narcissism, but fear. He's trying to get control over his health and future by trying to control others.

I say out loud what's been a whisper in my mind for days.

'I made a mistake. Jake's injury wasn't my fault.'

I have a choice whether to act now, even if it puts everything I've worked for at risk.

I remember a demonstration Elizabeth gave during her teaching session at college. She held out her hand and told us to imagine a butterfly in her palm. If we hold on to what we think is the right thing too loosely, the butterfly flies away. But if we are inflexible, if we treat our beliefs with rigid certainty and too tight a grip, we crush the thing we care about.

I've made up my mind.

I take out my phone, press play on the video Jake made, then turn it towards Harry. I'd been so unsure of whether this was the right thing to do but now it's clear. There's more than one way to make a difference. I might be able to make Somni a safe place without risking it being shut down and losing a lifeline for patients.

'You need to step down from Somni and inform the board of your unethical practices, advising them to stop straight away. If not, my brother will release this video at midnight to his thirty thousand followers online and I will send it to the inspectors ahead of their visit.'

Harry's mouth hangs open as watches the small screen. Off-key music fits the images that Jake spliced with facts about the dangers of unethical practice in the field of sleep engineering. There are brutal images of brains in jars, patients writhing in hospital beds and old photographs from long-closed mental health institutions that are a far cry from what has actually been happening but serve to strengthen the message that Harry has overstepped the mark.

I let my hand rest loosely on my lap, not a fist or fully open.

'For the greater good,' I say, and I don't apologise.

42

FRIDAY, 21 JUNE

I thought I would need this final supervision session with Elizabeth so she could tell me what to do about Harry, but instead I've been able to update her on what I've already achieved.

'Now Harry has taken some sick leave and Heidi is acting up into his role.' She listened calmly to the details of my ultimatum with Harry. In the end, I gambled that he'd choose to leave over risking the future work of Somni. I can't be sure yet if what I've done will work out. There's still a lot to agree with Heidi and the board for me to be assured of future standards. They could still find a way to discredit and threaten me.

'It sounds like you had a difficult decision to make over whether to report the anomalies or not. Tell me how you came to your conclusion of the best way ahead.'

She makes it sound as if I'd been sure of the choice but it was messier than that. I could see the arrows of experience that pushed Harry along a route to speed up trials and bypass consent, how his desperation to avoid his father's fate led him to try protective methods even though they caused the very symptoms that he feared. Fortunately, Heidi was shocked enough at Harry's framing of Ben, and his absolute conviction that he should continue to self-medicate and use brain stimulation that she realised the Board would have to be informed. With Harry off sick, he can no longer use the labs to continue his programme of trying to better his brain with electrical stimulation. I've done everything I could to do what's right, whatever shade of grey that is.

'We can't change the past. In order to have the future we want, Somni has to continue to exist. But with new rules.'

Elizabeth's head tips to the side in that way she does before she tries to untangle something. I'm unsure how she could make this relate to me.

'What were Somni's old rules, may I ask?'

'Well, Silence for Somni, as in don't tell anyone what's happening. And Smile for Somni – don't show any underlying feelings, only the glossy magazine version.'

'Are these rules written in the contract? Discussed in meetings?'

I hesitate. Where did I get those phrases from that show up so clearly in my mind, capitalised and intrusive?

'No. I'm not sure. It's just how things operate here.'

Elizabeth nods. 'Well it certainly seems so from all you've described.' I sigh out my tension as she agrees with me. 'Would it be fair to say that these have also been *your* rules for living?'

Silence. Smiles.

Yes, for almost all of my life.

She continues, her voice gentle and kind. 'And if you were to accept that you can't change your past, but you chose to rewrite your rules for the future, what would they be?'

I tell my patients to use their values as a compass to guide them in their decisions. I hold out my hand as if there were a compass in my palm. What would the arrow point towards?

'Act with kindness. Make a difference. Connect.'

Elizabeth looks to my palm too as if she understands what I'm doing.

'Does that include kindness towards yourself? Making a positive difference to your own life as well as to others? Connecting in a deep sense even if that brings up strong feelings and fears?'

I wipe away a tear with the back of my hand.

'Yes. I'll try my best for it to be for me as well.'

Elizabeth sits back, satisfied.

'If you were to choose to act according to those rules right now, what would we use this time together for?'

I've been avoiding the fact that this our last meeting. I told Heidi I needed this final supervision without being totally sure what it was I wanted to say other than to thank Elizabeth. There's so much I haven't had answers about yet: her role in Somni, her future research, what it is that connects us.

'You don't seem rattled today but you were last time we met up. I guess the threat of Harry has gone but I didn't understand why you put Somni first and not me. You left the supervision session when I needed you.' Elizabeth doesn't break eye contact as I speak. 'I'd like you to explain your role in Somni to me, why you didn't say you were leaving, what it is you're doing next and if it has anything to do with our work together.'

'I'm glad to hear you ask from the heart, Christie. I've tried to gauge what you were ready for as you have a pattern of hiding from truths. In what way do you think my future research has anything to do with you?'

I think back to the event at the museum, that one word that stuck out and has stayed with me since: longitudinal.

'You said you were going to follow some people across time. I was wondering if you've done that before. With me.' My cheeks warm with embarrassment in case I'm completely wrong. It seems arrogant to even consider it but I can't shake the feeling that Maximus wasn't the first time Elizabeth studied me.

'I'm happy to share that I was part of the Maximus trial once you were in recovery, Christie. I wanted the best for you, and Shadow seemed like the perfect opportunity for you to understand yourself and what resources you have inside you.'

'And before that? Before Maximus?'

She beams. Her response surprises me.

'I know you worked so hard in your studies to be a therapist. I was proud of you and how much you allowed yourself to grow and develop.'

Elizabeth remembers me! I was one of fifty or sixty in her lectures and never spoke with her directly. Was she involved in my journey earlier than I ever guessed? Did she get me into Somni?

'What about before that? I know longitudinal research can last years. Your specialist area is recovery from trauma. Did you already know what I'd been through? Did you select me *before* I worked here?'

Elizabeth's eyes sparkle with tears of admission. She stands up.

I copy her action so we stand opposite one another.

She loosens the scarf around her neck. A gentle glow emanates from beneath.

'You already know the answers, Christie.'

I realise that I do.

Her skin ripples. The truth unfolds into a map. I can barely breathe. Joy and sadness bathe me.

'I'll miss seeing you, Elizabeth.'

My version of Elizabeth. She reaches her arms out.

'You won't have to miss me if you don't let me go.'

I take a step towards her, clutch her slight body as it wavers, until I absorb her into me.

I wake up in the therapy chair, shaking slightly.

My Elizabeth isn't the same Elizabeth who will be getting on an aeroplane next month. She is part of my mind just as my patients were: an internal supervisor, based on a real person who inspired me with her compassion. No wonder my version of Elizabeth hadn't aged in all those years. I laugh to myself as I recall all the clues that she gave me along the way.

From now on, I'll be my compass. I need to safeguard Somni. And then I need a long, honest conversation with Ben, my brother and the ghost of my mother.

NINE MONTHS LATER

'Time to set up,' shouts Julia from the window.

I rub my fingers along the uneven sandstone of the clinic. Looking out on to fields divided by stone walls and clusters of trees, it feels further from Manchester than a few miles. A restful place. Although the Board offered us space on floor six at Somni to replace Zed that was dissolved, I think we made the right decision to come up here instead.

I savour the early spring air for a moment, then stride back indoors to prepare for our first training session. The large screen is set up at the front of the room ready for Heidi to join us remotely from London for her slot later.

'You can let the delegates in now, I'll be ready to start in five minutes.' Julia leaves to collect twenty psychotherapists.

I sneak out of the side door as I hear the audience chatter their way towards the room. At the end of the corridor, I peek into lab three. Ben is utterly focused on the computer screen, reading the lines of the somnograph like it's a musical score.

'Hey, shouldn't you be off home soon?'

He doesn't turn his head but I can tell from his profile that he's smiling.

'I will as soon as I've finished scanning through these. It was a great idea to make the lab look like the Evergreen Care Home, the dementia patients were much more settled last night. Now we wait to see the daytime ratings from staff and family.'

We're all hoping that the data will show that our sleep intervention has had positive effects on behaviour and memory, how life-transforming that would be for the patients and their families. But one step at a time.

I lean over to kiss his cheek.

'It'll be worth waiting for. The only thing we can control is how well we design our procedures at this end. Doing our best is enough. Now, get yourself home to sleep so I don't feel too guilty waking you when I get in.'

Ben tears his eyes away from the screen.

'Yes, good luck today. I have no doubt that you will be excellent. It's the next important step for Shadow.'

'You mean for the Kaleidoscope project.' I didn't want to use the name Shadow any more, we need a fresh start to take the ideas forward with a properly organised research trial. 'Maybe we should update Harry when we know the results of the Alzheimer's study. Not in detail, just a summary to send to him at home. I think it would mean a lot to him even though it's not focused on the same illness his dad had. Catch you later.' Reports from Heidi updated me that Harry is actually doing really well without access to unnecessary medication and harmful electrical stimulation – his brain and body are now in recovery, he was never actually unwell.

Back in the training room, I place my notes on the lectern in case my mind goes blank with nerves. I'd originally asked Heidi to do the training introductions during our weekly telephone meeting.

'It's your project to lead on now, Christie. Just talk from

your heart – every person in the room will feel the passion you have, you'll inspire them.'

It was good to get her support as the new chair of the board for Somni. Even better to feel like I had my friend back.

A hush falls as the rows of therapists look at me expectantly. I take in a cleansing breath through my nose, straighten up and speak without looking down at my notes.

'I'm so pleased to see you all here at our Somni North headquarters. Many of you will know about helping your patients who have sleep problems by teaching them sleep hygiene techniques or working on any underlying mood issues. You're all here today to think about a new, exciting way to work with patients that uses sleep as one of the tools for therapy.'

I click the handheld button and show a collage on the screen that Jake designed. It's a drawing of a head with all kinds of fascinating images inside that he'd drawn to represent aspects of the self: angry faces, outstretched arms, figures clinging to one another, angels and devils.

'Freud said that dreams are the royal road to the unconscious. Therapy used to involve a so-called expert attempting to decode a patient's dream for meaning. Many of us had one of those books from the cut-price bookshop that you could look up what your dream meant with your friends, right?'

There are nods in the audience, a few laughs. It's good to speak as myself, not just with my own accent but to talk about my own experiences without worrying about other people's judgement.

'The amazing news is, our patients don't have to wait to see what their minds make up or be told by somebody else what their own thoughts mean. They can take some control and use their dream world to understand themselves better, if they choose to. Before I tell you how, I want to set you a task. Turn to the person next to you and describe your own personality in three words. Don't overthink it.'

I don't want to encourage the therapists to think of their patients as being different to them. It's how all humans are made – many parts to make up a whole. They'll benefit from thinking about themselves as much as about those they work with, just as the real Elizabeth taught me. How would I have described myself a year ago?

There's an energy in the room that buzzes as all the delegates join in wholeheartedly. I overhear some of the descriptions: bubbly, driven, a worrier. I can't help but wonder where these words came from in the first place, how hard they've clung on to them, whether they even know that they are more than the sum of their labels.

'Next, I want you to pick one of those words and think about a time that you were the opposite. Let's have an example. Anyone at the front want a go?'

A woman raises her hand. She looks smart in a pearl-white shirt over wide trousers, a leather file balanced on her lap in which she's written handwritten notes.

'I was just explaining to this man next to me that I'm a planner. It works for me. I like to know what I'm doing and when, and I love lists.'

'Thank you, yes. Can you think of any time when you didn't plan, that you were spontaneous?'

She frowns in concentration then her face brightens.

'On holiday in Spain for my fortieth. I ran into the sea to my knees in my sequin dress, high heels in my hands. No idea why.'

'What was it like?'

She laughs. 'It was funny. Everything's different on holiday. The water was warm and the girls thought it was hilarious, they couldn't believe it was me.'

'It was you, though. And did that mean that you're not a planner?'

'God, no!'

'Thank you. So, there's just one example. We have other parts to ourselves that may only show themselves in certain situations, or maybe we don't allow them to show at all. We're not always the same. But we may be telling ourselves that there's only one version of us that's acceptable or the real version. Do you find that your patients do that? Behave in a particular way with you and you get the feeling there's more to it? Shout out some examples.'

'Like when someone tells you they don't ever feel frustrated with their kid or partner because they're not an angry person. But you think they do have those feelings underneath. That's just normal, isn't it.'

I nod and try to encourage others who've been quiet to speak up.

'When I set a homework task to do some self-care and then someone says she didn't have time or forgot. Sometimes I think she really wanted to do it then bottled it.'

'Yes, great. So, imagine if in therapy with a patient, you could talk to different parts of them. Find the parts that are healthy, compassionate, free, wise, and ask them what to do next. You wouldn't have to be an expert telling someone what to do. They could work it out for themselves with your guidance, listening to your questions as they sleep and use dreams as a way to see how another part of themselves answers. There's even the potential that some creative patients may be able to dream more than one aspect of themselves at a time, like taking part in group therapy. Watch the video now to see how this works in practice with lucid dreaming training and medication.'

As the training video plays on the large screen, I feel a little nostalgia thinking back to my part-of-me patients. I wiggle my toes in the red shoes I treated myself to when I got the promotion to lead researcher. They're low-heeled and comfortable, but the colour is a throwback to my younger days when I dared to break away from what my mum taught me a young woman should look like. I don't need to take it to the extremes of five inches and red lips to match like the Mia part of me did – I feel loved by Ben and my brother even after admitting the truth of my past deceit.

I don't think I could have let myself enjoy being a part of this project if I hadn't made my peace with Mum. Letting go of guilt started with my discussions with Mike. Accepting love and anger toward the same family member came from understanding Isobel. It's not that far to drive from here to visit Mum's grave. I've taken flowers every couple of weeks and spoken to her while I'm there. I feel sad that I didn't try harder to talk openly with her while she was still alive, but the past is done. I can only change what happens in the present, which gives me a new future.

As the final scene plays on the screen, a surge of warmth rises up through my chest. I imagine faint silver lines linking all of us in the room like a spider's web. The delicate strands spread outwards through the windows, past the fields to connect to all the patients whose lives we can impact together, which in turn stretches out to their own networks of people who care about them.

'Now you'll hear from Heidi Lawton, chair of Somni, via video link to welcome you to this pilot programme of Kaleidoscope and share with you our plans for the next six months of the research trial. After that, you'll be taken through the protocol manual by our Head of Research, Dr Julia Winnow. I'll see you all later today for a reflective session.'

Heidi comes into view on the big screen. Over the last few months she's looked healthier without the strain of worrying about Harry, who accepted early retirement to protect the reputation of his beloved company. Under Heidi's positive leadership, the board has agreed to national standards around ethics with staff no longer required to take part in studies.

I retreat to the French doors while Heidi talks to the audience about next steps in the project. I'm glad she encouraged me to go with a different name. It took me days to think of a suitable title but once it hit, I knew it was perfect.

One Christmas, Jake got a tiny kaleidoscope in a cracker from a box the neighbours gave us.

'The telescope's broke,' he said, passing it over to me.

'No, Jake, look. This is how it's supposed to be. Turn this and watch what happens.'

He was utterly fascinated by the ever-changing dance of jewels and their reflected beauty. We took it in turns holding it to the light, each pattern as different and special as the last.

The kaleidoscope wasn't broken and now I realise that neither was I.

All the parts were inside me the whole time, waiting to be seen.

THE END

ACKNOWLEDGEMENTS

Thank you to all those who shared their time to read early drafts of Shattered. In particular, the sound advice and enthusiasm from my writer friends Sophie van Llewyn, Steve Campbell, Judi Walsh, Helen Rye, Hannah Persaud, Victoria Richards, Patricia Adrian and Joely Dutton. I also received invaluable expert professional input from Lizzie Huxley-Jones, Sabhbh Curran, Shelia Crowley and Dr Bernhardt Staresina. Thank you to the Bloodhound Books team including Betsy Reavley, Tara Lyons and Abbie Rutherford for turning my Word document and dream into a real book.

A NOTE FROM THE PUBLISHER

Thank you for reading this book. If you enjoyed it please do consider leaving a review on Amazon to help others find it too.

We hate typos. All of our books have been rigorously edited and proofread, but sometimes mistakes do slip through. If you have spotted a typo, please do let us know and we can get it amended within hours.

info@bloodhoundbooks.com